CAT BURGLAR

At one a.m., Helma's telephone rang. She grabbed the phone, instantly awake.

"Yes?" she said. "May I help you?"

She heard the faint movement of breath, then a squeak like a squeezed rubber duck. The crescendoing yowl of a meow sounded in her ear. She pulled the phone away and stared at the receiver.

"Who is this?" she demanded.

The voice was gravelly and at the same time a monotone, something mechanically disguised. She couldn't tell if it was a man or a woman. "I have your cat," the voice growled. "Mind your own business or the cat dies."

"That's not my cat," Helma said.

"It is too."

"Could you make him yowl again, please?"

Silence. Then, "Hurt him again? What are you, a monster?"

"I'm sorry," Helma explained, "but I do not negotiate with terrorists."

"You're right. You *will* be sorry. Say bye-bye to kitty-kitty."

And the connection was broken.

Books by
Jo Dereske

BOOKMARKED TO DIE
FINAL NOTICE
MISS ZUKAS AND THE STROKE OF DEATH
MISS ZUKAS AND THE ISLAND MURDERS
MISS ZUKAS AND THE LIBRARY MURDERS

BOOKMARKED TO DIE

Jo Dereske

AVON BOOKS
An Imprint of HarperCollins*Publishers*

AVON BOOKS
An Imprint of HarperCollins*Publishers*
10 East 53rd Street
New York, New York 10022-5299

Copyright © 2006 by Jo Dereske
Excerpts copyright © 1994, 1995, 1995, 1998 by Jo Dereske
ISBN-13: 978-0-06-079082-0
ISBN-10: 0-06-079082-2
www.avonmystery.com

First Avon Books paperback printing: June 2006

Printed in the U.S.A.

10 9 8 7 6 5 4 3 2 1

For the men: TP, AP, EJ

Contents

BOOKMARKED
TO DIE

Chapter 1

Awakening Crisis

On that fateful Monday morning when Miss Helma Zukas awoke to her clock radio playing a Boston Pops rendition of "Louie Louie," she realized in that peculiar awareness of the rudely awakened that not only was it the morning of her forty-second birthday but that she was suddenly and inexplicably . . . *in crisis.*

She lay rigid, squarely in the center of her queen-sized bed tucked between white sheets, covered by a pale blue blanket, her eyes squeezed closed. The word *crisis* might as well have been written on the inside of her eyelids, it was that apparent.

"Louie Louie" played on, cheerfully blaring into the morning, trumpets seeming to blast from inside Helma's head. She would have switched off the radio except, at that moment, her arms were frozen across her breast like the effigy on a medieval tomb, a modern *gisant.*

A disquieting sense of dread bound her to her mattress, a peculiar numbness with a touch of, yes, hopelessness.

Helma Zukas was unaccustomed to emotions that sprang from the unknown. She didn't experience mental states that couldn't be traced to a concrete source: a rude driver, flawed library cataloging, admiring library patrons.

"Oh, Faulkner," she whispered and sat straight up in bed without using her hands. She couldn't lie in bed any longer, contemplating sensations that were assuredly temporary. Her day at the library began in one hour, barely enough time to get ready.

Her bed covers fell back smoothly from her body; her comforter was still folded neatly on the foot of her bed, so obviously she hadn't thrashed in frustration during the night.

As she reached for her clock radio, accidentally hitting the wrong button and sending screeching beeps through her apartment before she connected with the Off switch, she glimpsed black in the hall outside her bedroom door.

Boy Cat Zukas, who wasn't allowed beyond the wicker basket just inside the sliding glass doors to her balcony, sat in the doorway. Instead of slipping out of her sight as he usually did when she caught him out of bounds, the former alley cat calmly gazed straight into her eyes as if sensing that her state of mind granted him special indulgence.

He was right. Helma ignored him as she felt the floor with her bare feet, missing her strategically placed slippers, then somehow slipping them on the wrong feet. Her robe tie twisted into a knot and by the time she untangled it, Boy Cat Zukas was deliberately licking a paw, keeping her warily in his peripheral vision.

She stood in her shower overlong, soaping and rinsing and soaping and rinsing again. The bar of soap squirted out of her hands and slithered around the floor of her tub until she recaptured it, but her usual sense of the passing minutes—so accurate, she routinely timed her showers within thirty seconds—had deserted her.

When she'd finally pinned her grandmother's cameo straight on her collar, it was too late to eat breakfast.

Helma looked longingly at the place setting she'd arranged the night before at her dining room table, facing Washington Bay, but resignedly grabbed a banana from her fruit bowl.

The morning felt, as her Aunt Em would say, "scratchy," or off-kilter, even ominous. Holding her banana in both hands, she took a calming breath, then jumped as her phone rang in the midst of a measured inhale.

"Hello?" Later, she would concede she *might* have sounded impatient.

"Helma?" The man's voice asked, hesitant, as if he was uncertain it was her voice. "This is Wayne Gallant."

The chief of police, her . . . well, her friend of course. At least. And more. She glanced at her clock. Yes, she was going to be late.

"I'm going to be late," she blurted into the phone.

"You're going to work?" he asked.

"Of course"—she was squeezing her banana to mush—"but I'm late."

"Tonight, then," he said. "I'll be . . ."

"All right," she interrupted, dropping her banana in the trash. "Good-bye." And hung up.

As she locked the door of her third-floor apartment Helma remembered she'd neglected to let out Boy Cat Zukas, and after she did that realized she'd forgotten her blue pumps on the counter and had to return to her apartment yet again.

After that she stopped and took two breaths, actually shaking her head to banish the curious heaviness.

"Top o' the morning, Helma." It was TNT, Helma's next-door neighbor. The grizzled retired boxer bounced his way up and down the three floors of the Bayside Arms every morning precisely from 7:45 to 8:15.

"Good morning," Helma responded, and something in her voice or demeanor brought TNT to a full stop. He bounced in place, his feet thumping against wood. Perspiration dotted his face and the center of his gray sweats. He unwrapped the towel from his neck and mopped at his forehead. "Are you doing okay, girlie girl?" he asked, too much concern on his face for Helma to be offended. "You've got the look of the glum about you."

"Just a low morning is all," Helma told him, shocked at her own candor. She had never been a person who inflicted her moods on others, especially people she hardly knew.

"Then you gotta concentrate on going the distance," TNT told her, jabbing the air with a right hook. "Keep your dukes up, stay off the ropes, and before you know it, you've knocked your opponent out of the ring."

When TNT's talk wasn't punctuated with Irishisms, it carried the salt and punch of the boxing ring. He still boxed at the YMCA. "Have to spar with the kids," he'd told Helma once. "Not many guys my age can dodge these fists."

She nodded and descended the staircase that led to the parking lot, each step an unaccustomed effort, even in descent.

"Loosen your hips, lighter on your feet," TNT called after her. "Give the blues the big KO," and he began humming the theme from the *Rocky* movies, already beginning another lap down the steps past Helma and around the parking lot.

Normally, Helma would have taken deep pleasurable breaths of the crisp October morning. She'd have noted the blue skies over the deepest bay in the most northwest corner of the lower 48, and the reddening fire bushes that lined the sidewalk. She might have glanced up at the squawking seagulls soaring above her building or tipped her head at the watery bark that sounded like a seal. But today was not normal.

Her twenty-five-year-old Buick coughed once before the engine caught. "Your car's been more loyal to you than most men are to their women," her friend Ruth had once told her. Helma didn't know about *that*, but it *was* a good car.

Helma turned from her parking lot onto the boulevard that curved Washington Bay, and gasped at the blare of a horn, slamming her brakes. A red pickup swerved around her, tires squealing and horn blaring. The driver—a woman—shook her fist at Helma.

She backed up and waited a few moments in the Bayside Arms driveway, her car in neutral and foot on the brake, catching her breath.

After her near miss, she concentrated on her drive to the Bellehaven Public Library, hardly glancing at the curve of Washington Bay where an early morning sailor already tacked to the breezes and a tugboat chugged toward the mouth of the bay and beyond to the open water leading to the big blue Pacific Ocean.

The news announcer on her car radio warned of a scam artist, and then cheerily said, "Bad news on the Bellehaven city budget front!"

She flicked off the radio, bruising her knuckle on the knob.

"It's my birthday," she said aloud.

Speaking to herself was also an uncommon occurrence, and she pressed her lips together so no other words could escape, turning her full attention to her entrance into downtown Bellehaven, Washington.

School children walked to school, their huge backpacks bending them like gnomes carrying bundles of wood. Cars lined six deep at the five espresso stands. Little traffic drove in the opposing lane, most were on her side streaming toward the downtown area that held the library, city hall, courthouse, police station, jail, and hospital. "Bureaucracy in a box," she'd heard it referred to.

She braked behind a green Mustang pulled crookedly into her parking space, her front bumper just barely touching the Mustang's rear. She'd waited seven years to earn a parking slot in the tiny library lot, and that had come only eleven years ago, after the cataloger prior to George Melville had been indicted for tax evasion

Helma backed up, leaving enough room for the owner to back out the Mustang and relinquish the parking slot, then turned off her engine and removed her purse and blue pumps from her car seat.

The desk of George Melville, the bearded cataloger, sat nearest the staff entrance. He slouched in his chair with his feet propped on an open desk drawer, casually clicking his computer mouse.

"Hi, Helma," he said, glancing up. He took a swallow from his "Born to Read" cup. "Hold on. I'm just downloading the MARC cataloging record for that new set of Norwegian philosophy." He clicked the mouse again and shoved it away, his grin widening. "By the way, happy birthday. You look exactly the same as the day I unwittingly stumbled into this institution."

"Thank you. Where's Gloria?"

George's face softened. "Glory? She was already here when I dragged myself in this morning. Working away at her little desk like the proverbial. Last time I saw her, she was in the mail room sorting publishers' catalogs, the job everybody loves to hate."

Helma found Gloria Shandy kneeling on the floor of the mail room, surrounded by stacks of brightly colored publishers' catalogs.

Gloria "Call me Glory" Shandy was Bellehaven Public Library's newest reference librarian—petite and pert with a sleek fall of hair almost too red to be true. Freckles dusted her nose in childish blotches. As if to emphasize the effect, Glory dressed not exactly childish but in clothes that a twelve-year-old girl who hadn't yet discovered rock music might wear, including a myriad of girlish beaded bracelets and sparkly hairbands. Men's eyes went dewy at the sight of Glory Shandy, even

George Melville's, as if they were reminded of youthful lost chances and latent possibilities.

Glory raised her head, concentration breaking in her green eyes. "Oh, Helma," she said in her breathy voice. "I didn't expect you to come in on your birthday."

"It *is* a work day," Helma reminded her.

"Well, happy birthday. I hope it's just the most wonderful, happy, happy day you ever had in your whole life. You certainly don't look fifty."

"That may be because I'm forty-two."

Glory gave a tiny, perhaps embarrassed, laugh. "That explains it, then. You don't look forty-two, either."

"I wonder if you might move your Mustang from my parking space," Helma asked her.

Glory's mouth formed a round O which she covered with her hand. "I'm sorry. Of course I will. It's all my fault. Totally. You see, I was so positive you wouldn't come in that I grabbed your place before anyone else could. I'm so tired of parking six blocks away." She jumped up from the floor, publishers' catalogs cascading willy-nilly from her lap. "I'll get my keys."

"It can wait until you're finished here," Helma offered.

"Oh no. I'll do it right now. I wouldn't inconvenience you. I'd never ever do that." She brushed off her gathered skirt as if dust had settled there, which it might very well have since it had been so long since the catalogs had been sorted. "It's no problem." She took two bouncy steps, then stopped. "Oh. I had a phone call from a citizen about our Local Authors project. You weren't here so I handled it for you."

Helma couldn't help it. She stood silent, stunned. Impossible as it was, the Local Authors project had

simply evaporated from her mind. She had been planning the Local Authors project for a year. Tonight's
launch had been coordinated and programmed down to
the ice water, coffee—regular and decaf—and non-
crumbly snacks. Brochures were printed.

Helma's carefully prepared and rehearsed remarks
still sat on her kitchen counter, forgotten. The fact that
the grand launch of the project fell on her birthday had
been unavoidable, the Iva Grover Room in the library
was booked months in advance.

She gazed over Glory's head at the wall clock. She
was only twelve minutes late, the library wouldn't
open for two more hours. "You didn't ask them to call
back when I was here?"

Glory shrugged, the lines deepening between her
eyebrows. "Did I do something wrong? I didn't think
you were coming to work. I told her about your launch
tonight and she said she'd be there."

There'd been a grant for the new collection, a tasteful article in the *Bellehaven Daily News*, attention from
the library world and authors. But horribly, over night
she had forgotten it all. It was an unfathomable situation. Once again that word invaded her vision: *crisis.*

Glory stepped closer to Helma, frowning. "Are you
all right?"

'I'm fine," Helma told her. Even in her distracted
state, Helma felt Glory's intense gaze, *inspecting* her.

"Because if you don't feel well, I'll handle the
launch of Local Authors for you tonight. I've already
thought of a few things I could say to, you know, create
more excitement for the project, like offering awards.
Maybe medals on little plaques." She blinked, looking
upward as if stars shone on the ceiling. "We could be-

come as big as the Booker, or the Edgars, even the National Book Awards."

"I'll be there. I'm prepared," Helma assured her, unable to recall a single word she'd written and rehearsed.

"I only want to help you and the library in every way I can," Glory said, raising her hand and fervently pressing it against her heart.

Chapter 2

The Art of Extortion

For the first time in her career, Helma inadvertently missed the beginning of her shift on the reference desk. Harley Woodworth, who George Melville called "Hardly Worthit," cleared his throat at the entrance to Helma's cubicle, and when she raised her eyes in inquiry, he ducked his head apologetically and pointed to the oversized watch he'd recently purchased because it had a sweeping second hand that made it easier to check his pulse rate. "You're up."

"Oh my," Helma said, rising so quickly the flyer she'd read five times without comprehending either the advantages of one more online citation database or its cost, slipped from her grasp and fluttered into her wastepaper basket. Harley frowned at the flyer, glancing from the wastepaper basket to Helma, opening and closing his jaws without parting his lips, but saying nothing.

The public area of the Bellehaven Public Library buzzed with activity, the usual on Mondays, belying the statistics that claimed, for the first time in fifty-eight years, library use was slipping downward. Unblinking patrons stared into Internet computers, the newspapers were gone from their racks, even the three remaining antique microfiche readers were in use by genealogy fans. The line at the reference desk was too long for Helma to discreetly search the online catalog for a timely book on personal crises.

During her shift, Helma fumbled to find the time zone of Afghanistan, mistakenly sent a woman looking for eighteenth century clothing to a book titled *Dressing for the 1800s*, gave a man who wanted an Interlibrary Loan form a change-of-address card, and admitted to a student that, of course, he was right—Samuel Clemens was Mark Twain *not* Lewis Carroll.

The staff cast curious glances her way, and one of the circulation clerks walked uncertainly toward her, stopped, and returned to the counter. Despite a ridiculous but distinct feeling of impending doom, Helma bravely carried on, making incremental progress against whatever had surfaced that morning Although it would be unusual, she attributed it to nervousness over the Local Authors launch. Yes, that was it.

"Miss Zukas?" a timid voice asked, and Helma looked into the face of a library patron she recognized as Molly.

Molly wasn't one of the "behaviorally unpredictable" patrons notorious for disruptive behavior, but the staff treated her with careful tenderness. Molly was thin, her demeanor fragile, haunted. Her pale hair was pulled severely back from her face, where a birth-mark like a splash of ocean water stained her left cheek.

Molly had been a library user for years, but a month ago she'd begun intensely frequenting the library, sitting for hours at a table near the atlases and filling pages of lined paper, writing with pencils she kept in a plastic zippered case decorated with Snoopy cartoons. She didn't appear unstable, only someone who'd sought the sanctuary of the library during a difficult period in her life. It wasn't unusual.

"How may I help you today?" Helma asked.

"Can I look at the newest *Writer's Market*?" she whispered, stumbling over the words, requesting the directory shelved behind the reference desk because pages tended to disappear from it.

But after Helma gave it to her, Molly remained at the desk, gripping the book with both hands, her knuckles white. Her lips nervously twitched. Helma waited, nodding once to encourage her.

Molly cleared her throat. Her light skin flushed and the birthmark grew more vivid. "I want to . . . I mean . . . Can I come to the Local Authors launch tonight?" she asked in a trembling rush. "I'm not a published author."

"Of course you can," Helma assured her. "You're more than welcome." She doubted the room would be full and the larger the audience, the better.

Molly smiled, absently raising her hand to her face to cover the bluish birthmark. "Oh. Thank you. I'll be there early."

Glory Shandy passed by the reference desk in a stroll that swirled her skirts. "Two books came in already for the Local Authors collection," she announced, holding one up so Helma could see *Papier-mâché Jewelry.* "Isn't that great? I'll put them on your desk, okay?"

"Thank you," Helma agreed, and Glory flounced away, trilling, "Isn't this *fun*?"

No sooner had Helma returned to her cubicle, feeling like her reference desk stint had been comparable to an underwater dive in a silted swamp—if she were a diver, that is—than Ms. May Apple Moon, the director of the Bellehaven Public Library, appeared at the entrance of her cubicle.

"May I speak to you, Helma?" Ms. Moon asked. Ms. Moon rarely entered a cubicle; she leaned into it, keeping her feet firmly planted on territory she considered her sole domain.

"Come in," Helma invited, pointing to the chair beside her desk.

"I believe we'd be more comfortable in my office."

"I'm quite comfortable," Helma told Ms. Moon, whose creamy pink face flushed to red near her ears. "My office, if you please," she snapped and turned around.

Helma followed the director toward her darkened office, newly painted a deep green, "conducive to polite conversation and thoughtful exchange." The walls were hung with fabric art and pictures of warm and friendly beings: cavorting bear cubs, headlight-struck wide-eyed fawns, open-mouthed baby birds, naked babies curled inside flowers. Ms. Moon kept an oak-encased ticking metronome and two baseball-sized crystals on her desk.

A container of yogurt and a bag of chips sat beside a small pyramid of sliced roast beef, enough for three generous sandwiches, remnants of Ms. Moon's no-carb diet.

She'd lost thirty pounds but they'd crept back as the carbohydrates stealthily returned to her meals, although her clothing suggested she might not be aware of that fact.

Helma sat in a chair beside Ms. Moon's desk, instead of across the desk from her, and folded her hands in her lap, waiting. Vaguely Celtic music issued from hidden speakers.

Ms. Moon cleared her throat and caressed one of the crystals with her fingertips. "When someone has an emotional imbalance it's important to deal with it immediately." Ms. Moon smiled and Helma pressed back against her chair.

"I understand," Ms. Moon went on, "that you're feeling distracted today, that you've been unable to maintain the quality of excitement and centeredness vital to every librarian who serves the public"—Ms. Moon hesitated and, as if planned, a cymbal chimed from her recorded music—"that you've been making *mistakes*."

She leaned forward and searched Helma's face. "Helma, what's wrong?" she asked in a deep, liquid voice.

"Nothing's . . ." Helma began but realized denial was useless. "It's just a difficult day, that's all. Everyone has them."

Ms. Moon brought her hands together and raised them to her chin, nodding as if Helma had proffered deep wisdom. "Everyone *does*." She sighed. "But I've never seen *you* like this. Your fellow staff members are deeply concerned. Are you worried about the Local Authors launch tonight?"

"I'm prepared for it," Helma told her.

"Is it because of the library's budget crisis?"

The Bellehaven city budget was experiencing a serious shortfall, and the library had been mentioned as an attractive victim. One city council member had claimed, "Everything's on the Internet, anyway."

"Naturally, I'm concerned about the library budget," Helma said, "but . . ." It might be more advantageous for Ms. Moon to believe that she *did* have budget worries.

But it was too late. "So, it's *not* the budget," Ms. Moon said, nodding as if satisfied. "Tell me, what steps do you intend to take to regain your equilibrium?"

"I'll simply wait until the mood passes, as it will. I see no need to 'take steps.' "

Ms. Moon laughed her tinkling laugh and absently rolled a slice of roast beef into a long tube. "That's far too passive for someone like you. We must be more aggressive."

"*We*" Helma asked, her heart sinking even further.

"I'd never allow an employee to flounder when I've had so much more experience turning life from ordinary to exquisite, from troubled to passionate." She squeezed her eyes closed and her bosom rose in a deep breath. "I'm going to help you."

Helma stood. "No, thank you. Help is not necessary." Then at the sight of Ms. Moon's face, she added, "But I appreciate your interest."

Ms. Moon rose, too. She glanced at her watch, which hung around her neck on a gold chain. "I'll make a few phone calls. Please return to my office in exactly forty-five minutes."

"I . . ." Helma began but Ms. Moon playfully shook her finger at her. "Forty-five minutes. Be here or beware."

"This is unnecessary," Helma protested, "and unwanted."

"Forty-five minutes," Ms. Moon said with finality, dismissing her.

This was not good. Helma left the office but turned back just outside her door. Ms. Moon was already punching buttons on her telephone, and when she spotted Helma gazing at her, she raised her hand and made brisk, cheery, go-away motions.

For a wild and shocking moment, Helma Zukas envisioned ripping the telephone from Ms. Moon's hand and demanding the director cease and desist. But there was the crux, wasn't it: Ms. Moon *was* the director. Her nails bit into her palms. She took three steps away from Ms. Moon's office and nearly bumped into Eve, the fiction librarian.

"Oh, Helma, are you all right?"

"I'm fine," Helma said for the fourth time that morning. That summer, Eve had cut her bushy yellow curls into a tight cap and now, as her hair grew, curls bounded from her scalp in every direction. She gazed into Helma's face, her blue eyes wide and one corkscrew curl standing straight out above her right ear.

"Glory's practicing to take over the launch of Local Authors tonight," Eve said, "so I thought you had to be *really* sick to give that up."

Eve's eyes actually teared up, but then Eve wept over harp music, crying babies, and women who asked for books on surviving divorce.

"I haven't changed my plans about tonight's launch at all," Helma assured her. "Glory misunderstood."

Eve's smile beamed back at her. "What a relief. After all the work you've done. I'll tell Glory—she's so worried about you, she's telling everybody."

George Melville, the cataloger, stepped out of the staff

lounge with a fresh cup of coffee and two chocolate chip cookies. "These are great," he said, holding up the cookies. "Glory brought them. They melt in your mouth."

Glory brought freshly baked sweets every few days. "Just something I made last night," she'd said at a staff meeting. "Baking helps me think." Then laughing and turning to pat her small bottom until George and Harley's eyes glazed, saying, "*I* sure don't need to eat them."

"What's going on?" George asked, biting into his cookie and waving the remainder toward Ms. Moon's office. "You were sequestered in the inner sanctum and Glory said you're sick."

"I'm not sick," Helma told him. "Ms. Moon wanted to discuss library programs,"

George nodded sagely, concluding she meant the Local Authors project. "Ah yes, our local talent. What a hornets' nest that's going to be."

"We're prepared. The guidelines are clear."

"Hah. Don't you believe that for a second. You're going to be dealing with egos the size of Cleveland and excuses for inclusion the size of gnats' nu . . . knees."

"Are you attending tonight?" Helma asked.

"Wouldn't miss it. Is the Moonbeam?"

"If you mean Ms. Moon, she hasn't said." Hopefully Ms. Moon would be engaged elsewhere. The director had a way of turning the simplest activity into a complicated exploration of motives and implications, her speculations rising to loftier planes than most people imagined existed.

"She's got some size to her again," George said. "Such goes the way of faddish diets," and he took another bite of his chocolate chip cookie. "Hey, what do you hear from your buddy Ruth?"

"She's still in Minneapolis," Helma told him. "Painting and living with her friend, Paul."

"No marriage in sight?"

"Not that she's mentioned."

George shook his head and brushed cookie crumbs from his beard, a soft look crossing his face. "This town could use a Ruth. Her disruptiveness wasn't all that bad, you know. Remember her purple phase?"

Helma nodded. Purple clothes, purple paintings, purple eye shadow, none of it quiet or subtle.

Helma recalled Wayne Gallant's phone call that morning. She didn't normally call him, but she *had* been distracted, perhaps even abrupt. She phoned the police station.

"Oh, Miss Zukas," the receptionist said when Helma requested the chief. "He's not here. He was planning to stop by the library sometime this morning."

Helma hung up, sat down at her desk, and absently sorted her morning mail by size, waiting for Ms. Moon's forty-five minutes to end.

And, exactly forty-five minutes later, Helma knocked on the doorjamb of Ms. Moon's open office. The music had been switched off and Ms. Moon hummed what sounded like a cheery Rodgers & Hammerstein tune. She nodded to her own music, smiling, beckoning Helma inside.

Helma entered but remained standing. She thought better on her feet.

"You're going be very pleased," Ms. Moon announced. She held out a sheet of paper to Helma.

Helma took the paper. A bluebird flying over a rainbow decorated the top of the page. Beneath it, in Ms.

Moon's round handwriting, the *i*s dotted with empty round circles, was written:

An Age of Certain Years: Tues, 7:30
    Legion Hall
Battery Cables for Your Career: Wed,
    7:30 Sandy H.S. Library
Commitment Issues: Thurs, 7:30 Public
    Market basement
Dealing with Troubled Pets: Fri, 3 P.M.
    Pet Barn

"Starting tomorrow. And don't worry," Ms. Moon said as Helma puzzled over the paper, "you can leave early on Friday."

"What is this?" Helma asked, reading the words over and over, trying to make sense of them.

"Opportunity," Ms. Moon said, her voice dropping in sincerity. "Opportunity to explore every issue troubling you. I chose them based on the major aspects of your life. Your career, your love life, your cat, and even that today is your birthday and you're statistically over halfway through your life-span, a time when many women feel confused and benefit from guidance."

Only one phrase in Ms. Moon's list penetrated Helma's mind. "My *love life*?" she replied.

"Or lack," Ms. Moon said sanguinely. "Everyone knows you and the chief are unable to get to"—she

waved her hands and winked—"second base. This will
help."

Ms. Moon spread her arms as if to embrace Helma.
Helma stepped backward until she felt a chair against
the back of her legs.

"I've managed to reserve a place in each of these
sessions for you. You'll be with other women who
share your concerns, who assist each other on the journey of self-discovery. You'll emerge a more fulfilled
and self-aware woman."

Helma could only stare dumbfoundedly at her director. What was she talking about? Ms. Moon, still beaming, leaned back and flicked the button of her CD
player. As whale song moaned into the office and
Helma studied the days and times beside the four top-
ics, one day after another, beginning the following
night, it finally dawned on her.

"You have registered *me* for group-counseling sessions?" she asked in what she knew was a low voice,
but outside Ms. Moon's office, beyond her open door,
the normal rustle and clatter of the library workroom
went dead silent.

Ms. Moon nodded and clasped her hands together.
"Yes. It wasn't easy getting sessions one night after the
other at this late date, but fortunately I have a long association in the field. They're all held right here in
town; isn't that exciting?"

Helma set the sheet of paper on Ms. Moon's desk
beside the ticking metronome. "I don't attend group-
counseling sessions."

The director's face pinked, her smile faltered, then
recovered. "Perhaps not in the past," she said in her

softest, most dulcet, most dangerous voice, "but this, as you can see, is now."

"And now is exactly the same as in the past," Helma told her. "I don't attend groups."

"This is in your best interest *and* in the best interest of the library. I recognize the warning signs of some-one in the early stages of crisis."

Helma's heart leaped as Ms. Moon spoke aloud the word that had been pursuing her all morning: *crisis.*

"Of course, I'm not unreasonable," Ms. Moon went on, her smile widening. "If you prefer not to attend, you don't have to."

Every fiber of Helma's being went on alert.

"Another option would be to take a few days off, travel to the islands and walk the beaches, listen to the waves, and translate the music of your soul." Ms. Moon shook her head, considering the beauty of it.

Helma remained silent, knowing there was more to come.

"I happen to know there's a ferry for San Juan Island that leaves this afternoon at three ten. You have plenty of time to pack a bag, make reservations at that pleas-ant bed-and-breakfast overlooking the harbor, and be on your way to a relaxing few days."

"Tonight is the launch of the Local Authors project," Helma reminded her, thinking of her arrangements, the radio spots and circulars, and burgeoning community interest.

Ms. Moon only smiled.

Helma bit her lip, her back straightening. Anyone glancing into the director's office at that moment would have spied a tableau of two women facing each other as rigid as stone, the air between them as electric as an imminent Midwest thunderstorm transplanted to the Pacific Northwest.

Ms. Moon was the first to speak. "Glory Shandy has been following the Local Authors project, always willing to help, learning from you, full of admiration for your organizational skills. Why, I believe she looks up to you as a mentor, isn't that gratifying?"

"I will not—" Helma began

"You've put tremendous effort into the Local Authors project," Ms. Moon interrupted. "If it's successful, it'll raise the public's awareness of the library. It could even help with our funding"—she lifted the piece of paper from her desk and held it out toward Helma by two fingers—"but I'm sure Glory could step in with very little preparation on her part."

Helma kept her hands at her sides.

Ms. Moon waved the paper as if a breeze had caught it. "It's your decision, of course. Both or neither. But Glory would do a *wonderful* job. You could leave her your notes, and I'm sure she'd *love* to have you serve as her assistant when you return."

As if she had no will, Helma's arm slowly reached for the paper. "This is blackmail."

Ms. Moon's smile relaxed into beatification as Helma removed from her fingertips the paper ordering her to attend four back-to-back, night-after-night counseling sessions.

"Now don't you feel better?" Ms. Moon called after Helma. "Have fun, fun, fun at your launch tonight."

Chapter 3

The Launch

At five o'clock, Helma drove back to her apartment to retrieve her remarks for the opening night launch of the Local Authors project, taking a few minutes to set food on her balcony for Boy Cat Zukas, and retrieve her mail. Boy Cat Zukas, glared down at her from the overhang of her roof, his back raised as if he were warming up to pounce. The day was still crisp, but high wispy clouds stretched across the western sky, blunting the late afternoon sun.

Three square envelopes—birthday cards—sat on top of ads and window envelopes. One from her nephews in Michigan, one each from her mother and Aunt Em, even though they both lived across town and were attending tonight's launch "to support your career, dear."

No card from her friend Ruth in Minneapolis, although she wasn't surprised. Ruth was likely to call in the middle of the night three weeks from now and ask in a puzzled voice, "Did you have a birthday? Did I miss it or something?"

None from Chief of Police Wayne Gallant, either. No call during the day, no discreet gift like last year's bottle of Elizabeth Arden Spiced Green Tea perfume, no roses like the year before. What had Ms. Moon meant: "*Everyone* knows you and the chief are unable to get to second base?" Aside from the crude baseball analogy, *everyone* knew?

He wasn't obligated after all, it wasn't as if they had an *understanding*, although of course there had been moments when they'd nearly agreed to come to an agreement.

Still, there was the aborted phone call that morning and the police receptionist's assertion he planned to stop by the library. But he hadn't.

Helma started—she'd wasted six minutes *standing* there, as if she were in a trance.

Boy Cat Zukas had already wolfed down his food and now stared in at her through her sliding glass door, one eye squinted. Helma had reluctantly adopted the stray cat when he lay unclaimed and near death after an automobile accident. He'd obviously never lived with well-mannered people and she herself hadn't desired a pet, especially a cat, since she was twelve years old. She and Boy Cat Zukas had formed an uneasy relationship based on propinquity and a truce of mutual tolerance.

She cast a last glance around her apartment, mentally checking that her furnishings were in order, the twenty-five-watt bulb over the stove turned on, her curtains closed. All this she did automatically, missing the little stab of pleasure she normally felt at leaving order in her wake.

It wasn't a crisis at all, she thought as she tucked the piece of paper listing Ms. Moon's group sessions into her slotted mail holder where she filed specious solicitations for money. It was unaccustomed nervousness over the Local Authors project. Once tonight was over, her life would return to normal, the crisis would evaporate, and she would toss Ms. Moon's list into her trash.

The sign over the door of the Iva Grover Room in the library warned that its official capacity was limited to 135 people. Helma hoped for forty or fifty at most. To be safe she had ordered refreshments for sixty. By 6:20, everything was in order: folding chairs in rows, refreshments, fresh-brewed coffee, brochures beside the door. A sign balanced on an easel in the hallway read LOCAL AUTHORS.

Titles for the campaign and the new collection of local authors' books, had been offered by the staff including "Bards of Bellehaven," which George Melville had immediately amended to "Bards & Nobles," then "Local Talent," again offered by George, but finally, the simple "Local Authors" had stuck.

"Isn't this nice?"

"She's so organized."

Helma looked up from straightening the first row of chairs to see her mother and Aunt Em standing by the refreshment table. They each carried library books.

"We're early, dear," Helma's mother said, "so we could bring you these. Happy Birthday." She offered Helma a bulging brown bag with handles. Bows and gaily decorated wrapping paper peeked over the edge.

"But I thought we were celebrating this weekend," Helma said. Her mother's hair was a new, brighter shade of blond and she wore yellow slacks that were surprisingly snug.

"We will, we will," Aunt Em said in her lingering Lithuanian accent, "but it's not right for such a day to escape." In a month, Aunt Em would be celebrating her own eighty-eighth birthday.

Through a series of unsettling twists and turns, first Helma's mother had moved to Bellehaven from Michigan, then Aunt Em. Now they lived on the opposite side of Bellehaven in a retirement home with a reputation among the senior set for "fast living."

Helma's mother led Aunt Em to two chairs directly in front of the podium, directly in Helma's line of vision. The first thing Helma would see each time she raised or lowered her eyes would be her mother.

"You might be more comfortable in the back in case you want to leave early," Helma suggested. "If you get tired."

"Hah," Aunt Em said as she settled into the metal chair. "Not me. I want to hear your every word."

A woman in a heavy wool sweater peeked uncertainly into the room, then picked up a brochure and gave Helma a happy nod. It was only 6:30, still a half hour before the meeting.

"Could you keep this until after the session?" Helma asked her mother, tucking the brown bag of birthday gifts beneath her mother's chair

Her mother nodded, pushing the bag further beneath her chair with her foot. "Don't open it until you get home. Em's gift"—she glanced to the left and right, then rolled her eyes—"is private, not for the library to see."

By 6:50, in a town where being on time was considered rudely eager, every chair was taken and library pages were pressed into service to set up more. The coffeepot was empty, only crumbs remained on the trays. Both the coffee and ice water were gone.

Helma's mother and Aunt Em moved forward into the new front row of chairs and now sat at arm's length from the podium whispering to each other as they watched the room fill, every now and then raising their fists at Helma in rah-rah motions.

All Helma's brochures had disappeared.

"I'll photocopy more for you," Glory Shandy offered, suddenly appearing at Helma's elbow. "Isn't this great?"

Helma surveyed the growing crowd, taken aback. Bellehaven had gained a reputation as a writers' and artists' haven, along with luring in the active to its water and mountains, and wealthy retirees to its pricy waterfront. Native Bellehavenites were a rarity. The city on the bay was growing by over one thousand a year, but could there possibly be *this* many authors in Bellehaven? Conversation swirled around her.

"Who's publishing her now? I thought her stuff was poison."

"Can you believe he called that *writing*? You know what Dorothy Parker said."

"She said her publisher was Posers' Press. Never heard of them."

By 6:55, not another chair could be squeezed into the room. It was worse than standing-room only; people were jammed up outside the doors, lining the hallway and craning to see inside.

"I'm getting you a mike," George Melville the cataloger said as he pushed the podium so close to the back wall there was barely room for Helma to squeeze behind it.

"A microphone?" she asked dumbly.

"I'll hook up a speaker in the hallway for the overflow, like we did when the Pets Are People Too speakers were here."

When she continued gazing at him, George paused and awkwardly patted her shoulder, leaning closer so she could hear him over the noisy crowd. "Buck up, kiddo. You're gonna be a star."

"I didn't expect . . ."

"Who knew what writers lurked in the depths of Bellehaven's closets, eh?"

Helma stood behind the podium busily sliding one paper over another, not seeing what she was doing, in reality keeping her eyes closed and performing the breathing exercise that had never failed her: inhale for a count of four, hold for four, exhale for eight, ignoring the rising cacophony of voices, the bustling library staff, the advancing clock, the knot of iron that had appeared that morning and still refused to vacate her stomach.

Suddenly, silence forced her to raise her head. George Melville stood five feet to her side, his arms raised like an old photo of Richard Nixon. The crowd, a blurred backdrop of faces, waited, the air taut with expectancy.

George glanced over at Helma and although his role was unplanned, began to speak: "This is the launch of Bellehaven Public Library's Local Authors project," he said. "Just in case you're in the wrong place, you can leave now."

A few laughs, but no one moved.

"Okay, then. All right. Everybody's an author. We have contact." He pointed and bowed to Helma like a ringmaster making way for the high-wire act. "So let's hear what Miss Helma Zukas, who's the instigator of this project, has to say,"

Helma cleared her throat and the sound bounced back at her from the speakers. "Welcome," she said, glancing down at her notes. "Here at Bellehaven Public Library, we plan to recognize . . ."

A wildly waving hand from two rows back interrupted her. Twenty minutes had been scheduled at the end to answer questions but what could one matter now? She nodded to the mustachioed man. He stood as if this were a presidential news conference. "Can you define the term 'local author'?" he asked and sat down.

"Certainly," Helma said graciously. She'd anticipated this question. "We're defining a local author as a published author who lived in Bellehaven longer than three months."

A woman near the door popped up and without waiting for acknowledgment called out, "Well, *I've* lived in Bellehaven for twenty-two years and my son wrote a book. If you add up all his visits, it equals more than three months."

"We're defining this as an established residency," Helma clarified.

"Do books have to be written *while* you live here or can they have been written any time, and then you have to live here for three months?"

"Ken Kesey lived in my backyard in the sixties for a summer," a man with a long gray ponytail said.

"He was a nationally known author," Helma told the crowd. "I believe we have all of his books."

"He never did give me back my sleeping bag," the man continued.

"The Local Author collection will be housed on designated oak shelving made by a fine local carpenter," Helma interjected.

"What about e-books?" a voice called from the back. "I've had two books published on the Internet. Are you prejudiced toward Internet books?"

"We have Internet computers," Helma tried.

"That doesn't mean they were good books," someone else said. "You can put *anything* on the Internet."

"What if we don't have a publisher yet?" a woman asked, raising her hand at the same time. "I know it's going to happen soon, though. Will you accept unpublished manuscripts?"

"Oh, don't do that," another woman warned. "Somebody could steal your ideas."

"Hey!" a youthful voice called. "Your library could be like that Brautigan book, where you collect all the manuscripts that people can't get published."

Beside Helma, George said softly, not realizing how close he stood to the microphone, "Library, hell. For that we'd need to be a Costco warehouse."

Murmurs and buzzes rose from the crowd and George leaned closer to the microphone, grinning apologetically. "Sorry. Just joking."

"Each book will have a Local Author bookplate and a special designation in our online catalog," Helma said. "We'll also publish an annual listing, a bibliography, both online and in print, of all the local authors and their works. These will be available in bookstores, tourist offices, and to other libraries. They'll serve as models to libraries across the country."

"You mean books published by *real* publishers, not self-published, right?"

To the side, a woman stood up, holding a sheet of paper so nervously the page fluttered in her hands. Helma recognized Molly, their shy library patron who'd asked if she could attend. Her hair was down now, the left side covering her birthmark. She looked terrified but resolute.

Molly's soft but quavering voice cut through the others, drawing attention by its uncertainty. "Will you include poetry?" she asked.

At last, a safe question. "Yes, we will include poetry," Helma said, to the immediate response of someone saying, "Well, there isn't much of *that* that's not self-published."

"I'm glad," Molly said, taking a deep breath, "because I've dedicated my life to writing poetry," and in her trembling voice she began to read from the sheet of paper she could barely hold steady.

> *My heart lies in this pit*
> *As dead as ancient lit.*
> *Forgotten by you,*
> *Not a page of it new.*
> *Oh why oh why did you leave me?*

The crowd fell silent, uncertain. By the last line, a few titters floated through the room, then Molly ended in barely a whisper, "By Molly Bittern," and dropped back into her chair. Scattered hands sympathetically clapped, nearly drowning out the voice that said, "What's so special about being in a collection with *that*?"

Helma saw Molly lower her head. "Thank you, Molly," she said quickly in a voice that cut off any further comment from listeners.

A young woman in glasses and short hair stood politely waiting until Helma acknowledged her. "I am a published local author." She said it defiantly, raising her chin. "My work is aimed at the adult audience." Here, every male in the audience turned considering eyes toward the plain woman.

"Where can I buy it?" a man sitting behind her asked, and she turned, gazing at him just as appraisingly.

"I'm sorry," she said politely, "but it's not illustrated."

More titters and guffaws.

"Do you intend to *censor* this collection?"

"I write magazine articles. Why doesn't that count?"

"My advertisements have been seen nationwide. I qualify as an author."

Helma suddenly was overcome by profound exhaustion. Her eyes threatened to close even as she stood at the podium, her useless notes before her. She struggled to recall how she'd intended to close this meeting. Something about submitting published books to her for inclusion, about telephoning her with any questions. She couldn't open her mouth to say a single word. The crowd seemed to be surging forward, pressing against her.

And in a horrified moment, she realized her mother was holding her arms out, struggling to rise from her chair and come to her daughter's rescue.

Helma raised her hand to stop her mother, and was

distracted by a disturbance at the doorway to the Iva
Grover Room. Heads turned. Voices trailed off. Helma
squinted toward the rear of the crowd. Now what?

It wasn't that the crowd parted; it didn't. There was
no need for it to because, there, towering inches above
everyone in the doorway, her bushy dark hair electric
with a Bride of Frankenstein streak, her lips upturned
in glee and eyes bright, stood Ruth Winthrop. Her big
voice rang out, cutting off a question about the library
offering money to compensate local authors.

"Am I missing some kind of public coup?"

Chapter 4

—Crossed Signals

The crowd's attention shifted from Helma to the arrival of Ruth. More than one local author reached for pencil and paper and began to take notes.

Ruth made no move to enter the room but stood where she was, seemingly—but definitely not, Helma knew—unaware of her impact. She waggled her fingers hello at Helma and smiled, nodding once as if in encouragement.

Helma felt a shred of lightness enter her troubled heart. And not just because the crowd, which had been closing in on her, faltered as if a challenge had been issued from the castle to a pitchfork-wielding mob.

There were people on earth who somehow managed not exactly to trivialize problems but who put them in perspective merely by their presence. And although Ruth lived in a cyclone of problems of her own manufacture, Helma had to admit Ruth was one of those people.

They had known each other since they were ten years old in Scoop River, Michigan, when Ruth's frustrated parents had sent her to St. Alphonse Catholic School in vain hopes the nuns would instill a modicum of decorum and common sense in their daughter. From enemies, Helma and Ruth had developed a bewildering friendship. Being in Ruth's company longer than an hour left Helma as disoriented as if she'd been trapped inside one of those rooms filled with balls and small children. And after an hour in Helma's presence, Ruth began to tap her feet and blow upward from her lower lip as if she were attempting to cool her forehead.

They'd made their separate ways to Bellehaven, Helma for her first professional librarian position, Ruth following a rock musician lover who'd moved on without her.

Over a year ago Ruth had moved to Minneapolis, following the only man Helma had ever seen her cry over: a calm and reasonable man with whom Ruth held absolutely nothing in common. She and Ruth had continued their friendship through phone calls, emails, and the dead art of letter writing.

And now here she was back in Bellehaven, unannounced as usual.

Beside Helma, George Melville's smile stretched so wide his beard rose. "Ah," he said. "Just in the nick of time, a diversion."

Helma spotted Glory Shandy by the door holding a stack of photocopied brochures, gazing up at Ruth with open mouth.

Helma had read once in a well-researched and excruciatingly documented history of the Peloponnesian War that a commander's well-timed decision to withdraw while his troops were still able to fight could ultimately not only win the battle, but the war as well.

So with her lips only a half inch from the microphone, Helma announced in her silver dime voice that left listeners without rebuttal, "Thank you all for coming. On your way out, please pick up a brochure that fully explains the Local Authors project."

"Amen," George said, letting out a deep breath.

The assembly obediently rose and headed in a muddle for the door at the back of the room while Ruth made her way against the flow toward the front. Helma waited, knowing she'd be lost in the milling crowd whereas Ruth would effortlessly sail through it.

Ruth was just over six feet in her bare feet, and as a child had alternately wept or resorted to fists over names like "Daddy Long Legs," and comments such as "How's the weather up there?" But once Ruth had discovered the pleasures of attention, no matter what the source, she'd embraced her height, increasing her stature with high heels, bushy hair, and clothing that accentuated not only her length but her presence. She never slouched, didn't lower her head to speak to those shorter, and only stepped out of the visual line of children. "Good posture will get you anywhere and anything," she liked to say.

What Helma had observed was that it mainly got Ruth trouble.

"Helm," Ruth said now, her voice easily carrying over the heads of the intervening fifteen feet of people.

"Helma," Helma automatically corrected, but quietly, unheard by even her mother and Aunt Em, who still sat in their front-row seats craning their necks to see what was going on.

"I came to wish you a happy birthday in person. Are you surprised?"

"Definitely. And pleased."

Ruth wore red leggings and what might have been a dress on a shorter woman but was a black tunic on Ruth. With her strappy high heels, her legs appeared to begin at Helma's shoulder level.

Ruth gazed after the departing throng. "Who'da thunk a bunch of writers could get so excited?"

"Were you here for the entire meeting?"

Ruth shook her head and metal earrings tinkled like distant bells. "Just enough to see the crowd turn after that impromptu poetry reading. What were you thinking, shutting all these creative types in the same room?"

"This project recognizes *their* talent and accomplishments. I thought they'd be more . . ." Helma stopped, hearing the querulous note in her voice.

"You expected gratitude? We rarely are, you know. Ever alert for the trick clause that stops us dead in our tracks." Ruth was an artist whose bright, confusing canvases had earned her a name in the Northwest and an erratic living in Bellehaven.

Ruth peered more closely at Helma and said in a quieter voice, "Don't worry, it'll sort itself out. Recognition is a new and refreshing idea, and it takes awhile for appreciation to sink in."

"How's life in the Heartland?" George asked Ruth.

"Why George," Ruth said, lightly touching his shoulder. "I can't believe you even noticed I was gone."

.

"Once or twice," he said, still smiling.

"It's good. Life is good," Ruth said. "Yes, it is."

Even in her distracted state, Helma noticed the shadow that passed over Ruth's face.

"Where are you staying?" George asked.

"With Helma."

Helma couldn't remember a single time Ruth had stayed at her apartment when it hadn't led to disastrous results.

"You haven't capitulated and given Boy Cat Zukas your second bedroom yet, have you?" Ruth asked Helma.

"No. It's available."

"Oh, hey. Look who's here," Ruth said, waving toward the front row of chairs where Helma's mother and Aunt Em gathered up their books and bags and eyed Ruth, both smiling, if Helma's mother's smile was a little more strained.

"Ruthie!" Aunt Em exclaimed as Ruth *did* bend down, to hug Aunt Em. "You look as bright as sunshine," she told her. "We've missed you."

"Did you come alone?" Helma's mother, who was both appalled and avidly curious about Ruth's love life, asked.

"Just me," Ruth said in a bright voice that closed the subject. "You two are as beautiful as the last time I saw you."

"She still tries," Aunt Em said, nodding toward Helma's mother, who unconsciously pulled back her shoulders and smoothed her blouse. "I've gone to seed. Beauty is for the young, like you two."

"Don't you believe it," Ruth told her. "Is Helma giving you a ride home? Let me carry some of this stuff for you."

"Oh no, thank you," Helma's mother said. She handed Helma the brown bag holding her birthday presents. "Here comes Jason to help us. We came over in the minivan." She held up her hand and whispered, "Isn't he a doll?"

A tall young man in slacks and a T-shirt stepped forward. He was nearly as tall as Ruth, and she gave him an appraising glance as she did every man no matter his age who fell within her height-compatibility range.

"You gave a nice talk, Wilhelmina," Aunt Em told Helma. "Don't pay any attention to the rude ones."

"That's right," Helma's mother added. "You were very professional. Where would they all be without librarians?" She frowned at Helma. "Are you all right, dear?" Then, as if Helma were eight years old instead of newly forty-two, she placed the back of her hand against Helma's forehead. "You're so quiet."

"I'm just tired," Helma assured her.

"Ready, girls?" Jason asked, holding an arm out to Aunt Em. The room had nearly cleared.

"Bye now," Aunt Em called over her shoulder as she smiled up at Jason and took his arm. "You come over with Helma, Ruthie, and I'll make you *kugelis*."

"I'm counting on it," Ruth told her, waving before she turned back to Helma. "So what do you feel compelled to clean up here before we can leave?"

"Nothing, really. My purse is . . ."

"Yoo-hoo, Wilhelmina."

Helma looked up, saw Aunt Em holding up one hand, using it to block people's view of her. She jabbed her index finger in the direction of Chief of Police Wayne Gallant, standing in the doorway talking to

Glory Shandy. Glory nodded vigorously in assent to something the chief had just said.

At Aunt Em's "yoo hoo," the chief looked up and grinned, then left Glory and joined Ruth and Helma. "Good to see you back in town, Ruth."

"Thanks. It's only a social visit. No murders or criminal misconduct." Wayne Gallant was six foot three. And Ruth couldn't help it—she moved closer to him, as if basking in his comparative height, a smile of satisfaction on her face.

"Excellent." Helma felt his cool policeman's eyes appraising her. "Hello, Helma. I heard you had an active crowd here tonight."

Helma nodded. "The local authors are very interested in this project," ignoring Ruth's guffaw.

"You've taken on a big assignment," he said, eyes still unusually intent on her face, his hands in his pockets. Above the sound of the departing crowd, she heard the jingle-jangle of coins in his pocket.

"Perhaps bigger than I realized." Was it Helma's imagination or was Wayne Gallant's manner growing cooler the longer he spoke to her?

"Did you have a pleasant birthday?" he asked. Curiously, his blue eyes narrowed. He tipped his head slightly and a wave of his graying hair fell forward, covering his widow's peak.

"My mind was on the Local Authors launch, so my birthday was actually unremarkable," Helma told him.

"Well, thanks," Ruth interjected.

"Except for Ruth's appearance of course," Helma amended. "That was definitely the highlight."

"Nothing unusual that required a response from you?" he asked Helma.

It was a puzzling question. "Nothing as important as tonight's launch," she told him, watching as Wayne actually seemed to pull back from her.

"Well, the day's not over yet, right?" Ruth said, glancing from Helma to the chief.

"Twenty-four hours," he said coolly, "just like any other day."

Ruth's lips pursed and Helma blinked long enough to see the word *crisis* flash on the inside of her eyelids.

"How are the kids?" Ruth's words fell into the silence and the chief's face softened a little.

"Doing good," he said, a smile finally tweaking his lips. "Both wrestling with high school life. They'll be here for Thanksgiving."

"Hey, Wayne," Bailey Tompkins, a City Council member, called. "When you're finished there, can you settle an argument for us?"

"Be right there," he said. If this were 1938 and he had worn a hat, he would have undoubtedly tipped it to Helma and Ruth. "Have a good visit, ladies."

As they watched him walk away, Ruth repeated, " 'Ladies?' What's going on, Helm?"

"I didn't believe anything was," Helma said, watching as Bailey slapped Wayne Gallant's back in greeting.

"Don't tell me he forgot your birthday?"

"Obviously he didn't because he asked if it had been pleasant."

"But nothing else?"

Helma shook her head. They stepped aside as Jack the Janitor carried a stack of chairs past them.

Ruth whistled and then said brightly, "But the day isn't over, he said so himself." She glanced at her watch. "That's right. We still have nearly four hours left. What's say we go to Joker's and celebrate? I'll buy you a mildly alcoholic drink."

"Thanks, but I prefer to go home. You go ahead. I'm sure there are a lot of people who'll be happy to see you."

"No doubt. But if you don't mind, I'll spend your birthday with you. That's why I'm here, after all. Besides, I bet the policeman of your dreams is planning a late-night surprise."

"Excuse me," a bald man who Helma had noted standing to the side said, "I have a comment about the local authors' books."

"Yes?" Helma asked, preparing for a new challenge.

"Congratulations," he said. "It's an excellent idea, very supportive of the writing community."

"Thank you," she said in relief and pleasure.

Still he stood in front of her. "My ex-wife wrote a book," he said. "It's not true, what she says. I just want to say that." And he walked away.

Helma tucked her notes into her manila folder. The room was nearly back to order. Chairs were stacked, the podium pushed to the side. Glory Shandy busily cleaned off the refreshment table, George at her elbow, eagerly holding out his hands for the cream and sugar containers.

"I'm ready," she told Ruth. "Do you have a rental car?"

"Nope. I took a taxi from the airport."

"Where did you leave your luggage?"

Ruth patted the gray leather purse she carried. "This is it."

True, the purse was large but definitely a purse not a suitcase, and hardly even bulging. "You traveled across the country without any luggage?"

"It was a spur-of-the-moment decision," Ruth said, shrugging, not meeting Helma's eyes.

"My plane landed just before dark," Ruth said as Helma pulled her car out of the library parking lot. "O Little Town of Bellehaven has grown this past year."

"That's what our newspaper keeps telling us. The city's stretched to the max financially, trying to keep up with infrastructure."

Ruth yawned. "Yeah, yeah, same old story. So they're threatening to cut budgets again, I bet, right?"

Helma nodded. "The library has been mentioned."

She slowed her Buick. A block ahead of them, along Cedar Street, emergency lights flashed.

"Uh oh," Ruth warned, peering through the windshield. "Must be something big. Look at all those lights."

"The city sends police, ambulance, and fire trucks to every emergency call they respond to," Helma said. A more enticing candidate for budget cuts than the library, she thought.

"Let's check it out," Ruth told her. "Pull over."

"We'll take Forest," she told Ruth, turning to the south, one block before the flashing lights. It would add only three minutes to the drive from the library to the Bayside Arms.

"Too bad," Ruth said wistfully, gazing back at the receding lights. "I haven't seen those guys in a while."

After they'd toasted Helma's birthday with the last of Helma's red wine, Helma opened her gifts from her mother and Aunt Em: a cookbook, *Cooking for Two*, and a sweater from her mother; a bottle of wine from both of them, and in the last small package from Aunt

Em, a black matching set of underwear constructed mainly of lace.

"Your Aunt Em has got some taste, doesn't she?" Ruth asked.

The label was expensive, slightly risqué, the fabric feather light. Helma ran her fingers across the delicate seams, thinking she and Aunt Em shared surprisingly similar, but very private, tastes.

Ruth lay sprawled on Helma's sofa with Boy Cat Zukas on her belly, his eyes closed. "Nothing's changed here," she said, gazing around Helma's apartment. "Consistency in an inconstant world. I was counting on this."

"Are you in some type of difficulty, Ruth?"

Ruth laughed her big laugh. "I might call it . . ."

"Is that Ruth?" The voice came through the screen door from the balcony of the next apartment. The October night was pleasantly cool and Helma had left the door open an inch.

"TNT?" Ruth asked, dumping Boy Cat Zukas on the floor and getting up in one long movement. She banged open the sliding glass doors and stepped onto Helma's balcony.

Through the open door, Helma heard TNT say, "So you've come to cheer her up? Good," and then their voices dropped too low to hear even though Helma bent down on her knees beside the sliding glass door to be sure no crumbs from the snack she'd fixed had scattered to the floor.

It was 10:30 and her phone hadn't rung. She'd checked it twice, once in case she'd accidentally unplugged it, and once to be sure there hadn't been any interruption in service. Both times, the dial tone had buzzed back at her.

Ruth returned from the balcony, leaving the door wide open, and yawning. "TNT told me that you're, as he put it, 'on the ropes.' What's up?"

"I was worried about the Local Authors launch," Helma told her as she slid the balcony door closed. "That's all."

Ruth shook her head. "You? I don't believe that for a second. It's the man, isn't it? Without my guidance, you couldn't keep the romance alive. You two have been push-me pull-youing around each other for years. Somebody's *gotta* make a move here." She reached for the telephone. "What's his number? I'll call him."

"No, Ruth."

"Nine-one-one ought to do it," Ruth said, punching buttons.

As she hit the second 1, Helma reached out and un-plugged her telephone.

Ruth gazed at her calmly, holding the dead phone. "You are a coward," she said in a withering voice.

"I simply don't conduct my life as you do," Helma told her.

"From what I can see, you don't conduct your life at all." Ruth dropped the receiver on the phone with a bang and yawned again. "Damn, I'm still on Minnesota time. I'm going to bed. Let's talk in the morning."

"I didn't know you ever paid attention to the time," Helma said. Ruth could paint all night long and sleep or eat according to an unfathomable internal clock.

"That's what a regular life will do to you," Ruth said drily. She swept up Boy Cat Zukas and headed for the second bedroom. "And thanks for taking me in, I mean it."

Helma reconnected the phone. After she'd rearranged the cushions and pillows and refolded her afghan, she sat on the sofa and gazed out her window at the dark swath of Washington Bay. A buoy blinked back at her. To the north, in downtown Bellehaven, she glimpsed the distant emergency lights from whatever had detoured them. One by one the lights in homes along the bay clicked off while night closed in.

At ten minutes after midnight, after checking her landing to be sure nothing had been belatedly delivered, Helma went to bed. Her birthday was over and her telephone had not rung. The only sound she heard as she closed her bedroom door was Ruth's snoring.

Chapter 5

A Poet Remembered

"Helma. Wake up! You've got to see this!"

Helma sat bolt upright in her bed, fumbling for the bat-shaped "fish wacker" her nephew had made for her in sixth grade shop years ago, and which she moved from beneath her bed to her bedside table every night.

It was when she felt the smooth wood of the handle that she remembered Ruth had spent the night in her spare bedroom, and that the screeching voice belonged to her. She leaped from her bed, forgetting her slippers and robe, running from her bedroom. Had something happened to Boy Cat Zukas?

Ruth stood in brief red underwear, waving a can of diet cola toward the television. "Can you believe it?" Her hair bushed out in every direction. "I came out here looking for something caffeinated for breakfast and flipped on the news to make sure the world was still intact. And look at that, would you?"

"What?" Helma asked, trying to hear Gillian Hovel, who always slowly and deliberately pronounced her name, "Ho-vell," the indefatigably cheery local news anchor. The woman valiantly tried to appear serious and concerned but still looked like she was practicing "Sad" in front of a mirror.

"There. See?"

A woman's photo appeared over the newscaster's left shoulder and Ruth started in again. "Isn't that the woman from your thingee last night? You know, the broken hearted 'heart-in-a-pit, dead-as-lit' poetess?"

The woman had shorter, better-tended hair than Molly the poetess, plus she wore eye-enhancing makeup and was a few years younger. The birthmark on her cheek was only a light shadow. But yes, it could very well be Molly. If only Ruth would be quiet so Helma could hear the details.

"There! Did you hear that?" Ruth went on. "Milieu? Who names their kid Milieu?"

"I believe she said Molly Lou," Helma said, trying to see around Ruth's waving arms.

"Just as bad," Ruth scoffed. "And Bittern? A bittern's a bird, isn't it?"

"It's a freshwater wading bird," Helma answered automatically. "Rarely seen."

Gillian the newscaster brightened to her normal perkiness as she switched to a story about two children who parlayed their allowance and sweet faces into three cases of chicken noodle soup for homeless men.

Ruth took another swig from her cola can. "Isn't that something?" she asked as she wiped her mouth.

"Ruth, I did not hear one single word of that story."

Ruth rolled her eyes. "Why do you think I called you out here? So you could."

Helma let it go. "What happened?"

Ruth drew her finger across her neck. "Dead. Hit and run. On her way home from the library last night."

"After the launch of Local Authors?" Helma was horrified. "Molly was killed after the meeting in the library?"

"Looks that way. Crossing Sixth and Cedar."

Helma remembered Molly shyly approaching the reference desk the previous morning; her sorrowful uncertainty as she asked if she could attend the launch, the thin woman's quavering but determined voice as she read her—even Helma had to admit—amateurish poem at the launch. But dead? A tremor of sorrow for Molly forced her to take a deep involuntary breath.

"Did they arrest someone?" she asked Ruth.

"Nope. Where'd you get that nightgown?"

"My mother. Those must have been the lights we saw on our way home. That was near Cedar and Sixth."

"I *told* you to stop." Ruth rubbed her arms as if they were cold. "I didn't think her poetry was *that* bad."

Helma handed Ruth her shirt, which she'd left hanging over the rocking chair. "Ruth, Molly's poetry may have lacked a professional writer's polish but it had nothing to do with her death."

"Says you. I know better than you how these things work. She stole some teenager's coffee shop musings. A girl, I bet. Not many guys get quite so plaintive, at least in my experience. And when she heard Molly reciting her deep, dark wrenching rhymes, she followed her and killed her. I wonder if . . ." She stopped and looked closely at Helma, frowning. "Oh God, Helma, I'm sorry. Did you *know* her?"

Helma shook her head. "No, but I had association with Molly through the library."

"She worked there?"

"She was a patron. For the last month or so she's been spending a lot of time in the library, writing all day long."

"She was one of your weird ones?" Ruth asked and drained her can of cola.

"Not at all. My impression was that Molly was recovering from a personal difficulty, wanting to be among people. She was very well-behaved."

"Some guy dumped her," Ruth said, "that was obvious." Ruth clapped her hands together. "I've got it! Call him." She held up two fingers. "One, get the details of Molly's death, and two, demand an explanation for his goofiness last night. Two birds with one call."

Helma stepped closer to her telephone in case Ruth tried to duplicate last night's attempt. "I don't believe I'll call him at this time," she told Ruth.

In light of Wayne's rude behavior the night before, not to mention completely ignoring her birthday, the onus was on him to contact her, not the other way around. It wouldn't be sensible.

Ruth crossed her two fingers. "From your letters I thought you guys were like this." Her eyes narrowed. "Is there another woman?"

"We're really not in a situation in which, if there were, she would be considered the other woman. It would be his personal business."

"The woman last night?" Ruth persisted.

"What woman?" Helma asked, her question ending in an unbecoming squeak.

"Forget it. Just my overactive imagination." Ruth clicked the remote and turned off the television. "No sense leaving this on. It's not exactly a news story to interrupt your regularly scheduled programming. Maybe the killer was at your launch. I can't wait until they arrest the disgruntled local author."

"Don't make light of death," Helma said, attributing Ruth's "other woman" sighting to Ruth's unfortunate tendency to anticipate trouble and upheaval. "A woman is dead and I'm sure the hit-and-run driver was someone who panicked, not a local author."

"Like, if you know how to put words on paper you can't panic? A few writers I've known have been in a life-long panic."

"By tomorrow the police will have made an arrest and everything will be sorted out," she said, then returned to her bedroom for robe and slippers. Helma *did* believe that. The Bellehaven Police Department was award winning, efficient and effective, even if they could benefit at times from listening more carefully to an outsider's observations.

She didn't need to conduct a personal inventory to recognize that the dread feeling she'd awakened with on Monday morning was still present, and now even intensified by the death of Molly. Resolutely, she showered and dressed, refusing to allow its intrusion to slow her morning preparations.

When she returned to the living room, Ruth stood gazing out the sliding glass doors at Washington Bay and the humpy blue islands leading to the horizon.

Low banks of fog drifted across the water toward land. It was that time of year.

"I have so missed this. Maybe it'll rain today," Ruth said hopefully, turning back to Helma. "Now, by dawn's early light, I can see that TNT was right. You *are* in a state of some kind. Is there more going on than our buddy Wayne's male funk?"

Helma picked up Ruth's cola can, rinsed it out, and dropped it in the recycling box beneath her sink. "I awoke yesterday morning feeling . . . uncertain," she told her honestly. "It seems to be apparent to others."

Ruth swung Boy Cat Zukas to her shoulder. "You never were a good actor. I get those sometimes. A new man fixes me right up. Maybe it's just your birthday: forty-two. One of those midlife blips. Forty-two isn't so bad, I'm forty-two and look at me. Forty-two is the answer to life, the universe, and everything, hadn't you heard? Who said that, anyway?"

"Douglas Adams," Helma told her, never having read the book, but like any good librarian, she'd seen references to it.

"Good for him. What are you going to do about this little . . . uncertainty, then?"

"I intended to let it run its course." She paused, then admitted, "but Ms. Moon became involved."

"Since when did you start taking the Moonbeam's advice?" She pursed her lips. "Unless she tricked you or blackmailed you. Which was it?"

"Blackmail," Helma conceded. "She threatened to hand off the Local Authors project."

"Who to?"

"Gloria Shandy. She calls herself Glory."

Ruth shook her head. "Never heard of her."

"She's a new librarian, very . . . eager, hired after you left town." Helma pulled cereal and muffins from her cupboard, then set out eggs, butter, and jam from her refrigerator, adding a small frying pan so Ruth would have a choice for breakfast. It was easier to leave food out for Ruth than risk her rummaging in abandon through Helma's cupboards.

Ruth absently petted Boy Cat Zukas who was rubbing his head into the palm of her hand. "Mmm. So what did the Moonbeam blackmail you into doing?"

Helma retrieved Ms. Moon's list of group sessions from her Specious Solicitations file and gave it to Ruth.

Ruth scanned the page, her lips moving as she read, saying the last entry aloud, " 'Dealing with Troubled Pets?' " She shook the paper. "These are group sessions. She's sending you to one, two, three, *four* group sessions?"

Helma nodded glumly. "One night after another, beginning tonight."

"That's ridiculous. Just say no."

Helma pulled plates and glasses from her cupboard beside the sink. "I've worked for months on the Local Authors project."

"Geeze . . . *Work,*"—Ruth held out to her side one fist, then held out the other on the opposite side of her body—"*Life.* It's like separation of Church and State. She can't *make* you do this."

When Helma didn't answer, Ruth sighed and held up her "work" fist like a winner.

"Ruth," Helma countered. "Why are you here? It's not just because of my birthday."

Ruth breathed a dramatic sigh and sat on the arm of Helma's couch. "I was homesick."

"And Paul?"

"Keeping the home fires burning." She tipped her head to gaze up at Helma's ceiling. "The painting's been slow so I figured why not get away for a few days, visit my old friends in the far Far West."

An alarm sounded in the back of Helma's head. Memories of Ruth unable to paint and in her frustration stirring up trouble and, yes, even pandemonium in Bellehaven, still lingered. "Since you didn't bring any luggage, you'll need clothes." She motioned to Ruth's red underwear. "Rather soon."

"I'm borrowing TNT's jeep and driving to that consignment store in Linden."

Linden was a Dutch community twelve miles from Bellehaven noted for its unusually high population of tall women. With a few embellishments, Ruth could turn the most sedate clothing into, well, something that would never hang in Helma's closet and probably not the original owner's either.

"Take the day off and come with me? Or better yet, you could drive and I wouldn't be putting TNT's jeep in jeopardy."

"I doubt you could hurt his vehicle," Helma told her, thinking of TNT's bare-bones jeep.

"Remember my Saab?"

Helma did. An aged, periodically running car without any real color that always smelled of the salmon Ruth had once taken in trade for a painting and forgot to remove from her trunk. "What are you driving now?" she asked.

"Paul bought me a VW. New. Blue. I look like one of those circus clowns when I get out of it. He washes it for me every Saturday." Ruth's voice dropped and she turned her face toward the view of Washington Bay. "Inside and out. You'd like it. There's nothing mysterious under the seats anymore."

When Helma arrived at the library, Ms. Moon was changing the saying over the staff bulletin board. "Books are the basis of all social progress," read the quote which Ms. Moon had printed on colored paper decorated by daisies and sunflowers.

"Isn't that a quote from Karl Marx?" Helma asked.

"Most definitely not," Ms. Moon said. "I doubt this could be a Marxist sentiment."

Helma wasn't so sure about that, but she resolved to look it up and give the author proper credit.

"Congratulations on the turnout for the Local Authors launch," Ms. Moon said as she pressed in the last push pin, moving it inward from the corner to avoid a sunflower's petal, and turning to face Helma. "Hopefully the public will recognize one more aspect of library service and rally in support of our budget needs."

"It was well attended," Helma agreed, surmising from Ms. Moon's calmness that she hadn't made a connection between Local Authors and the death of Molly Bittern. But then, Ms. Moon avoided serving time on the reference desk and wasn't familiar with Bellehaven Public Library's more steadfast patrons.

Helma's relief was short-lived as George Melville entered the workroom, whistling the work song from *Snow White and the Seven Dwarfs*. He stopped and pointed a pencil at Helma, shaking his head, "I heard about Molly. What a damn shame. Think it was the case of a local author being permanently censored?"

Ms. Moon jumped as if she'd been pinched. "What?"

George nodded. "She was killed leaving Helma's launch meeting last night. Hit and run."

"It was an unfortunate accident, that's all," Helma said, speaking to Ms. Moon in the soothing voice she'd once used to dissuade a frustrated young man from bashing his fists into the side of a computer. "Nothing whatsoever to do with the library or the Local Authors project."

George raised a hand and crossed his fingers. "We can hope. Not that poor Molly sounded like serious competition to Bellehaven poets."

"An author killed her?" Ms. Moon's voice rose. She clasped her hands to her bosom, her eyes staring into the shocking middle distance. "Authors killing authors in *our* library?"

"Nah," George said. "Authors killing authors on our *streets.*"

Glory Shandy suddenly appeared beside George, touching his arm and rendering him momentarily befuddled.

"We all knew Molly as a regular patron," Glory told Ms. Moon, who appeared ready to swoon. "Helma's right, it was an unfortunate accident that had nothing to do with the library."

"I hope not," Ms. Moon said darkly, recovering herself. "It would be an untenable situation if a murder were connected in *any* way to the Local Authors project. *That* would naturally mean the end of the program."

"A death knell, so to speak," George agreed, nodding gravely. "Now we *all* have a reason to be depressed," then he ducked his head at Helma. "Sorry."

When Ms. Moon and George left, Helma told Glory, "I appreciated you photocopying extra brochures last night."

"You're welcome. Wasn't it exciting? All those writers in one room? I could hardly breathe being so close to them all. You did a fantastic job." She shoved her hands into the pockets of a girlish pink jumper. "The whole project is fantastic: you and everything you know about the community and the library. Your institutional memory is such a help to all us younger people hired after you."

Helma nodded, deciding it was best not to examine Glory's fulsome admiration too closely and watched Glory's forehead wrinkle.

"The death *was* accidental, wasn't it?" Glory asked. "A *real* writer would never kill another writer, would they?"

"Why ever would they?" Helma asked, rhetorically of course.

A half-filled book truck already awaited Helma in her cubicle, all the books entries from local authors for inclusion in the collection, plus a small stack on her desk. She'd developed a plan to logically sort them, but they were arriving faster than she'd expected. She had just lifted the first book from the truck: *Learning to Live with Your In-laws*, when her phone rang.

"I only live a block outside the city limits. Why can't I qualify?" Then another call. "If you get a book from Telly Graff, that's a pseudonym. If somebody's too ashamed to use their real name, I don't think they should be included, do you?" "My mother wrote a lot of cute stories about her grandchildren in longhand. Can I

send it? . . ." Until finally Helma stopped answering
and only glanced, now and then, at the furiously blinking red light on her telephone as her messages mounted.

At eleven o'clock she relieved Harley at the reference
desk. Harley looked up at her arrival. "A sad day," he
said, and morosely nodded toward the atlas case.
"That's where poor Molly Bittern always sat, right by
the atlases. Writing her poems with all those yellow
pencils."

"I know."

"I never saw her quarreling with anybody, did you?"

"No, I didn't either."

"That's what I told the chief."

Helma stopped straightening the pencils. "The
chief?"

"The chief of police. Wayne Gallant. He talked to
you, too, didn't he?"

"When was he here?"

Harley busied himself picking up his scattered papers, one of which held a chart of blood pressure numbers. He didn't look at Helma. "About an hour ago.
Last time I saw him he was talking to Glory."

Not since she'd first met him had Helma known
Wayne Gallant to visit the library without at least stopping by to tell her hello.

Chapter 6

An Unsettling Meeting

The man in front of the reference desk cleared his throat twice, then stepped back as if he might have offended Helma by standing too close.

"How may I help you?" Helma asked. Too many people were reluctant to "interrupt" the librarian sitting at the reference desk even though the sign hanging above the desk clearly read, "Information/Reference."

"Be approachable to your patrons," Ms. Moon liked to admonish. "Be a beacon for their information needs." And then she'd add slyly, "But don't use it as an excuse to neglect library-related work."

"I'm a local author," the man said and Helma braced herself for one of the stickier questions about the project. He was slender, in his mid-forties with graying hair and leathery, rough features that contrasted with long-lashed dark eyes.

His jeans were sharply creased and his denim long-sleeve shirt tucked in and belted, giving him a look of being from Somewhere Else.

"Do you have a question about the project?" she asked.

"Not really. I came to the meeting last night out of curiosity. No offense, ma'am," he said, pulling at his shirt cuffs, and Helma heard the twang and drawl of a western accent, "but I write under a pseudonym, and while I greatly admire what you're doing, I'd just as soon not be limited by a 'local author' status."

"Don't you believe it's an honor rather than a limitation?" Helma asked. She noted one of her favorite patrons, Ezra Vedder, aiming his motorized wheelchair toward the reference desk. The elderly man listed to the left side of his chair, his useless arm tucked close to his body.

"Depends," the man in front of Helma said, and he smiled so widely at Helma that for a moment Ezra Vedder and his wheelchair disappeared. When he smiled the roughness of his features vanished and he looked . . . well, if not Bellehavenish, at least coastal.

"Go ahead. I can wait," the man said, stepping aside for the whirring wheelchair. Ezra, who with local fanfare had recently celebrated his ninety-fifth birthday, glanced from Helma to the waiting man, then nodded his head as if something satisfied him.

"Here's your paper, Mr. Vedder," Helma said, handing him the *Wall Street Journal*, which, strung on a special stick each morning, made for easy reading by a one-armed person.

He balanced it across his lap, thanking her, then

paused to squint at the waiting man. "You live around here?" he asked.

"I do," he said. "I've seen you."

Ezra nodded. "Yeah, I'm hard to miss," and motored off to his favorite spot near the windows.

"I'm Boyd Bishop," he said, offering Helma his hand.

Library patrons didn't normally shake hands with librarians at the reference desk, but Helma held out her hand, and he shook it formally. "Is Boyd Bishop your given name or your pseudonym?" she asked.

"Given. Last night," he said, and the smile left his face, "I sat next to the woman who was killed." Boyd Bishop touched the left side of his cheek, at the site of Molly's birthmark, then jerked his hand away, flushing.

"Molly Bittern," Helma supplied.

"That's right. Did you know her?"

"Only through an association here in the library."

"I might have contributed to her death." He shoved his hands in his pockets and rocked back and forth on his feet.

Helma leaned back in her chair, away from him. Library patrons sometimes made startling confessions to librarians, especially across a desk. "I feel like a bartender," George once said, after a man asking for a book about writing country-western music volunteered that his wife had skipped town with his business partner.

"You need to talk to the police," she told Boyd Bishop now as she reached for a pencil and paper. "I'll give you their telephone number."

"No, no, not that way. I didn't have anything to do

with her actual death. In some eyes, what I did was just as bad." He took a deep breath. "Remember when she read her poem?"

Helma nodded, recalling Molly breathlessly reading the awkward phrases, the plaintive, "Why oh why did you leave me?"

"Well," Boyd Bishop said, wincing. "I laughed."

Helma Zukas was neither a writer nor an artist. Her closest acquaintance with a creative person was Ruth, and she recalled how after a bad review of one of her shows, Ruth had gleefully plotted for months before wreaking a humiliating revenge on the reviewer.

"And you believe by laughing you contributed to her state of mind so she was distracted on her way home and stepped in front of a moving vehicle?" Helma guessed.

Boyd Bishop smiled wryly. "Put that way, it sounds pretty arrogant of me, doesn't it? To think I had that much power?"

"It sounds more like misplaced guilt."

He laughed shortly. "Always trying to recover from my Catholic upbringing, I guess."

"I have one of those," Helma said, being shockingly indiscreet.

"It's like living in a subculture, isn't it? You seemed to know her last night so I decided to ask if she was the kind of person who might become, as you said, distracted."

"She may not have heard you laugh," Helma told him. "People are often oblivious to their surrounding in a public situation like that."

Boyd Bishop's shoulders relaxed. "Thanks. I know

you're being kind, but I appreciate it. It's one of those spontaneous stupidities that haunt you. Did I or didn't I?" He glanced down at Helma's bare left hand. "The other librarian referred to you as *Miss* Zukas last night. Is that . . ."

They were interrupted by Ruth stepping up to the reference desk. Heads turned as they often did when Ruth made an entrance. But this time she'd surely outdone herself.

"What do you think?" Ruth asked, twirling in a circle.

A red striped skirt with the deep slit worn in the front, a thigh-length burgundy cotton jacket over a V-necked green silk T-shirt, a black and rose scarf bumped by dangly gold earrings. She'd even found shoes in her size: ankle-high black boots with two-inch heels.

"I think you had a successful shopping trip," Helma said diplomatically.

"Thank you," Ruth said, looking proudly down at her outfit, tipping her feet to the side like a child with new shoes.

Ruth towered over Boyd Bishop, who wasn't short. He grinned up at her and said, "And I thought you stole the show *last* night."

"Who are you?" Ruth asked.

"Boyd P. Bishop," he said, offering her his hand before he turned back to Helma and said, "Thanks for your help, Helma. I'll be talking to you soon."

Ruth watched him walk away, one eyebrow raised. "That man is vedddy interested in you, my dear."

"You can tell that from a handshake?" Helma asked.

"And my highly attuned skills of sexually charged

observation. I'll wager you hear from him before the week ends."

"I don't make wagers," Helma reminded her.

"Just you wait and see. I'm going to run my loot back to your apartment, give TNT back his Jeep, and take Boy Cat Zukas for a walk."

"People don't walk cats."

"Well, he's getting one from me. You obviously haven't noticed his size lately. He's a major porker, destined for a kitty heart attack." She rearranged her bags. "Have you heard any more details about the dead poetess?"

"Molly?" Helma asked, wanting Molly's name to be said aloud; it was too soon to turn her into a description or a statistic. "No, nothing. The police have been asking questions."

"Did he talk to you?" Ruth asked, not saying who "he" was, but Helma knew.

"Not at this time," Helma told her.

Ruth sniffed. "I know just the trick to end your descent into the Slough of Despond."

"I didn't claim I was sliding into Bunyan's slough," Helma told her.

"No need to. But listen to this: You figure out who killed Molly; Wayne is bowled over by your clever, clever mind, and sweeps you into his arms. You're back on track and everybody lives happily ever after."

"Except Molly," Helma amended.

"Yeah, there is that." Ruth made a face. "But the idea's foolproof. I could help."

As if encountering a scene that couldn't be approached head-on, Glory Shandy advanced at an angle toward the reference desk, casting sideways glances at Ruth and her finery.

Ruth, who was never unaware, gave Glory a quick appraising once-over. Helma had seen it before: that on-the-spot dislike between two women seemingly based on absolutely nothing. "That's her," Ruth muttered unaccountably.

Glory stood beside the desk, staring.

"Ruth," Helma said, "this is Gloria Shandy. Gloria, this is Ruth Winthrop."

"The artist?" Glory breathed, putting her hands together in tiny little claps. "Please, call me Glory. A friend of mine has one of your paintings. I love it, just love it. I see it every time I pull in."

Ruth raised her eyebrows, unable to resist a comment that had anything to do with her art. "When you 'pull in'?" she asked.

Glory nodded eagerly. "She hung it in her garage. The colors are so vibrant." Sweeping her eyes across Ruth's attire, she added, "like you. You have such a sense of . . . color. What an asset to Bellehaven. I'm so thrilled to meet you, I really am." She gave a wave and a giggle and continued on her way to the circulation desk.

Ruth watched her darkly. "So sweet you'd like to see her spread across a piece of bread," she said.

"Glory *did* help me at the launch last night," Helma said, to be fair.

Ruth opened her mouth as if she were about to speak, and then closed it tight, shaking her head at Helma.

After Ruth left, Helma found the newest dictionary of pseudonyms in the reference collection. The book listed authors' names both by pseudonyms and given names so a reader could search by either name and find a cross reference. Helma found it very enlightening reading and a work of commendable, if tedious, research.

There was no listing for a Boyd P. Bishop, so either he wasn't very well-known or Boyd P. Bishop wasn't the man's actual name, either. Helma doubted she would ever cross paths with Mr. Bishop again, but it had been an unusual conversation.

She helped a young woman find information on Caspian terns, tried to explain to a college student why there weren't any reliable statistics on which citizens lied when they claimed they voted for a specific candidate, then gave an elderly woman a website that listed statistics on deaths of older men who used, as she said, "grow drugs" during encounters with younger women.

She answered questions competently and accurately, no doubt about that, but the thrill of ferreting out elusive details eluded her. Where was her usual pleasure, the gratification in beholding beaming, satisfied patrons?

Local author questions continued to come Helma's way. She developed a response that flawlessly covered 90 percent of the inquiries: "Send me your submission, along with a short description of your eligibility and we'll consider your work for inclusion," rather than argue over the definitions of books, citizenship, and quality publishing.

"Ah, Helma," George Melville said after overhearing her explanation to a high school student holding an elaborately rendered and hand-sewn comic book titled *Teachers Suck*. "At this rate we'll bust the budget just for enough shelving."

* * *

"Police to see you," the circulation clerk told Helma, who bumped her pencil holder, sending it rattling to the floor and banged her knee on her desk drawer as she tried to grab for it.

"I'll be right there," Helma said.

He stood beside the circulation desk, slapping a notebook against his pant leg, idly watching Curt, the library page, fill a book truck with materials to reshelve. Curt kept casting nervous glances toward the police chief.

"You wished to see me?" Helma asked.

Wayne Gallant turned, and she saw from his smile that whatever had caused the coolness after the Local Authors launch unfortunately remained. The mysterious heaviness that now stubbornly accompanied her day and night, swelled in depth and breadth.

"Let's sit down for a minute," he said, pointing to two unoccupied chairs in a more private corner of the library foyer.

"We're talking to everyone in the library regarding Molly Bittern's death," he said as he sat and casually opened his notebook, smoothing down a page before he looked at her.

"I doubt if there's anything I can add that hasn't already been said," Helma told him. "Molly frequented the library almost daily, quietly reading and writing. We all knew her, not personally but as a library patron. Whenever I saw her, she was alone."

"Someone referred to her as 'sad,' would you describe her that way?"

Helma preferred not to ascribe emotions to people, but she had to agree that "sad" did apply to Molly.

"Last night, from your vantage point at the podium,

did you notice anyone argue with Molly Bittern?" Wayne Gallant asked her. He was deliberate, he was polite, he was professional, he was a policeman coolly inquiring about a crime.

"No. I understood she died in a hit-and-run. Are you saying her death was intentional?"

"We're investigating all possibilities."

"Here in the library, we *do* have an interest," Helma reminded him. "If we knew exactly what the police were looking for, we could provide additional, valuable help, even be observant to clues you're investigating."

"We always appreciate citizen input," he said stiffly, "but the police are trained for these investigations." He wrote in his notebook without glancing up. "Did you notice anyone watching her, perhaps sitting near her?"

Despite years of association and occasional discussion of difficult cases between them, Chief of Police Wayne Gallant had just dismissed Helma Zukas as if she were a meddling old crank.

And no, theirs *wasn't* only a professional association. Definitely not. Helma straightened her spine and met his eyes, feeling a hot spot burning at the back of her neck. He looked down at his notebook. His pen moved, and from its motions she could tell he was merely drawing circles.

"Did you notice anyone watching Molly, perhaps sitting near her?" he asked again.

She thought of Boyd Bishop's confession that he'd laughed at Molly's poetry. She *hadn't* seen him. "No, I did not," she told Wayne Gallant.

The chief frowned. His raised his head as if he'd caught scent of her hesitation. "You're sure?"

Helma rose. "I would not have said so otherwise, Chief Gallant. Is there anything else?"

"No. That's all," he said. He half rose, then hesitated, opening his mouth to speak. "But I wish . . ."

He was too late. Helma had already turned her back and left the foyer.

It wasn't until she was tidying up her cubicle, preparing to go home that Ms. Moon appeared, blocking Helma's exit. "The police have spoken to me regarding our library patron's death," she told Helma.

"They've spoken to the entire staff," Helma told her.

Ms. Moon stroked her hands over the front of her dress, two, three times. "I trust any connection between the Local Authors program and this death won't be in the newspaper," she said as if Helma had influence over the *Bellehaven Daily News*.

"I don't believe Molly was a published author," Helma assured Ms. Moon, "so I doubt Local Authors will be mentioned."

"We won't benefit from negative publicity, not now, not with the current budget situation."

"Not ever," Helma clarified.

"You could talk to the chief of police," she said as if she'd just thought of it. "Ask him to request that the editor . . ."

Seeing Helma's face, she stopped. Then, dropping the subject as if she'd never mentioned it, Ms. Moon's face smoothed and she folded her hands at her waist. "I know your evening at the Age of Certain Years session will be beneficial, Helma. You'll be in the company of fully realized women."

"If that were true, I'd doubt they'd be attending these sessions," Helma pointed out.

Ms. Moon smiled benignly at her. "Maintenance, it's called. Once our goals are reached, it's all about maintenance. You're in for a treat tonight." She clasped her hands together in prayerful pleasure. "I spoke to Sunny Reese, your guide for tonight's session. If only my mother had thought to name *me* Sunny, wouldn't that have been delightful? She has a very special guest for you to meet, someone who will make a difference in your life."

"Who is it?" Helma asked.

She shook her head. "Oh, I can't tell you. Definitely not. It would just be too naughty."

"All right," Helma said, declining to fish for clues, "then I'll see you in the morning."

Ms. Moon turned to leave, saying, "She'll open the world for you, I promise."

There would be no last minute reprieve. Helma drove back to the Bayside Arms for a quick dinner before the Age of Certain Years session, her thoughts as gray as the waning day.

Ruth was gone. An open jar of salsa—not from Helma's supplies—sat on the counter beside a carton of chocolate milk, again not from Helma's refrigerator. Sections of the *Bellehaven Daily News* lay scattered across the kitchen table, printed too soon to contain more than the barest details of Molly's death, not even her name.

Helma automatically tidied up, straightening cushions, placing Ruth's plastic bags of new consignment clothing in the spare bedroom, wincing as a four-inch wide school bus–yellow belt fell out. What did Ruth intend to pair with that?

She bit her lip, gazing at her telephone, then entered *69 to retrieve the phone number of her last caller. Helma Zukas did not own an answering machine, certain that anyone with an important message would continue calling until they reached her. The electronic voice droned Helma's mother's number.

She hung up, donned a sweater and sat on her deck, watching the light grow dusky, silver-gray muting to pewter. Beyond Washington Bay the islands were shadows of varying darkness, without definition. A speedboat sedately chugged toward the marina, its lights piercing white and its engines audible to Helma. Beneath her in Boardwalk Park a few people jogged or walked dogs along the curving sidewalks. Helma idly watched their progress. Tonight all of it was merely weather, water, and movement.

Boy Cat Zukas was nowhere to be seen, so either Ruth had actually taken him for the threatened walk or he was off on one of his mysterious rounds that sometimes brought him home with a bloodied ear or bulging stomach, or both.

Sitting quietly, she contemplated the dark and confusing sensation that had descended upon her, a feeling without cause and which felt as impervious as concrete. "Keep busy. Just keep busy," Helma's mother always cheerily advised against low periods, as if you couldn't be caught if you were on the move.

So Helma glanced at her watch and saw there wasn't time to fix dinner. She ate five round crackers with a half slice of yellow cheese on each one, brushed her teeth, patted down the stubborn curl on the left side of her head, checked her shoes for smudges and her purse for tissues and emergency pay phone change.

It was time to go.

Chapter 7

Bad News Bearer

The Age of Certain Years group met on the third
floor of the Legion Hall, two blocks off Bellehaven's main street. The brick building contained
an elevator that had an out-of-order sign taped to
the door, but Helma Zukas avoided elevators
whenever possible. She climbed the steep flights
of stairs without pausing and without needing to
catch her breath before she reached the third floor.
A spiral notebook was tucked beneath her arm so
she could sit at the back of the room and work on
politic answers to the unexpected questions that
had arisen regarding the Local Authors collection.

A dozen women, who Helma judged to be in
their forties and fifties were already present in the
wood-paneled room that stretched across the entire third floor, as if it once had been a ballroom.
Voices echoed against the tile floor and high ceiling. A portable bar and upright piano were pushed

against one wall, along with stacks of folding tables and chairs.

American and Washington State flags hung on upright poles that could be carried, and for an instant, Helma saw her father, for once solemn, his mischievous eyes grave, exhorting a group of teenagers to stand and salute the passing flag during the Color Festival parade in Scoop River, Michigan. At the time, it had just been another of his embarrassing antics. But now . . .

Metal folding chairs were arranged in a circle in the center of the room. So much for sitting unobtrusively in the back and working on the Local Authors project.

A slightly overweight dark-haired woman separated herself from the group and approached Helma, her hand outstretched. She wore black glasses shaped in stylish round circles and deep red lipstick.

"Welcome to the Age of Certain Years group," she said. She spoke in a modulated voice, reminding Helma of Ms. Moon, a voice intended to sooth. "I'm Sunny Reese, and I'm your facilitator tonight. You're Helma Zukas. May Apple called me about you." Sunny was a woman of scarves. Two circled her neck: a thin black silk and a deep-patterned cotton that picked up the colors of her suit, ends draping down breast and back. She played with the fringed ends as she spoke.

"I'm very surprised to be here," Helma told her.

Sunny nodded. "I know. May Apple said this was her idea, not yours. I hope we can help you retouch your center tonight." She winked. "Bring sunniness into your life." She made as if to elbow Helma in the ribs. "That was my little joke."

Helma chose not to see it and waited politely, stepping out of range of Sunny's elbow.

"Well," Sunny said, clearing her throat. "Yes. You'll find this a nourishing group of women. Help yourself to a cup of tea or a bottle of water. We'll begin in five minutes."

Helma chose the chair furthest from the seat Sunny had claimed. The other women made their way to chairs in the circle, some nodding to Helma. She recognized two women as library patrons and saw on their faces that they were puzzling out who she was, seeing her out of context.

"Hi," said an athletic-looking woman with short brown hair dropping onto the chair beside Helma. "I'm Pepper Breckenridge, and yeah, before you ask, Pepper's my real name. You're new."

Helma nodded and the woman patted her leg. "Don't worry. This is painless. Kinda fun, really. You get what you need, then move on." She held a roll of candies out to Helma. "Breath mint?"

"No, thank you." In Helma's experience, a proper diet and preventative dental care made breath mints unnecessary.

Pepper snapped her fingers, her face opening in recognition. "I know. You're the librarian. I was at your meeting last night."

"You're a writer?" Helma asked warily.

Pepper—Helma couldn't bring herself to say her name aloud yet, although the image did fit the animated woman, more than the name Sunny fit the group's facilitator—tucked one leg beneath her and shook her head. "Nah, I could barely scribble out college papers. I was looking for books on CD in the library and saw this horde of people. So I followed them. Hot time."

"People are very passionate about their art," Helma explained.

"Egos, you mean." Pepper shuddered. "And then that poet got killed like that. Did you know her?"

"Ladies," Sunny Reese announced, leaning forward to take command of the group, holding both ends of her black scarf so it tightened dangerously around her neck. "This is going to be an unusual and exceptional evening so let's first begin with our Greeting of Admission. I'll start."

She considered the group, pausing at each face before she said in the impassioned voice of a confessor, "I'm Sunny and I'm forty-seven years old."

The woman next to her did the same, saying "I'm Catherine and I'm fifty-one years old," and the woman next to her declared in a defiant voice, "I'm Janey and I'm forty-five years old."

"Janey, Janey," Sunny gently admonished, and the woman named Janey blushed and amended, "I'm forty-seven years old."

"Thank you, Janey. Now doesn't that feel better?"

Janey nodded but not enthusiastically, Helma noted.

After Pepper, next to Helma, chirpily announced, "I'm Pepper and I'm forty-one years old," it was Helma's turn. She remained silent.

"Helma," Sunny said, "wouldn't you like to share your Greeting of Admission with us?"

"No, thank you," Helma told her. "I don't see the need for it."

Sunny smiled sadly. "It's a step toward self-acceptance. We don't force anyone here, but when you feel comfortable it *is* a step toward becoming a member of this group."

Helma refrained from replying she had no intention of becoming a member, that she was present under duress, and this was her first and final appearance.

The chair next to Helma was empty, although a plastic yellow rose lay across the seat. Sunny took a deep breath before saying, "And there's where our dear Molly sat every Tuesday evening."

"Molly Bittern?" Helma asked aloud.

"That's right, the poetess whose life so tragically ended last night, which brings us to the first exceptional portion of this evening." Sunny nodded toward the chair in silent homage as if the shade of Molly Bittern hovered there, and removed a sheet of folded paper from the black briefcase leaning against her chair leg.

At that moment a hand reached down and snatched the rose from the chair seat. In a flurry and a flourish, Ruth dropped down beside Helma. A gasp rose from the group of women and Ruth, twirling the rose in her hand and turning her head between the shocked women, asked, "What? Is this chair taken?"

Sunny smiled uncertainly at Ruth but motioned for her to remain. "I have here," she continued, "a poem of Molly's. We all knew how bravely Molly struggled with her sorrows. In her memory, I'd like to read this poem, which she wrote during one of our creative imagery sessions and presented to me."

Ruth leaned toward Helma and whispered, "Are we talking about Molly the Dead?"

Helma nodded. "What are you doing here?"

"I have to tell you something."

"Excuse me," Sunny said, pointedly looking at Ruth. "May I read?"

"Be my guest," Ruth told her.

"Thank you." And Sunny read:

Insomnia

I don't sleep at night no more
Since I lost your rousing snore
You left me feeling flat
I'm not old, I'm not fat
I only wanted in us to believe
But me you did deceive
Oh why oh why did you leave me?

A sniffle and sigh rose from the group. "This is a woman who nursed her grief to keep it warm," Ruth commented, paraphrasing Robert Burns and shrugging her shoulders at the looks cast her way.

"We'll always remember Molly," Sunny said. "She was a gentle creature with a troubled heart, yet a shining beacon in a darkling world." She held up the paper, "But we have these words to remember her by. And as long as she's remembered, she'll continue to live on past her brief tenure on earth."

Sunny's words were warm, perfectly generous, but there was an edge to her tone. Helma was always uncomfortable with overexposed emotion, but still she thought she detected a note that didn't quite ring sincere.

"Methinks she doth profess too much," Ruth commented, exactly what Helma was thinking, if not quite in those terms.

"Because Molly didn't have to work, she spent her life creating her poetic legacy," Sunny finished.

"Good golly, Miss Molly was *rich*," Ruth whispered. "Isn't that what she's saying?"

The door at the back of the room opened and closed and Sunny clapped her hands together once, lifting the somber mood. "Ah, our guest," she said, smiling and nodding toward the rear.

Everyone turned to look at the slight woman entering. She appeared carefully constructed, "put together," as Aunt Em might say—her makeup and perfectly highlighted blond hair flawless, subtle and expensive suit unwrinkled, store-fresh high heels, a tasteful brooch pinned to her suit lapel.

"This is Tanja Frost," Sunny said and a few women, including Pepper next to Helma, gasped in pleasure. "Tanja's a fellow counselor, a dear friend, and author of *Women in Jeopardy,* her remarkable book of how women have overcome seemingly insurmountable odds at mature ages. She's recently moved to Bellehaven, and we're fortunate to have her with us tonight."

So this was the woman who Ms. Moon said was "absolutely gifted." Helma jotted down the author and title and raised her hand. "How recently did you move to Bellehaven?" she asked.

"Just six weeks ago," she said, and Helma sat back, relieved. Less than three months, so her book wasn't eligible for Local Authors, at least not in this first crush.

Beside Helma, Pepper whispered, "This is so exciting. I'm going to the bathroom so I don't have to get up while she's talking. Her book is a groundbreaker—you should have it in the library." She half stood, hunched over, and headed for the exit.

And on the other side of Helma, Ruth said, "I've got to talk to you, Helma. Let's get out of here."

"After this."

Ruth blew out an exasperated sigh and Sunny added, "Soon Tanja will publish another groundbreaking book, and if we're lucky, she'll share a few pages with us tonight," immediately complicating Helma's Local Author guidelines.

Tanja Frost stood before them, a vision of good taste, smiling, her voice warm and heartfelt. "My book is packed with stories of women your age . . ." She laughed lightly, appealingly, "*our* age, who looked the word *NO* in the face and refused to accept it. Growing older means nothing, I want you to believe that. We are as vital and active and capable as our younger counterparts. We can love. We can compete. We can win."

"Excuse me."

Ruth stood, towering in all her misguided finery, glancing around the room before she said, "This is no horse race. It's time to face up to one thing: we're not young. We're a garden of pears. Our bodies are going to hell no matter how much exercise or surgery we can afford."

Tanja smiled kindly but indulgently as if Ruth were a charming but ill-behaved child. "But *age* is immaterial. Younger women are no more beautiful than we are. With healthy diets and proper exercise . . ."

To Helma's horror, Ruth lifted her shirt and exposed bare breasts. "See these," she interrupted Tanja, cupping her breasts and raising them. "They don't stay all perky on their own anymore." She turned her back to the circle and slapped her buttocks. "And neither do these."

As the group stared speechless at Ruth, who appeared about to raise her skirt and show her bottom, which was probably also bare, Helma jumped up and grabbed Ruth's arm.

"Excuse us but we have to leave," she said and pulled Ruth toward the door.

No one protested, not even Ruth.

At the front of the room, Tanja reached out a hand toward them in puzzled concern, much like Helma's mother had reached out to Helma during the launch, then let it drop.

As she led the way past the broken elevator and down the steep stairs, one hand to the railing, Helma asked Ruth over her shoulder, "What on earth were you doing?"

Ruth hummed the "I wish I were an Oscar Mayer wiener" song and Helma stopped on the steps and turned. Ruth was smiling down at her.

"You made a spectacle to get us out of the session, didn't you?"

"It worked, didn't it?"

"Yes, it did, but it was unnecessarily disruptive."

Ruth unconcernedly restraightened her shirts and jacket, which had been rucked up during her display. "Admit it. You're glad to get out of there."

Helma never denied the truth. "You're right. I am, but I'd have preferred a more subtle exit."

"I'd have preferred a more subtle exit," Ruth mimicked. "Let's go.

"What was so important to tell me?" Helma asked,

continuing down the steps, pausing once to push a small pebble to the side of the tread with the toe of her shoe.

"Oh. I had to tell you . . ." Ruth stopped and Helma turned to see Ruth's stricken face. Her breath caught. Aunt Em. Her mother.

"Tell me what? What's happened?"

"Oh, Helma. I lost Boy Cat Zukas."

Chapter 8

Gone Missing

"What do you mean?" Helma demanded, turning to face Ruth, standing six steps up from the doorway. "How could you *lose* Boy Cat Zukas?"

"Careful. Don't fall. Let's go outside and I'll explain." Ruth passed Helma and opened the wooden door onto the street. Moist night air flowed into the entry, carrying the odor of briny decaying things.

On the sidewalk, they faced each other. "Please explain to me how you could possibly lose a cat," Helma asked.

Whistling caused Helma to turn her head. Two men strolled toward them. One of them tossed a set of keys back and forth between left and right hand and then straight up into the air. The other man reached out and snatched the keys. They slowed, watching Ruth and Helma with interest.

"Look," Ruth said, glancing at the two men,

then at Helma's Buick parked in front of the door. "Here's your car. Get in and I'll tell you on the way home."

"How did you get here?" Helma asked, glancing up and down the street for TNT's jeep, still trying to digest Ruth's words: Boy Cat Zukas? Lost? He wasn't the kind of cat one associated with the word *lost*. Ruth had to be mistaken; she just wasn't used to the casual manner with which Boy Cat Zukas treated his adopted home.

"I hitched a ride. Don't worry Helma. We'll find him."

Helma unlocked the passenger side, then the driver's door. "Boy Cat Zukas frequently leaves my balcony," she assured Ruth. "He climbs over the roof of the building and down the steps to hunt mice—or whatever cats do. He's not lost. Where did you last see him?"

Ruth climbed into the passenger side of Helma's car and slammed the door too hard. "Look," she said. "I'm fastening my seat belt."

"Congratulations. Where did you last see Boy Cat Zukas?" she asked again.

Ruth kept her head down as she buckled her seat belt. Helma couldn't make out her mumbled response. "Where?" she asked.

"At Joker's."

Helma pulled her hand away from the ignition. "Joker's? The bar? Boy Cat Zukas was outside Joker's?"

"Well, actually, inside the bar. I took him for a walk, remember? Because he's fat?"

"You took Boy Cat Zukas *into* a bar?"

"You wouldn't want me to leave him outside, would you? Maybe tied to a light pole where a mad dog could have torn him to shreds? Of course I took him inside.

He was okay until some guy's motorcycle backfired, then he was out the door like a streak of . . . like a wildcat."

"Ruth, Joker's is two miles from my apartment."

"I know, I know. I called and called and checked everywhere. Under cars, behind garbage cans, in the bushes. He's smart. I mean, he's a retired alley cat. He'll be okay until we find him, or he comes home on his own."

"We're going to Joker's right now," Helma said, turning onto Chestnut.

"I figured you'd want to."

Helma swerved her car around a man and woman on a bicycle-built-for-two traveling in the bicycle lane but without lights. "That was weird, wasn't it," Ruth said, looking back at the bicycle, "the way Molly Bittern popped up at your group session tonight? Not literally, I mean, but her poetry."

"It's not *my* group session; I won't be attending again. But you're right, I *am* surprised Molly was a member, but more by the coincidence of it. She was obviously seeking help beyond what she could find in the library."

"Imagine that," Ruth said absently. She rolled down her window and pulled back her hair. "Two poems about being dumped. Maybe there's a wife or girl-friend out there who ran her down. Wham. No more competition. Did the chief come around today and make nice?"

"He was very professional," Helma told her. "He asked if I'd noticed anything unusual about Molly at the Local Authors launch."

"That's all?" Ruth asked, turning on her seat to face Helma. "Why don't you just *ask* him what the cold shoulder's all about? It's easy. You just purse your lips and say, 'What's going on?' "

"He did remind me that the police department was perfectly capable of solving a crime without citizen interference," Helma said, seeing again Wayne Gallant jotting in his notebook, not meeting her eyes.

"Uh-oh, the gauntlet's been thrown, right?"

"I don't know what you're talking about."

"The stage is set, don't you see? He's challenging you to find Molly's killer. It's a mixed message because he's incapable of saying what he means."

"Mixed messages," Helma asserted, "negate the intent and purpose of language. We might as well quit speaking altogether."

"Yeah, or go into politics. Slow down. What's that?"

But Helma had seen it, too, a glare of animal eyes, and already slowed her car. But the car lights flashed on the glass eyes of a carved bear lawn ornament.

"False alarm," Ruth said.

They were silent the rest of the ride, both of them, Helma was sure, thinking of Boy Cat Zukas, not their private lives.

The low-tide odor was stronger near Joker's. The skies had clouded over. It wasn't raining, but it smelled of moist weather mixed with the scent of the sea. Joker's bar had once been a fisherman's bar, but commercial fishing had ended in Bellehaven and Joker's still hadn't discovered its new customer base. Ferns stood in one corner, a big-screen television in another, a pinball machine in another, and a few tables between.

Helma had only been inside a few times and each of those times was due to trouble involving Ruth.

Kipper, the bartender, looked up and shook his head. "No sign of him yet, Ruth. Sorry. But we're looking every time we take out the empties."

"Then we'll search for him," Helma said, ignoring the man sitting at the end of the bar who blearily asked, "Runaway husband?"

Ruth and Helma searched behind Joker's and along the adjoining streets, Ruth calling, "Kitty, kitty, kitty?" Three cats answered the call but none of them Boy Cat Zukas.

Helma rarely called Boy Cat Zukas. He was either there or not there, but she tried it now. "Come, cat," she called two times without response.

After an hour of searching through the darkness, probing in nooks and crannies, squinting up tree branches, checking in the backs of pickups, and calling into open garages, they gave up. "At least he's wearing a collar," Helma said. "My phone number's on it."

"I'll come back tomorrow morning while you're at work," Ruth said. "Or he could be waiting on your balcony when we get back to your apartment." She clapped her hands together. "Yup. That's where he is, sitting on your balcony wondering where the heck you are."

Ruth grew increasingly nervous as they approached the Bayside Arms, wringing her hands, tapping on the dashboard, fidgeting in her seat; and as Helma unlocked her apartment door, Ruth actually pushed past her into the kitchen, sweeping something off the counter and jamming it into her pocket.

"What's that, Ruth?" Helma asked.

"Nothing," Ruth said. "What's to eat around here?"

"Ruth."

"Oh, shite," Ruth said and from her pocket she pulled out an object and held it up for Helma to see: Boy Cat Zukas's collar. "He slipped out of it when the motorcycle backfired. I had ahold of him, honest, but the little sucker . . ."

"He's out there without proper identification."

"But he's smart. He'll find his way home. He adopted *you*, remember? He'll be back."

Helma phoned the after-hours emergency number at the Animal Shelter and explained the missing cat.

"Bring a photo of him in the morning and we'll post it and also show the patrol drivers," the woman at the shelter told Helma.

"A photo?" Helma asked. "I've never photographed my cat."

"Some people do. What does he look like?"

"Black, but he had several bald spots that have grown in white. One ear, his left, is torn, and I think his tail was broken at one time; it has a bend in it. Plus he has a scar on his nose and two claws missing from his right front paw, not that it impedes his activities in any way. He was neutered—against his wishes."

The woman was silent a moment, then asked, "Do you live in a permanent home?"

"I beg your pardon?"

A pause, then, "Does this animal live on the street?"

"I am a professional librarian," Helma informed her.

"Sorry. Give me your name and address and I'll post this tomorrow morning. Check back tomorrow afternoon if you don't hear from us."

Helma hung up, her fingers holding light over the number pad, then closed her hand. It was excessive to phone the police department over a lost cat, but then, she thought, flexing her hand open and closed, the sooner the authorities were aware of the missing animal, the more likely it was he'd be found. Boy Cat Zukas might be noticed in passing and her report would be remembered.

Ruth slouched on the sofa, her long legs stretching out past the coffee table. She turned the cat collar in her hands, cocked one eyebrow, and said, "Go ahead. Call him."

Instead, Helma dialed the main number of the police station, the non-emergency number.

"This is Miss Helma Zukas," she told the policeman who answered, wincing as she recognized the distinctive voice of Officer 087 who'd once unfairly given her the only traffic ticket she'd received since she'd begun driving at the age of sixteen. She'd protested the ticket in court, leaving her and Office 087 at unspoken but bitter odds. He was a motorcycle policeman and Helma often spied him lurking behind hedges plotting to trap unwary drivers.

"How may I help you, Miss Zukas?" he asked in a professional voice, using the identical query the librarians used at the reference desk, all of them victims of the same city-sponsored public service workshops.

"My cat has gone missing in a high-traffic area near Joker's bar," she told him. "I'd appreciate it if the police would notify me should a black slender cat cause any difficulty in that area of town."

"You mean if it gets hit?" Officer 087 asked cruelly.

"That would certainly be one situation," Helma said in her iciest silver dime voice. "Another might be if he injured a police officer by attacking him from behind, or irrevocably scratched up the shiny leather of a policeman's motorcycle seat. Thank you for your time." And she hung up

"Ouch," Ruth said. "I'm guessing you weren't speaking to one of your favorite cops. Is Sidney Lehman still on the force?"

"Being in a position of authority is never an excuse for rudeness," Helma told Ruth. "And, yes, Sidney's still there."

Ruth licked her lips.

"But I believe he's engaged to a physical therapist at the hospital."

Ruth shrugged her shoulders. "Immaterial."

Helma realigned her telephone on the counter and sat down in the chair opposite Ruth. "Ruth, what's going on?"

"Going on? Nothing's going on." She grimaced at Helma. "Come on, I've hardly been here twenty-four hours; how could anything be going on?"

"You didn't come back just for my birthday."

Ruth dropped the cat collar on top of the latest *Time* magazine and unwound the black-and-rose scarf from her neck, draping it over the back of the sofa. Helma waited while she kicked off one shoe, then the other. "It's all so transitory, isn't it?" she said finally, wiggling her bare toes with their vermilion paint. "We just bungle along making our little messes." Then she looked up at Helma and laughed. "I sound like one of those inspirational marquees, don't I?" She raised her hands and made quotation marks in the air in front of her. " 'Cry me a river, build a bridge and get over it.' "

Helma remained silent, the only method she'd ever

discovered to keep Ruth from turning every word into a joke, going completely off track, or evading questions she didn't want to answer.

Ruth sighed. "I love the guy, Helm. I really do. It kills me to be away from him. He built me a studio, did I tell you that, off our bedroom, so I can roll out of bed in the middle of the night and work if the urge strikes. We have gardens and a hot tub. He comes home every night, sometimes with flowers. I don't owe anybody money any more. He gave me an espresso machine for Valentine's Day."

Except for the hot tub, because she didn't believe in bathing in pre-used water, it sounded pleasant to Helma. Yet each fact Ruth totted up was spoken in a descendingly sorrowful voice. "But?" she supplied.

"I can't paint," Ruth said. She raised both hands to cup her face like the Munch painting. "Every time I try, it turns out shit. Maybe it's really gone, do you know what I mean? Maybe this time I've actually lost it and I may as well hang up my spurs and start making dried-flower bouquets or egg carton wastepaper baskets."

Helma thought either activity might be more comprehensible than most of Ruth's paintings, but Ruth was her friend so she said, "You believed if you returned to Bellehaven it might encourage you to begin painting again?"

"Right. Back here in the land of my triumph. Maybe this is where my muse hangs out, in the rain and mildew. People I know here *expect* me to be an artist. Back there, I'm an abnormally tall woman who dresses funny and lives off some nice guy who makes good money."

"What did Paul think of you coming back to Belle-haven?" Helma asked.

Ruth bit her lip.

"He doesn't know?" Helma guessed.

"I left him a note."

Helma stood on her balcony before she went to bed, listening and watching, spinning around once when she heard a noise on the roof of the building. A breeze had sprung up from the south. Rain tomorrow, she suspected. She left a fresh dish of food and changed the water in Boy Cat Zukas's bowl, surprised that since Ruth had told her of the cat's disappearance she'd barely thought of the Local Authors project, Molly Bittern's death, or her scheduled and dreaded group sessions. And not much of Wayne Gallant, either. Hardly.

She slept fitfully, waking several times to sounds she normally wouldn't have noticed: the refrigerator turning on; a slamming door in another apartment, a car horn.

At 2:43 A.M. she was brought wide awake by the slamming of her own apartment door. She grabbed her robe and found Ruth fully dressed in her kitchen.

"Are you going out?" she asked Ruth.

Ruth shook her head and pointed to the grocery sack on the counter. "Coming in. I brought you a few supplies." She pulled out two large bottles of red wine, a bottle of expensive port, and two bags of garlic-and-onion potato chips. "It's nice to be back in the land of the all-night grocery store. Hugie's is going a little downhill, though, don't you think? I swear I saw two overweight checkers and a French bottled water display that was asymmetrical." She pulled a water glass from Helma's cupboard. "Where's your corkscrew?"

Helma handed it to her and as she popped the cork from a bottle of Shiraz, Ruth said, "I searched up and down those damn streets for two hours and didn't catch a single glimpse of the little wretch."

Chapter 9

Fall from Grace

When Helma's clock radio switched on, the first thing she heard after the moaning cries of pan-pipes was a television voice. And as if Ruth had heard Helma's radio and knew she was awake, Ruth called out in a weary voice, "You'd better come see this, Helma."

The now familiar oppresiveness froze her supine for a moment. Perhaps Boy Cat Zukas had returned and was staring in through the sliding glass doors, hungry and contrite. She sat up and shrugged her shoulders to shed the dread feelings but nothing happened. So, just as wearily as Ruth's voice sounded, she donned her robe and slippers and joined Ruth in the living room.

Ruth wore a man's blue and gray plaid bathrobe and was pointing a cup toward the television screen. "This is too weird, isn't it? It gives me the creeps."

Helma glanced first toward her balcony. No cat. Then at the television screen where once again Gillian Hovel read the news, gazing sadly out at the audience. "Police are not saying whether this second death in two days was accidental or, in fact, may be somehow connected to the hit-and-run death of Molly Bittern two nights ago."

And there on the screen was a professional publicity photo of Tanja Frost, the author and guest speaker at the An Age of Certain Years group session the night before. The photo showed a beautifully made-up blond woman very much like Tanja Frost, except for the brushed-out facial lines and more dramatic hairstyle.

"Death?" Helma asked. Again.

Ruth nodded as a shot of Molly Bittern shared the screen with the blond author, Molly utterly plain in comparison. Two dead women. "She fell—or was pushed—down the stairs at the Legion Hall. They kind of look alike, don't they, Molly and Tanja? Blondes do, like a species apart. I wonder if Tanja wrote poetry, too."

"It must have happened right after the meeting ended," Helma said. "There had to have been witnesses to her fall, at least a few members of the group. Sunny wouldn't have let a guest speaker leave the building alone."

"Who's Sunny?"

"Last night's group leader."

"You're joking. Her name's *Sunny*? What's that, some kind of therapy joke, like in 'Sunny days are here again?'" Ruth rolled her eyes. "Yeah, but you're right: Sunny must have been with her. She was ready to wag her tail over Tanja. I'll bet it was an act."

"Sunny called her a 'dear friend,'" Helma reminded Ruth.

"That doesn't mean a thing. Movie stars call other movie stars their dear friends when you know they hate each other's guts." She took on Gillian the newscaster's fervent tones. "Sunny, in a fit of professional jealousy, toppled Tanja down the stairs after having killed Molly who drove her crazy with all that whiny poetry."

"But that doesn't create a connection between Molly and Tanja, except that Sunny knew both women."

"I rest my case. Maybe Sunny's next."

"The police will be questioning her, I'm sure," Helma said. "She was probably the last person to see Tanja alive."

"She was alive when I pushed her, officer," Ruth said in falsetto.

"It was most likely an accident," Helma told her. "Tanja slipped. Remember how steep those steps were?"

"I remember." Ruth tipped up her cup and drank the last of whatever liquid was in it. There wasn't any coffee made. "You missed the part where the police said they're looking for a blue car with a damaged front bumper in Molly's death."

"What make and model?" Helma asked.

"They don't know yet. Smallish, according to a witness. That's why you should call the man. Admit it. You're frustrated."

"I'm baffled," Helma said, untying, then retying her robe. "His behavior is highly unusual, but I'm not calling him."

"Well, *I'm* frustrated," Ruth told her. "If it were me, I'd cut this off at the pass."

"I don't believe a cowboy expression applies to this situation."

"You don't think little Miss Gushy Giggles is hot on the trail of *your* chief?"

"Ruth, please speak in plain English."

"That simpering pseudo-teenager in your library who wants everybody to call her Glory."

"Glory Shandy? You only met her once. I know you didn't like her comments about your art, but why would you believe she's interested in Wayne?"

"I may have only met her once, but I *saw* her at your authors' launch gazing all starry-eyed at Wayne. I *know* that look."

"Undoubtedly," Helma said. "You saw her for five seconds while she helped pass out brochures. You're wrong."

"Am not."

"That's ridiculous."

Ruth melodramatically sighed and said, "Okay, then. Forget it. What do you think will happen tonight?"

"What do you mean?"

Ruth held up two fingers. "Two meetings two nights in a row, two deaths. Both attended by Miss Wilhelmina Zukas who also has three more group sessions on her social calendar. What if some nutso is out there bumping off women who get together in little secret groups and talk about . . . well, he lets his imagination run wild. Maybe he's threatened by what he sees as women getting too uppity. Retro idea, I know, but he could be old school." Ruth was warming up. "Can't get any woman for himself, believes he's becoming superfluous in the mating game. He'll show everybody. So he begins reducing the female population; they piss him off anyway. Random, these might be random hits—and there you are out there trip-trapping from meeting to meeting directly in the line of fire."

"Ruth, you're blathering."

Ruth held up her hand like a policeman stopping traffic. "Think of it as brainstorming. You have to examine every angle. Sooner or later you hit on the answer, just like all those monkeys who typed the Declaration of Independence."

"I believe it was a Shakespeare sonnet, and it never happened. Aldous Huxley was theorizing on the concepts of chance."

"Well, you get my drift." Ruth considered Helma. "You're really not getting involved in these murders? Library connections, psycho-session connections. Right up your alley."

"No one has claimed Molly and Tanja's deaths were murders."

"They will," Ruth shrugged. "So mope around and dig yourself into a deeper hole. I'm keeping my ears open. Dead people take my mind off my breaking heart."

"You left Minnesota," Helma reminded her. "Actually, you *fled* Minnesota."

"I'm through with Minnesota," Ruth said. "I don't want to talk about it."

Ruth stretched and Helma glanced away as she realized Ruth wasn't wearing anything under her robe. "I'm going to stop by the art store and buy two pencils and a pad of paper. Is it okay if I draw a little bit on your balcony?"

"Of course. Do you feel the urge to paint again?"

"Maybe a little. I don't know yet. I'll start with plain old pencil."

"That's wonderful. You—"

"Stop. Don't disturb the muse. We're talking eggshells and butterfly wings here." Ruth paused. "I should write that down: eggshells and butterfly wings. Sounds like a line worthy of our Molly."

A sparrow landed on Helma's deck railing, then hopped down to the lip of Boy Cat Zukas's water dish. Both Helma and Ruth watched it dip its beak into the water and then raise its tiny head to swallow. It was relaxed and curious, aware somehow that it had no enemies to fear.

"I'll go back to Joker's to look for him today," Ruth offered.

A few blocks from the Bayside Arms, Helma spotted a black lump in the street near a hill of fir and ferns. Ignoring the finger of the man who swerved around her in a squeal of tires, she braked her Buick and stopped alongside the black form, her heart pounding.

She rolled down her window and was immediately assailed by the odor of skunk, somewhat of a rarity in Bellehaven. Her relief was immediately replaced by guilty sorrow, that even a skunk could meet such a cruel end.

Ms. Moon might have been lying in wait for Helma. She stood near the workroom photocopier, her eyes half closed, holding a clipboard. Helma recognized her flowy, ample dress as one she'd worn prior to her weight-loss and regain.

Ms. Moon opened her eyes and heaved a sigh. "Ah,

Helma. Disturbance accompanied you again last night, I understand."

"I wasn't present when Tanja Frost's death took place, but, yes, it is very disturbing."

The photocopier hummed, warming up, and Ms. Moon sat her clipboard on top of the machine. When she saw Helma glance at the pale blue paper, Ms. Moon turned the clipboard upside down. "It's a terrible loss to the field of counseling, and a loss for all women. Tanja was an advocate for self-fulfillment."

"I agree," Helma said. "Did you know her?"

"Only by reputation and of course her life-centered book, *Women in Jeopardy.* I expected her to become my close friend, though. So many people in the field are."

Helma took a step past Ms. Moon but halted as Ms. Moon shook her head and said mournfully, "Another local author."

"Tanja Frost was *not* a local author," Helma clarified. "Neither woman qualified. Molly Bittern was unpublished and Tanja Frost lived in Bellehaven only six weeks. To be a certifiable local author she needed to live here three months. Three months is the cut off."

"But Tanja *would* have lived here the requisite three months if she hadn't died," Ms. Moon said calmly. "I think a display of her life and work would be appropriate once the Local Authors project is more established."

Helma maintained her silence, a tactic that was less effective with Ms. Moon than with Ruth. Ms. Moon viewed Helma's silence as assent and confidently went on, her voice rising in excitement. "Yes, something colorful, in the main case by the library entrance, where we currently have the origami display. Glory can help you. To think we have a vicious killer on the loose."

Helma shook her head. "Tanja's death was an accident."

Ms. Moon's face smoothed and her voice dropped in the way of those who get to be the first to relate really bad news. She slowly shook her head, watching Helma's face. "I just heard it. The police have declared Tanja's death a homicide." She paused and said, as if quoting, ". . . injuries inconsistent with a fall."

Murder. And, yes, hit-and-run was murder, too. Two murders in two nights, just as Ruth had said. And Ms. Moon had known before Helma. She tried to correlate these two deaths to Ms. Moon's sudden enthusiasm for displays.

"Originally, you felt that a murder connected with the Local Authors project would mean canceling the project," Helma said, smothering the little glimmer that maybe a library without a local authors project wouldn't be the worst thing in the world to happen.

"I admit I said that, but you know what they say: there's no such thing."

"I beg your pardon?" Helma asked. "No such thing as *murder*?"

"Oh no," Ms. Moon said, smiling mischievously and tipping her head like the bird on Boy Cat Zukas's water dish. "No such thing as bad publicity. These are financially complicated times and a dramatic rise in our gate count might bring us to the attention of the city government."

"You're saying that if we sensationalize a local murder, there's *money* in it for the library?"

Ms. Moon's voice smoothed and soothed. "Not *sensationalize*, definitely not. Merely . . ." She fluttered her hands. "Inform! That's what libraries do to fulfill their responsibility to their communities, they inform by making information available." Her eyes went distant as she contemplated her mission.

"But there's no *actual* connection," Helma pointed out, "merely a coincidental."

Ms. Moon nodded absently, then said, "May I ask you a question about last night?"

"Of course," Helma told her, bracing herself for questions about the life lessons she'd learned at An Age of Certain Years.

"When you saw Tanja Frost standing there so full of life in front of you," she began, lowering her voice and eyes as if in shyness, leaning closer to Helma, "did you notice anything odd? For instance, a glow of premonition or unusual self-awareness?"

"She was uncommonly well dressed and made up," Helma said, recalling Tanja's perfect countenance.

Ms. Moon nodded eagerly. "As if she had unconsciously prepared for a long journey. Perhaps you noticed an . . . odd light around her or a faint musical sound in the air?"

"One of the fluorescent lights in the ceiling was buzzing," Helma offered.

Ms. Moon smiled in satisfaction and walked off toward her office.

"Hey, Helma," George Melville said, lugging a cardboard box into Helma's cubicle. "Look what I found on the loading dock this morning. They're addressed to the Local Authors Librarian, so I guess that's you. Where do you want 'em?"

"On this book truck is fine, thank you," Helma told him. "No return address or note?"

"Nada," George said, hoisting the box into the wheeled cart. "Just books, it looks like. They're coming out of the woodwork. Maybe instead of Local Authors shelves we're going to need a Local Authors *annex*."

"The response has been more than I anticipated," Helma said, recognizing she'd made an understatement. "Did the police talk to you about the death of Molly Bittern?"

"Yep. Your very own chief grilled me but I couldn't help much, even though I did intimate that poor Molly's poetry might have done her in." When Helma didn't laugh, wondering when they'd all begun referring to Molly as "poor Molly," George said, "Yeah, the chief's response was pretty glum, too." His face went serious. "Bad habit to make a joke about the events you'd rather cry over. Poor Molly, she didn't deserve to end her life that way. I did confess I own a blue Blazer but the chief wasn't interested, so I guess we can rule out Blazers as the murder vehicle. Has he talked to you?"

"Yesterday," Helma told him.

"That's what Harley said." He held up his hand. "We weren't gossiping. Well, actually, yes, we were. You doing okay?"

"Fine," Helma said.

"And then the murder last night. You know anything about that? The news is trying to make a connection."

"Nothing. I . . ."

But George's attention was drawn to the woman being led by Dutch, the circlation manager, toward Ms. Moon's office. "Isn't that Maggie Bekman, crack reporter from our local rag?"

Helma studied the curly-haired petite woman whose byline in the *Bellehaven Daily News* was often accompanied by a flattering photo. They were unmistakably the same. "I believe it is."

They watched Ms. Moon greet the newspaper reporter as if she were a close friend and usher her into her office, closing the door behind them.

"Uh-oh, she closed her door," George said. "Whatever that's about, you can bet it ain't good."

After George left, Helma unpacked the box of books he'd delivered. Thirty-eight copies of a self-published book titled *I, Mother,* the story of a devoted mother whose family treated her like a robot.

"Howdy. Remember me?"

Helma looked up from the reference desk into the smiling face of Boyd Bishop, the pseudonymous local author who'd feared he'd sent Molly Bittern to her death by laughing at her poem.

"I do," Helma told him. A young woman holding a stack of open books stepped up behind him. He turned and nodded to the young woman, and for some reason Helma pictured him tipping an invisible cowboy hat. Again, he wore creased jeans and, this time, a gray cable knit turtleneck. He turned back to Helma. "I won't take up your time, ma'am, but will you have dinner with me tonight?"

She was so surprised that for a moment she just

stared at him. He gazed back, relaxed, grinning. The young woman behind him pretended not to listen.

"Unless it's against library rules to date patrons, of course."

"No, it's not," Helma told him, although it *was* one of her personal rules, "but . . ."

"But I could be a—or *the*—murderer, right? So how about if instead of me picking you up we meet at a well-lit restaurant. Six thirty?"

"I have a meeting tonight," Helma told him.

"Tomorrow night?"

"I have a meeting tomorrow night, too."

"This is starting to sound like rejection." He touched his heart.

"I'm committed to a series of meetings this week," Helma explained, despite her father's advice and her own belief that explanations only cluttered communication.

"Then how about a quick sandwich between work and your meeting tonight?"

"Tomorrow night would be better," Helma said, breaking the rule she'd faithfully followed for eighteen years, although it had rarely been tested.

"Great. Five thirty at Echo's?" he asked, naming an upscale bar and eatery. "I can pick you up."

"No, thank you. I prefer to meet there. And six o'clock is better."

"I'll see you then," he said, and nodded to the woman behind him.

He was gone in a moment and Helma distractedly helped the young woman decipher the conflicting information in three different books on growing orchids, confounded by what she'd just agreed to do.

Glory stopped briefly as she pushed a cart of books past the reference desk. She wore her long hair in a girlish ponytail and earrings of tiny gold teddy bears. "Helma, I have more Local Author contributions," she sang out, causing an older man at the atlases to turn and smile indulgently in Glory's direction.

"If you have time, could you leave them on the book truck beside my desk?" Helma asked.

Glory smiled and bobbed. "Oh yes. Of course. I'd be glad to. And if there's anything else I can do to assist you or to improve the Local Authors project, just tell me and I'll do it right away."

"Thank you," Helma said, curious how simply being in Glory's presence for a few moments could prove so exhausting.

In a lower voice, Glory asked, "Do the police think the same person killed those two women?"

"I'm not aware of what the police believe," Helma told her.

"Really?" Glory blinked. "Are you engaged?"

"Engaged in what?" Helma asked.

"Engaged to be married."

"Of course not," Helma answered in surprise.

"Oh, goody," Glory said and gaily set off, humming a cheery ditty and pushing her book cart toward the workroom.

When Harley materialized to relieve her at the desk, Ruth appeared at the same time. She carried a giant white paper cup of coffee and, in her other hand, a bulging plastic bag. "Hi, kids," she said, taking a sip of coffee and smiling. "Nirvana. Good coffee again."

"Coffee's not allowed in the library," Harley told her.

"I didn't see a sign," Ruth said.

"It's implied."

"I don't do implication."

"We're not a Barnes & Noble," Harley told her, "yet." He opened his jaws twice while keeping his lips closed.

"Harley," Ruth said sweetly, "when did you start wearing your glasses on one of those little leashes?"

Harley touched the silver chain that looped from the earpieces of his glasses around his neck and Ruth went on, "It makes you look like a man devoted to keeping track of small things—like paper clips."

Harley's jaw worked furiously and Helma interrupted. "Did you want to talk to me, Ruth? I'll walk outside with you." She knew Ruth wasn't there to check out any library materials since she was still banned for owing eighty-six dollars in overdue fines.

"Thereby making everyone happy in one fell swoop," Ruth said, leading the way to the front door. "Bye, Harley."

Glory suddenly darted from the stacks in front of Ruth. "Hi, Ruth," she said, her ponytail bouncing.

Ruth raised her paper coffee cup toward Glory. "Cute shoes," she said, not even looking at Glory's feet, which Helma noted were clad in unremarkable Mary Janes.

"Oh," Glory said, looking down at her feet in puzzlement. "Thank you." But by then Ruth was already pushing through the library's front door.

Once outside on the sidewalk, Helma took a deep breath of the moist air. The street lamps in the distance faded into a grayish mist as if a light fog was coming ashore.

Ruth held up her plastic bag. "I bought a few things

at the art store so I'm going back to your apartment to fool around. I heard—and you need to know this—the word on the street is that our royal chief of police has become the Royal Pain in the Butt the last couple of days. 'Cranky as hell and twice as hot,' is the way I heard it."

"His moods have nothing to do with me," Helma told her.

"Such warmth. No wonder your cat moved out." Ruth slapped her hand to her mouth. "Sorry, really," she said through her fingers. "I didn't mean that. *I'm* the one who lost him."

"Yes," Helma agreed. "You are."

"And I'll find him."

When Helma stepped back into the library, Ms. Moon stood contemplating the library display case, which still held brightly colored and fanciful creations of origami.

"I spoke to Sunny," she said when she saw Helma, "your group leader last night."

"Did she have more information about Tanja Frost's death?" Helma asked.

"No," Ms. Moon said, looking at Helma closely, "but she described your friend's unregistered arrival and . . . *exhibition*. I don't believe she has the proper attitude to accompany you to these sessions, not at all."

"You just missed Ruth," Helma said, nodding toward the front door. "You could have discussed it with her."

There wasn't time for a proper lunch so Helma took twenty minutes to rush over to Saul's Deli and order a roast beef sandwich and a plain leaf lettuce salad to go.

"It'll just be a minute," said the waitress, whose left ear was riveted with so much metal that the upper curl bent forward like a friendly dog's. She nodded to a large table of businessmen at the rear of the deli. "We're almost finished with their order. Would you like an iced tea while you wait? On the house."

"No, thank you," Helma told her. "I'll sit over here."

She sat at an empty table not far from the counter, wishing she'd brought something to read, like her friend Georgia who always carried a "traveling book" for moments like these.

The deli was busy as it usually was during lunch hours, drawing from downtown businesses and government offices. Diners sat at tables surrounding Helma, and she wouldn't have noticed the woman at a table opposite her except the woman glanced Helma's way and then turned back to her companion in such a sharp movement that Helma caught it in her peripheral vision.

The woman wore two scarves and Helma recognized that it was Sunny, the group leader who'd introduced Tanja Frost. She sat corner-to-corner with a brown-haired man in his forties dressed in jeans and hiking boots. He wore a zippered nylon jacket that served year-round in Bellehaven. A patch on his shoulder illustrated a leaping salmon encircled by the words *Restore Salmon Habitat.*

Sunny leaned close to him, her face tight, lips in exaggerated articulation. Gone was any attempt to appear calm and "sunny." The man listened, shoulders stiff and eyes downcast. His face was tanned and his hair a little longer than most men's, with the currently fashionable fine stubble shadowing his cheeks and chin.

Helma Zukas never pried into other peoples' business, but naturally she wished to express her sympathy for the death of Sunny's "dear friend." She stood and quietly approached the couple's table, noting as she did, how Sunny stiffened and backed away from the man. She looked up at Helma and smiled without surprise, adjusting the drape of her scarf. "Hello, Helma."

"Sunny. I'm sorry about your friend, Tanja."

Sunny nodded, her face sorrowful. "The group is holding a brief memorial session tonight if you care to join us."

"I already have a commitment, but thank you." She nodded to the man who distractedly returned her nod. An aura of physical fitness hung over his broad shoulders.

"I'm sorry," Sunny said hastily, noticing the nod. "This is Julius, an old friend. Julius, this is Helma Zukas, a Bellehaven librarian."

The man exposed well-cared-for teeth but not much of a smile. "Nice to meet you, Hilda," he said, glancing toward the door with what appeared to be longing.

He didn't really see her, Helma could tell, so she didn't bother correcting him. "But I've interrupted your conversation," she said. And waited.

"We were just . . ." Sunny began.

"Miss Zukas, your order's ready," the waitress unfortunately called from the counter, before Helma could say any more to either of them.

"It's good to see you, Helma," Sunny said, her smile

relaxing with relief. "If you change your mind about tonight, just drop in."

After her lunch, Helma dialed the Bellehaven City Police department. "I phoned last night regarding my missing cat," she told the officer who answered. "I'm inquiring whether you have any information."

"I see," the officer said. "One moment."

So perhaps they did. Helma listened impatiently to wobbly, irritating phone music while her call was being transferred, maybe to a policeman who'd spotted Boy Cat Zukas and perhaps even picked him up. It was several seconds before a new voice picked up the phone.

"Animal shelter. How may I help you?"

"A book your mother reserved just came back in," Dutch told Helma. "I can call her if you want, unless you want to take it."

"I'll drop it off on my way home tonight," Helma told him. "Thanks."

The book was a paperback romance titled *Loving Debts,* by Angelique d'Boudier, with the usual beautiful and partially clothed but troubled-looking people on the cover.

The library had only recently begun carrying a selection of romances despite some of the staff's protests that they didn't constitute literature. "Yeah," George Melville had said, "remember how libraries refused to carry Nancy Drew or the Hardy Boys? We lost a whole generation of readers on that decision." Helma had agreed: the selection was limited to paperbacks, many of them donations that were kept on spinner racks, and they flew out the door. Helma's mother and Aunt Em were devoted supporters.

"Helma, we've been waiting for you," her mother said, opening her apartment door and waving her inside.

Behind her mother, arranged on her dining table, were a collection of cookies on a silver platter, a dish of cut pears and orange sections, an open box of chocolate-covered cherries, and a pitcher of iced tea, along with napkins, small glass plates, and forks. It had only been fifteen minutes since Helma phoned to say she was coming.

Aunt Em wore a Christmas apron. She was holding on to the back of a chair for support, but beaming. "Sit down, Wilhelmina. We have fixed a little treat for you."

"I really don't—" she began, but her mother, whose name was Lillian, said, "I put out those chocolate-covered cherries you loved when you were a little girl, remember? You used to eat them with a spoon so you wouldn't spill any of the filling on your clothes. It was so cute. Lola sent me these for Easter."

"Mother, Easter was six months ago," Helma reminded her.

Aunt Em laughed. "They keep one hundred years, like those Twinkies. Come sit down now. Let's see the book."

Helma laid the paperback romance on the table and Aunt Em snatched it up, quickly scanning the cover blurb.

"Eat, eat," she told Helma, and both women waited, watching her expectantly.

Finally, when Helma sat down and placed a vanilla sandwich cookie and two pear slices on her plate, Lillian and Aunt Em exhaled deep breaths of satisfaction and sat down, too.

Aunt Em and Lillian had moved in together a year ago after Mrs. Whitney, Aunt Em's former roommate and Helma's former neighbor, died peacefully in her sleep one night. "She was a lucky ducky. That's what I want," Aunt Em had announced the very day Mrs. Whitney died. Helma's mother had nodded in solemn agreement.

So from two women who'd spent most of their lives needing a referee at every family event, they now spent a seemingly companionable twenty-four hours a day in each other's company. Still, Helma would never have dared tell them they were beginning to resemble one another.

"How is Ruthie?" Aunt Em asked after she bit into a chocolate-covered cherry and sucked out its center. "How long will she visit?"

"She doesn't know yet," Helma said.

"Ah," Aunt Em said, nodding, a smear of candy center stuck to her chin. "Love problems. I thought so."

Lillian sniffed. "Ruth's whole life has been problematic."

"If she paints, she'll feel good, love or no love," Aunt Em said.

"Oh my," Lillian said. "I never could understand why people paid good money for those paintings. They just look like big scribbles to me."

"Hush, Lillian," Aunt Em admonished. "They're lively, like"—she couldn't think of the word and waved her hands in front of her—"lively, like, you know, *life*." She looked at Helma, "Like life *should* be, anyway."

"And how *is* our chief of police?" Lillian asked, apropos of nothing, watching Helma closely and getting to her most abiding interest. "Busy with the murders? Those poor, poor women."

"Yes, he is," Helma told her.

That's all Helma said, just those three little words, but she saw her mother and Aunt Em exchange worried glances.

"I'm sure he appreciates your insight, as always," Lillian said, pausing so Helma could fill in the details, and when she didn't, adding, "but maybe this time he's working alone?"

"The entire police force is involved in solving the homicides," Helma said, looking down at her plate and forking her pear slice when she caught her mother pursing her lips in a tight, sympathetic O.

Aunt Em leaned closer to Helma and patted her hand. "Men have their ways, dear," she said. "Your mother and I know *that*."

"We've had our share," Lillian said with a touch of smugness.

"Ask your mother about *her* brush with the law," Aunt Em told Helma.

"You were stopped by the police?" Helma asked, grateful to turn the attention to her mother.

"Emily means Jackson. I've only dated him once." She dropped her voice and put her cookie back on her plate. "He's a senior volunteer with the police department. He knows the chief." She touched her hair. "Lawmen. I know how they are. Don't you worry."

"I'm not worried. There's nothing . . ." She stopped as again she saw that quick exchange of knowing looks between the two older women. She gave up and instead deflected them with, "both of the murdered women were interested in being writers."

"Love," Aunt Em said, picking up *Loving Debts* and fanning the pages. "Murder's always about love. Love of people or things. Love of revenge. Always love. That song tells how love makes the world go 'round," she said, nodding. "Love stops it dead, too."

Chapter 10

The Empty School Blues

When Helma returned from her mother's apartment to her own, TNT was just leaving his, a bluc gym bag in hand and a towel around his neck. He was dressed in sweats, as usual.

"I heard about Boy Cat Zukas," he said to her, his boxer face craggy with sympathy. "Give him a little more time. Life's too good here."

"I agree," Helma told him. "His former life was likely very chaotic."

"I think your friend Ruth has got her blues on the run," he said, winking as he passed Helma. "That girl's a blinger. And once that cat comes to his senses, you'll be fighting like a champ, too."

With TNT's words in mind, Helma cautiously opened her door. Her apartment was silent, nothing appeared out of order, the balcony was empty. Ruth must still be out.

What had TNT meant: Ruth was a "blinger"?

She skimmed through the *B*s in the dictionary she kept on her coffee table but didn't find the word *blinger.* It must be one of TNT's Irishisms.

Helma stood on her balcony for a few minutes in the moist air, examining other balconies, looking up to the roof of the Bayside Arms, even the fir tree beside the building. The bowl of cat food hadn't been touched. She picked it up to replace that morning's cat kibbles with a fresh batch.

Stepping back into her living room she froze, hearing a scraping sound from the rear of her apartment near the bedrooms. Helma tipped her head, listening. No, there it was again. Her heart pounded and she glanced at her telephone, calculating she was eleven feet away from dialing 911. She took one silent and cautious step toward the telephone, then another.

Then stopped as song burst from the back bedroom: "Roll me over in the clover, roll me over, lie me down and do it again."

"Ruth," she said aloud, but only as recognition, not greeting. She relaxed, forgetting the 911 call. Only Ruth.

"Hello," Helma called out, moving toward the second bedroom and not wanting to startle Ruth as much as she'd been startled. Ruth's voice stopped dead just as she began the second stanza. Helma knew this bawdy song but only because she'd heard Ruth sing it. She'd never researched to discover if it was an actual song. The good thing was that she'd only heard Ruth sing it when she was happy.

"Helma," Ruth answered. "I'm in my room."

Helma stopped in the doorway of the guest bedroom, too overcome to say a word.

"I'm painting," Ruth said. "I decided to skip the pencils." And for the first time since her arrival, Helma saw glee in her stance, her voice, lighting up her face. Aunt Em might be right. Ruth had tied her hair out of her face in a tail that stuck crookedly from the side of her head. "What do you think?"

Helma was uncertain what Ruth was asking about: the brilliant orange and green canvas tilted on a makeshift easel on top of the bureau, the tubes and pots of paints arrayed on the unmade bed, or the scattered boxes, bags, and papers from Ruth's shopping trip. The bedroom where Ruth had slept for two nights looked as if an unruly family of six had moved into it a week ago. Ruth, who'd arrived without even a change of underwear, now had possessions scattered on every flat surface and draped over any object that might be substantial enough.

"Is that paint permanent?" Helma asked, looking at the orange smear on the pale blue bedspread.

"I certainly hope so," Ruth said, leaning closer to a glob of orange on the lower right corner of her canvas. "This brand is usually pretty good."

Behind Helma the doorbell rang. She left Ruth humming to herself and, as was her habit, peered through the peephole before answering. She didn't recognize the face of the woman standing on her doormat.

Opening the door didn't give her any clue, either. The woman was disheveled, her hair partially red and part gray, demarked by a two-inch line where the dyed hair had grown out. She wore coveralls and a pink sweater. "Is this yours?" she asked, holding out a black cat beneath its front legs. It struggled to jump out of her grasp.

"No," Helma said, "I'm sorry but that's not my cat."

"Okay, then," the woman said, releasing the cat, which streaked down the steps toward the parking lot and disappeared beneath a row of cars.

"But thank you," Helma told her, catching a whiff of alcohol as she closed the door, wondering how the woman had known.

Five minutes later, while Helma pulled salad ingredients from her refrigerator, her doorbell rang again.

It was the same woman and this time she held Moggy, the manager's white Persian cat, which on pleasant days slept in an ornate cushioned box outside Walter David's door, and for which Walter had attached a specially constructed cat cushion to his Harley Davison motorcycle. "Is this it?" the woman asked.

"No, this is the manager's cat. Please return her to her box."

To Helma's horror, she glanced down the steps behind the woman and saw a man climbing upward holding a struggling black cat that looked suspiciously like the first cat the woman had brought. And there, ambling across the parking lot came a scraggly man carrying an orange tabby.

"They just want the five hundred dollars," the woman said, looking at them disdainfully.

"What five hundred dollars?" Helma asked.

"On the poster, the five-hundred-dollar reward. You're Helma Zukas, aren't you?" She pronounced it "Zuckas."

"Zukas," Helma corrected. "Yes, I am she, but I didn't hang any posters."

"Well, somebody did, and your name, and a five-hundred-dollar reward is on them, clear as gin, as they say. If somebody brings you your cat, you gotta pay up. That's what truth in advertising is all about."

"I appreciate that information," Helma said, "and I'm going inside now. Would you please tell those two men that neither of the cats they're carrying is my cat."

"My pleasure, but we'll keep on looking, you bet. Are you going to pay the reward in cash or a check? Because it's harder for some people to cash checks, you know."

"I'm going inside now," Helma repeated, gently closing the door on the woman.

When she turned around, Ruth was pulling a bottle of red wine from the cupboard. "Another cat hopeful?"

"Did you hang posters promising a five-hundred-dollar reward for Boy Cat Zukas?"

"I figured it couldn't hurt. Want some?" She held up the wine bottle.

"I do not. Posters, Ruth? You should have asked me before promising a five-hundred-dollar reward."

"Publicity is not cheap. You want to catch the public's attention, don't you?"

"But five hundred dollars?"

Ruth filled her tumbler with wine. "Okay, so what price do you want to put on his safe return? What? Twenty-five dollars. Fifty? How much is your cat worth? Seven dollars, ninety-two cents?"

They were interrupted by Helma's doorbell. Ruth answered with the wine bottle in her hand. Helma couldn't see who was at the door but Ruth said, "Sorry. Wrong cat again." She closed the door and, no longer holding a wine bottle, said to Helma, "See, people are really out there looking."

"Where are they finding all these cats?" Helma asked.

"It's not like there's a shortage of cats in this town."

"Yes, but Ruth, these cats may be taken from other homes."

Ruth paused. "Oh. You mean like we're creating a whole city of lost cats?"

"No. *You're* creating a whole city of lost cats. The responsible action is to remove the posters or at least change them to reflect reality."

Ruth narrowed her eyes at Helma and brushed her hand across her hair, leaving a streak of orange. "So, okay tell me, what's the reality?"

"Simple is always the best. A phone number, just the word *Reward* and a description of Boy Cat Zukas."

"I drew his picture," Ruth said indignantly. "Wait, I made photocopies." She went to her bedroom and returned to hand Helma a sheet of paper with the words *$500 Reward!!!!!* above an incomprehensible rendering with four sticks that might have been legs and the word *CAT* beneath it, with Helma's name and address under that.

"Okay, okay, I'll make a new one. What's the latest on the murders? I heard that's what they're both being called now. Told ya."

"Only that they're considered homicides."

"But they're connected, right?"

"No one's officially claiming they are."

"Mm-hmm. I told you I was going to help. So guess who I ran into today?"

"I don't play guessing games," Helma reminded her.

"Of course you don't, why risk being wrong? Anyway, my old friend, Officer Lehman." Ruth paused to smile to herself. "And *he* said that Tanja's unusual injury was an oval edged bruise right here." Ruth touched her left temple. "Nothing on the stairs could account for it. See the connection?"

"Not really," Helma told her. "Tanja's is the only intentional murder. Molly's death now ranks as homicide, yes, but initially it was an accident. It became a crime when the driver didn't stop. That doesn't make a connection."

"Come on, even in your current little dark cave, you've got to admit there are some creepy coincidences here. Literary, psycho, blondes. Both women were bumped, just with different implements: a car and an oval thingee. Deaths that could have almost been passed off as accidents."

"You're reaching, Ruth," Helma said.

"Bet not," Ruth said smugly, rolling up the reward poster in her hands.

By the time two more cat offerings were rejected, a new sign had been made, then hung in place of the old posters. Ruth announced she was accompanying Helma to her next group session: Battery Cables for Your Career.

"You're not registered," Helma warned as she drove to the Sandy High School, where the session was being held in the school library.

"C'mon. These kinds of groups have hit their crescendo, peaked, and are stumbling toward extinction. Everybody takes pills now, life is happy-happy. They'll be thrilled to have fresh blood."

The air was tense when Ruth and Helma entered the high school library where four rows of chairs were set up near a large globe. Around them, the school hovered unoccupied and unlit. "Schools have to be one of the creepiest places on earth when they're empty," Ruth whispered, "worse than cemeteries."

Helma agreed. A fanciful person might have expected to see youthful ghosts wandering the halls and drifting around corners.

Ruth bumped against a chair which clattered onto the linoleum floor, causing gasps and two screeches from the eight or nine women waiting for the meeting to begin.

"Sorry," Ruth announced. "My eyes are way up here and the chair was way down there."

One of the women separated herself from the group at the coffee table, and Helma recognized Pepper, who'd sat beside her the night before.

"Hi, Helma," she said, her eyes bright. She turned to Ruth, offering her hand, "I'm Pepper Breckenridge."

"As in salt and—?" Ruth asked.

"Right," Pepper said in a tone that conveyed she'd heard that association too many times. "All anybody can talk about are the deaths of Molly and Tanja Frost. Murder, can you believe it? I was right there in the same room with her last night. Maybe if I'd been the last person out the door instead of Tanja—"

"Maybe you'd be dead instead," Ruth finished.

"Did anyone see her fall?" Helma asked.

Pepper shook her head. "After we all left at the end of the session, I guess Tanja went back because she forgot her cell phone. Sunny was waiting for her at the bottom of the stairs.

"I heard that all Sunny saw was Tanja tumbling down the steps." Pepper lowered her voice and touched her left temple. "I heard she had a vicious bruise."

"The elevator was out of order," Helma remembered.

"I bet the murderer hid inside and jumped out after her. Let's sit over here," Pepper suggested, pointing to the third row from the front. She carried a bicycle helmet and a small pack to a chair. Her pant leg clip hung on her wrist.

"You some kind of counseling groupie?" Ruth asked Pepper.

"No more than you two, I guess," she said. "But I moved here a few weeks ago and my sister said it's a great way to meet people. She moved to a new town after an affair . . ." Pepper looked embarrassed but eager to share. "A political scandal, I guess you'd say. You meet people like yourself—and it's safe, usually."

"Where'd you move from?" Ruth asked.

"Near L.A.," she said with a touch of defensiveness.

Ruth nodded, her nose twitching. "California. That explains the draw to this pristine little corner of the world."

"I'm aware of some people's prejudice toward Californians," Pepper said to Ruth, gazing steadily up at her. Ruth stared back just as steadily, both of them pushing their heads forward and leaning in front of Helma, chins raising.

"We all come from somewhere else, don't we?" Helma interjected. "Ruth and I did."

"From Scoop River, Michigan, the back of beyond," Ruth said, sitting back, and the moment was defused.

"Did you know Molly?" Helma asked.

Pepper shook her head. "I knew she was in the Age group and I heard her read her poem at your Local Authors meeting, but I never talked to her."

At 7:35, the group leader, who introduced herself

to the nervous women as Gretchen, started by saying, "First off, I want to assure you all that we are perfectly safe here," which caused several women to exchange looks or glance over their shoulders at the door. Gretchen was nearly as tall as Ruth, just not so . . . vibrant.

"Wait," a thin woman said, standing up. "Before we begin, I'd like to expose a ringer."

Gretchen the leader looked at her blankly.

"A poser, a charlatan, a . . . *spy,*" the woman clarified.

"Is she talking about me?" Ruth whispered, sitting taller, preparing a counterattack.

Gretchen looked around the room. "And who might that be?" she calmly asked.

Like a specter of death, the woman pointed to a blond, bright-eyed woman perched on the edge of her chair and holding a notepad. "Her. She's a reporter from the *Bellehaven Daily News.*"

Helma hadn't noticed Maggie Bekman sitting so quietly among the Battery Cable women. It was the second time she'd seen the reporter that day, the first time when she'd entered Ms. Moon's office. Maggie sat with crossed legs, pencil poised in her left hand, the notebook on her knee tipped in that nearly upside-down fashion of left-handers.

Everyone stared at Maggie Bekman who smiled and said, "So?"

"You're not part of this group," her accuser complained. "You're just here looking for a . . . scoop."

"This meeting *is* being held in a tax-supported facility," the reporter said.

Beside Helma, Pepper bounded up from her chair and faced the reporter. "Are you hoping that if one of us gets killed tonight, you'll have inside info for the story tomorrow morning? Local color?"

"Shades of Lois Lane," Ruth muttered.

The reporter smiled unconcernedly and jotted in her notebook.

"Would you like to leave?" Gretchen asked her.

"I don't believe I would," the reporter responded calmly.

Gretchen chewed her lip, glancing from the reporter to the group of women. Then, she cleared her throat, stood, and resolutely announced, "Since our group is so small tonight, I believe we'll cancel this meeting and reassemble next week." She hesitated, then added, "Stay together as you leave. If anyone needs a ride home, I'll provide it."

Maggie Bekman jammed her notebook in her purse and left, slamming the door behind her.

Helma's heart lightened. She was now halfway through the required group sessions. Only two more to go and maybe those would be canceled, too, although naturally she hoped it wouldn't take another death to cause a cancellation.

"Let's go to Joker's," Helma suggested to Ruth.

Pepper turned wide-eyed and asked Helma, "*You* go to Joker's?"

"You have no idea," Ruth said.

"My cat was last seen there," Helma told her, "and there's still a little daylight left."

"You lost your cat? I'm sorry. What does it look like? I'll keep an eye out."

Helma described Boy Cat Zukas and Pepper again looked at Helma doubtfully. "If I see him, I'll call you."

The women stood in the hall while Gretchen locked

the high school library door, then as a tight group, they moved together, their voices hushed, down the empty high school halls, past closed lockers and unlit trophy cases and football banners into the dim school foyer, their voices rising to normal levels once they'd exited into the evening. It was still light but not for long.

Pepper unlocked a bicycle that was chained to the student bike rack and swung onto it.

"Would you like a ride home?" Helma asked her. "You could come back for your bicycle tomorrow."

"It's still light out and I cut across town on trails. I'm not concerned."

Helma and Ruth watched her ride away. "Hope we don't read about her in the paper tomorrow," Ruth said. "Hey, look!" She pointed at a plain blue car passing the high school. Wayne Gallant was at the steering wheel looking straight ahead. "Quick. Let's follow him."

"I believe I'll go to Joker's," Helma told her, opening the driver's door of her Buick.

"That's a bad sign when a woman chooses her cat over a man. That cat's no prize."

"But my cat can't help it."

Helma spotted Maggie Bekman standing beneath a parking lot light, her purse balanced on the front fender of a Subaru as she rifled through it.

Helma turned off her car's engine. "I need to ask her something," she told Ruth.

"I'm coming, too," Ruth said.

There were times when Ruth's straightforwardness was helpful and times when it hindered. This was one of those times. Helma rolled down her window. "Stay here, you can listen."

"Afraid I'll blow your plans?" Ruth asked, but she stayed in the car.

The hood of Maggie Bekman's Subaru held the contents of her purse: comb, wallet, notebook, fuzzy tissues, glasses, a prescription bottle, and loose candies. She glanced at Helma. "I *know* I had my keys," she said, her voice frustrated.

"Are they in your coat pocket?" Helma suggested.

The reporter felt inside both pockets. "No. I bet I left them inside."

"Would you like a ride?"

"No," she snapped. "I'd like my keys."

Helma glanced inside the Subaru. "I believe they're still in the ignition."

Maggie Bekman raised her hands as if questioning the heavens. "Oh, that's just great. Now what am I going to do? I don't suppose you have a coat hanger?"

Helma reached for the door handle. The door easily opened and the reporter smacked her forehead with the flat of her hand. "I feel like an idiot. Thanks. Not enough sleep, I guess."

"You've been working on the recent homicides," Helma said.

"Yeah. Looking for an angle."

Maggie Bekman was speaking to her out of gratitude and Helma dared to press the point. "Why did you attend this particular meeting tonight?"

But Maggie was sharp, despite being irresponsible with her keys. "What do you mean?" she asked, narrowing her eyes.

"Did someone suggest you attend this meeting in case another woman died?"

"Do I know you?" She began gathering up items from the hood of her car and throwing them back into her purse.

"I was curious whether someone at the library gave you the idea. The director?"

"My sources are my own business," she told Helma. "Aren't you familiar with the First Amendment?"

"The First," Helma assured her. "And the following twenty-six,"

"Well, good for you," Maggie said and climbed into the driver's seat, pausing to say, in only a slightly more gracious manner, "Thanks again," before she slammed her door.

Ruth and Helma searched the streets near Joker's and even down to the Dumpster near the fish-processing plant without any sign of Boy Cat Zukas, and as they headed back to Helma's apartment, Ruth glanced out at the bay and said, "Ten thousand lakes ain't the same as an ocean," softly adding, "no matter who lives there."

She sunk into her seat, chewing on her thumb, then suddenly sat up. "Stop the car."

Helma did. The brakes screeched. "What's wrong?"

"I want out, that's all."

"Why? Tell me where and I'll drop you off."

"Right here," Ruth said fiercely. "Right friggin' here. I want to walk."

"It's late."

"You're right it's late, too damn late." She already had the door open and was stepping out.

"Ruth," Helma began.

"I'm a grown-up, Helm," she said in a ragged voice. "Don't play mother. I'll see you later."

And the door slammed. Helma bit her lip and sat behind the wheel of her idling Buick. She put her hand on the door handle, then removed it, taking a deep breath and watching Ruth's shadow slip into the darkness.

It was Helma's habit never to wait longer than fifteen minutes for anyone, but with Ruth, she judged three to be sufficient time for her to change her mind. After three minutes and twenty seconds by her dashboard clock, she drove home to her apartment.

Helma sat on the edge of her bathtub and watched it fill, yearning to sink into the hottest water she could tolerate. Over the gushing water she caught the sound of her doorbell.

"Oh, Faulkner," she whispered as she drew on her robe. Ruth, properly, had second thoughts about any late-night ventures and now couldn't find her key.

But when she peered through her peephole she gasped and jerked open the door.

"Aunt Em! Come inside. It's the middle of the night! Where's Mother?"

Aunt Em stood on Helma's landing, holding an oblong casserole dish covered with aluminum foil. "I snuck away in a taxi," she said, nodding toward a taxi parked by the elevator. "This is *kugelis* for Ruthie."

Helma took the potato dish, its fragrance a wave of memory back to every family gathering in her Michigan past, and ushered Aunt Em inside. "Ruth isn't here, but . . ."

"It's *you* I am visiting," Aunt Em said, patting Helma's arm. She gazed into Helma's eyes, squinting and nodding as if what she saw there was exactly what she'd expected to find.

"Sit down, Aunt Em," Helma said. "I'll go tell the taxi to leave and take you home after you've had a cup of tea."

"No," Aunt Em told her firmly. "This is *my* trip. I will start and finish it by myself. Listen to *me* now."

"I will, I promise, but please, sit down." Helma held out a kitchen chair and Aunt Em sat. Her breaths jumped in little puffs and she dabbed her damp lips with a linen handkerchief from her purse. Helma's own heart pounded as she watched Aunt Em struggle to catch her breath.

"What is it, Aunt Em?" Helma asked as she sat across the table from her. "What's wrong?"

"Nothing with me, but I saw what's wrong with you."

"Me?"

Aunt Em nodded. "I am two times older than you, plus a little bit. I know about these times." Aunt Em slid her hand across the air like skimming an invisible table. "When our hearts go flat. Like a stone pressing."

Helma could not even begin to deny Aunt Em's words. They perfectly described the heaviness she experienced each morning: like a stone pressing. She stared at Aunt Em, nodding. "What is it?" she asked in a whisper.

Aunt Em shrugged. "Who knows?" She smiled at Helma. "It happens to people, to women. When I was young, we didn't talk about it, not like now. Then, I thought it happened to only me." She sighed. "I can tell you one thing," she said, her *th* turning into a *t*.

"Tell me."

Aunt Em leaned forward, her tired eyes intent. "It will leave you, the heaviness. Keep doing as hard as you can and it will one day disappear." She made poof-ing motions with her arthritic hands. "I promise you."

In a way, it was what TNT had told Helma. Go the distance, keep your dukes up, and stay off the ropes. They had both shared something they *knew,* from their own long lives.

"Now, I've done my godmotherly duty," Aunt Em said, using her hands to rise, "and I'll go home before your mother thinks I ran off with the new night watch-man. Oh, he's a juicy one."

Helma helped Aunt Em to the taxi and fastened her seat belt for her.

"Mylieu teva," Aunt Em said as Helma closed the taxi door. *I love you.*

"Mylieu teva," Helma told her and stood in the dark parking lot until the taxi disappeared.

Helma uncovered the *kugelis* and breathed deep its fragrance as she cut herself a generous slice of the salty potato dish.

She closed her eyes in pleasure as she chewed, see-ing for a moment her uncles, her father and grandfa-ther, all of them too loud, waving their arms and arguing in Lithuanian whether the first horse on her grandfather's farm had been named *Agutė* or *Zitelė*.

She slowly swallowed, positive that tomorrow would be a better day.

Chapter 11

Changing Priorities

On Thursday morning, Helma wasn't the least surprised to be awakened by Ruth's voice calling, "Uh-oh, Helma, you'd better come see this."

Not another death. Her thoughts flashed from Pepper, who'd ridden away alone on her bicycle, to Maggie Bekman, the reporter who'd driven away alone, or even Gretchen the group leader who'd stayed to usher every woman from the school library.

She pulled on her robe and walked to the living room, avoiding the disaster of Ruth's bedroom as she passed, first sweeping her eyes across the balcony in vain before she braced herself for the sight of the television playing out more grim news.

But a commercial for some softly lit and vaguely described personal contentment product lulled from the screen and instead of sitting on the sofa arm watching it, Ruth stood at Helma's counter, leaning over the open *Bellehaven Daily News*. Ruth wore the same clothes she'd worn the day before, only now they were more spattered with paint: black and yellow added to the orange and green. Her eyes were red and puffy. After her return, Ruth had most likely stayed up all night. She was eating a huge slab of *kugelis* with her hands.

Knowing Ruth was back to practicing her former bad habits was a comfort of sorts.

"You're not going to like this," Ruth said, closing the paper to the front page and tapping her finger on the lead story along the right-side column.

"Who died last night?" Helma asked.

"No one that anybody's announced," Ruth said, stepping aside so Helma could read the headline.

"Murder Theories Surface," and beneath that: "Literary Envy?"

Helma skimmed the first paragraphs of the article which rehashed the deaths of Tanja and Molly, the blue car, the injury to Tanja's head, then gasped as she caught the words, "May Apple Moon, Bellehaven Public Library Director." She glanced at the reporter's byline at the top of the page: Maggie Bekman.

She read Ms. Moon's quotes: "I can't deny the evidence points to a link between these terrible murders and the library's recently launched Local Authors program. Each victim was a local author whose work was to be added to our collection. They likely met frequently in our library, since the library is the beating heart of the art community's creative center. We're erecting a display to celebrate the lives of the two authors and their work."

"But neither one of these women are eligible as Local Authors," Helma said aloud.

"Keep reading," Ruth advised.

Helma turned to A3 where the story's heading was SERIAL KILLER STALKING OUR LIBRARY?

Helma gasped a second time. "Serial killer?"

"As head of this new program," Ms. Moon was quoted as saying, "anyone with questions about Local Authors or the library's role should contact me," and then the article gave the library's general phone number.

"I thought the Local Authors project was your baby and the Moonbeam wasn't exactly a fan of it in the first place," Ruth said. She licked her fingers and reached for another piece of *kugelis*.

What Ruth said was true, but Helma recalled Ms. Moon's comment about there being no such thing as bad publicity. *Lurid* publicity was hardly part of the library's realm, either.

A smaller article beneath the more sensational story was titled: "Therapist Remembered." It paid tribute to Tanja's influential book and followed her beginnings from Wisconsin, another Midwesterner who'd come through the gates of California to the Northwest, a route so typical Helma was sure that someday a name would be coined for it, like Pass-through Migration or Coastal Seekers.

She blinked as she read the last line: "Tanja Frost's ashes will be returned to Dells, Wisconsin, for a final service, said her husband, Julius Morgan."

Julius? How common of a man's name was Julius? In the deli, Sunny had been engrossed in conversation with a man she'd introduced as Julius. He'd been the correct age to be Tanja's husband, although he hadn't looked as . . . put together, as Tanja. Still . . .

"Look, Ruth," she said, one finger to the article and explained how she'd seen Sunny with a man named Julius the day after Tanja's death.

"Sunny, who introduced Tanja so lovingly?" Ruth asked, her interest perking. "With Tanja's husband, eh? Maybe she was just extending her sympathy."

Helma didn't gossip so she said nothing. Ruth raised her eyebrows. "But you didn't think you were gazing on a sympathetic exchange, did you?"

"I did detect intense conversation," Helma replied judiciously. "Perhaps even strong words."

"Got it," Ruth said.

"Got what?" Helma asked.

Ruth shrugged. "The first sweet scent of scandal, that's all."

Helma's phone rang and she answered it. "Hi, Helma," a man's soft voice said. "I'm looking for Ruth. Is she there?" She recognized the voice of Paul, calling from Minneapolis.

"Hello, Paul." And although Ruth was vigorously shaking her head, Helma did not believe in participating in blatant subterfuge. "Yes, she is. I'll give her the phone."

Ruth scowled but her face lit with a curious mixture of anticipation and dread. She took the phone and covered the mouthpiece with her hand, saying to Helma, "Why can't you buy a cordless phone like other people?"

"I have to get ready for work," Helma told her. "You have all the privacy you need," and she left the kitchen as

Ruth stretched the curled phone cord taut so she could sit on the couch, hearing as she reached her bedroom door, Ruth saying in a low, naked voice, "I had to, I just had to."

When Helma left for the library, Ruth was still huddled in a corner of the sofa, the phone to her ear, talking in low tones. She didn't look up and Helma gently closed the door behind her. As she drove past the entrance to Boardwalk Park, her mind on Ms. Moon's newspaper interview, a police car was waiting to pull into traffic, reminding her of Wayne Gallant's cold behavior. She bit her lip and firmly expunged his image.

Barely thirty seconds later, she glanced into her rearview mirror and was shocked to see the patrol car behind her, its lights flashing. She pulled over and waited, ignoring curious glances of passersby, including a group of pointing and giggling teenage girls.

Wayne Gallant approached her Buick. Helma didn't roll down her window until he made window-rolling-down motions, and then only halfway down, passing her drivers license and registration through the opening.

"I don't want these," he said.

"What law have I broken?" Helma asked. "I presume that's why you stopped me."

The chief's face actually reddened. "No broken law," he said. "I wondered if . . . well, if you've had more time to think about my suggestion."

"I assure you I have," Helma said, recalling his smug request that "citizens" stay out of police business. "I have no intention of contributing to, or complicating, your explorations."

He appeared to be struck dumb. His mouth opened and closed most unattractively.

"May I be released now?" she asked since he seemed unable to speak.

He nodded briskly, once, and sharply waved his hand toward town.

Helma placed her Buick in gear, and if perhaps a tiny spray of gravel flew up behind her rear tires, it was completely unintentional.

"More books for you, Helma," Glory Shandy said before Helma had even removed her coat. Glory held a stack of seven or eight paperbacks, all with similar black lettering in a gothic font. "There's a note inside the top one from the author. She's from near Seattle but says her library doesn't have a Local Authors program, so could she please be included in ours."

Glory set down the books and cleared her throat. "Ms. Moon asked me to help you with the displays."

"Displays?" Helma asked although she suspected she knew.

"For the dead authors," Glory said apologetically. "I'm going to clear out the origami display to make room."

"Please wait until I discuss this with Ms. Moon," Helma told her.

"Certainly," Glory said. "I felt . . ." She tipped her head and looked upward at Helma as she played with a red strand. "I only want to do what's best for the library."

"And that's exactly what's expected from all library employees," Helma responded to Glory's favorite refrain.

When Helma entered the staff lounge, seeking the fortification of hot tea before she confronted Ms. Moon,

Roger Barnhard the diminutive children's librarian, was saying, "I had a call from a parent who'd just read the newspaper, asking if local authors were allowed in the children's room and was it safe to send little Johnny to the library all alone. Geez, what was that woman thinking when she gave that interview?"

"She didn't *give* it," George Melville said, "she *requested* it. I saw it with my own eyes." He lowered his voice to a conspiratorial tone. "A source who wishes to remain anonymous said they overheard the Moonbeam phone Maggie Bekman, crack reporter, and invite her to the library for a story that would 'make' her career. She's angling to give us a high profile, turn us into the Community Crime Center."

At that moment, Ms. Moon passed the staff lounge, hugging a newspaper close to her heart. Helma left her tea steeping on the counter and followed Ms. Moon into her office.

"Excuse me," Helma said. "I'd like to discuss your interview in today's *Bellehaven Daily News*."

"And I wish to discuss it with you," Ms. Moon said gaily, setting the paper on her desk and tapping it once before she beckoned to a chair. "Sit down."

"No, thank you," Helma told her, and Ms. Moon went on as if Helma hadn't spoken, "The response has been gratifying already. Two calls from the mayor's office and," she held up three fingers, "three from interested members of the community."

"In the paper you made reference to the Local Authors project," Helma said. "As we discussed yesterday, neither victim qualified as a local author."

"Aren't you being a little too stringent?" Ms. Moon asked. "For instance, one of the phone calls was from an author who spent a summer sailing out of our marina. Don't you agree that makes him eligible for local authorhood?"

"Bellehaven has become a destination town," Helma told her. "Spending a night in a hotel in New York city doesn't make one a New York State resident."

"Of course not, but there are always exceptions. Now, tell me, are you finding the counseling sessions helpful?"

"Last night's was very satisfying," Helma told her truthfully.

"I knew it." Ms. Moon, who normally would have prodded Helma for more information, suddenly leaned forward earnestly. "There *is* one thing we must be clear on."

"Yes?" Helma asked guardedly.

"In the past, you've had a tendency to . . . become involved with various . . . crimes in Bellehaven and maybe you've occasionally had . . . insights that have *accidentally* helped the police solve those crimes." She paused and Helma said nothing, waiting.

Ms. Moon pulled one of the crystals on her desk closer and formed a tent above it with her hands. "But this time it's vital to allow life to play out to its destiny, to not redirect the currents away from their intended culmination." She looked at Helma expectantly.

"You're asking me not to get involved in any investigation of these murders," Helma translated for her.

Ms. Moon clapped her hands together. "You're so perceptive. Only to pay close attention to your role as a librarian and allow our magnificent police force to fulfill their roles. It's beneficial for all of us to stay in our own true spaces."

"These deaths are unrelated to the library or the Local Authors project," Helma averred as she'd done earlier.

"If that's true, then they're of no interest to you. Your sole mission is to be a librarian."

"I *am* a librarian."

Ms. Moon's jaw tightened. "I understand your cat is missing. I expect that to be the limits of any amateur investigation you partake in." Her smile stretched tight.

In a flash, Helma saw her nephew at three years old, hands on hips, staring defiantly at his mother and saying, "You're not the boss of me."

But instead, she calmly told Ms. Moon, "I assume I will continue managing the Local Authors project, despite your comments in the newspaper."

Ms. Moon let out her substantial breath. "Of course, of course. A collection of Molly Bittern's poetry was donated to the library today and I gave it to Glory."

"As manager of the Local Authors project, it would have been more appropriate to give Molly's poems to me," Helma said.

Ms. Moon shook her finger at Helma. "Now, now, let's be generous. You know Glory will share them with you. She's spellbound by the project."

It seemed to Helma that Glory was in a perpetual state of spellbindedness.

"You and Glory can begin designing the display to honor Molly and Tanja. I think it would be wise to use only two-thirds of the available space."

Helma had no intention of using *any* of the space, but she was too curious not to ask, "And the final third?"

Ms. Moon shrugged, blushing. "If this *is* a serial killer stalking Bellehaven's local authors, we might want to highlight the connection, tie up all the loose ends, so to speak."

"You're asking me to create a display for authors who don't meet the criteria and leave space for the next *victim*?"

"Only if the unfortunate person—or perhaps even the killer—is a local author, of course. It would give the public a place to gather for information or read about the dangers of the career and to honor the written word. Don't you agree how nicely it all ties together?"

Helma couldn't think of a single word to say. She could only stare at the director.

"And so you also agree," Ms. Moon said, watching Helma closely, "that it would be totally alien to the flow of events for you to become involved and do your . . ." Ms. Moon's hands stroked the air above her crystal, "sleuthing?"

Helma took a step toward the door before saying, "I agree that while I am in the library, my attention will be dedicated to being a librarian to the best of my ability."

"That's exactly what I assured the chief of police," Ms. Moon said.

Ruth phoned at 11:45, as Helma was attacking a stack of Local Author offerings. The cover of the first book was illustrated with an elephant, apropos of nothing as far as Helma could tell since the title was, *You Care and I Don't*. It was self-published and she rubbed her forehead before setting it aside.

The next book was also self-published, *One 11 Millionth of a War,* memoirs of a World War II Air Force pilot. She gazed on the face of the handsome young pilot on the inside cover. Self-published or not, breaking the guidelines or not, these were the stories that *shouldn't* be lost. She set it aside for separate consideration, imagining the creation of still another special project: local historical memoirs.

"Okay, it's set up," Ruth said into her ear. "High noon at the Wild Hare."

"What's set up?" Helma asked. The Wild Hare? The Wild Hare was on the "renewal" side of Bellehaven, above the docks and railroad tracks, a darkish local brewery known for its beer collection and oversized hamburgers. Helma rarely ate in darkish establishments, preferring to clearly see whatever she was inserting into her mouth.

"We're meeting Julius Morgan, Tanja's husband, so you can grill him about all things murderish."

"What?"

"I did a little snooping around—it didn't take much. An old friend here, a gossip there. He lives in the woods somewhere out there beyond the city limits, one of those eco-types with a missionary complex. *Tanja's* husband—can you figure it? There's a story there, I can feel it, and you're sunk in this dark hole so *somebody* had to take charge. Who better than me? Be at the Wild Hare at high noon. I'll arrive a few minutes earlier to make sure the atmosphere's conducive to his spilling his guts. Don't pull out that little notebook you carry, okay? This is not an interrogation, just a friendly conversation. See you."

"Ruth—" Helma began, but Ruth had already hung up, leaving Helma holding a silent phone.

"You okay?" Harley Woodworth asked, standing beside the bookcase that separated their cubicles. "You look a little feverish. I have aspirin if you need one. Or vitamin C. You could be coming down with a cold; this is an early flu season I heard." Harley turned his head and nodded toward someone Helma couldn't see. "Oh, hi," he said, his voice rising a register. "Helma's sick and I was just offering her an aspirin."

Glory, her forehead wrinkled and lips pulled into sympathetic concern, a little hum of solicitude issuing from her throat, leaned into Helma's cubicle. "Can I do anything for you?" she asked. "A drink of water? Or herbal tea?"

"There's nothing wrong," Helma told her.

"Are you staying home tonight?" Glory asked. "You should."

"I'm attending a meeting tonight," Helma said.

"Where is it?" Glory asked.

"I'm fine," Helma reiterated, ignoring Glory's question.

But Glory continued on, her voice deepening into melodious tenderness as her eyes took on a sparkling brightness. "It's the stress of the past few days. The murders and your personal uncertainties. It wears you down. Staying home in bed is the answer. My mother's that way, too. After a few days of stress, she collapses. But then, she might be a little older than you are."

Even Harley blinked at that. Helma swallowed twice and took two calming breaths before carefully saying, "I appreciate your concern. Now, if you'll excuse me," and she made her way past Glory to the women's rest-room where as she opened the door, she nearly bumped into Ms. Moon.

"Oh, Helma, I've asked Glory to download a few possible layouts for the Deceased Authors displays."

She chuckled and Helma detected a watchful expression in her eyes. "Why reinvent the wheel, I always say. I told her to search for something tasteful but dramatic, a layout that will draw in the eye and satisfy the wounded soul struggling with life's tragedies, the answers that can be found in their local library. I'll loan you one of my crystals to signify our dependence on fate."

Helma Zukas was not about to debate inappropriate library displays while standing in an open restroom door. However she did point out, "If the police solve these deaths and there's no literary connection, the displays will be moot."

Ms. Moon's eyes narrowed. "All the more reason to hurry then, isn't it?" she said as the door swung closed.

Helma stood for a moment in the doorway of the Wild Hare while her eyes adjusted to the gloom. Ruth's laughter boomed from an even gloomier corner at the rear of the brewery. At the other end of the Wild Hare, glass windows exposed a room of gigantic stainless steel vats where beer brewed. The air carried a not unpleasant malty fragrance. And beneath that the smell of what Ruth called "frozen-to-be-fried" food.

"Hey, Helma, this is Julius," Ruth said as Helma sat in a chair at the end of the booth rather than sliding across the Naugahyde seat.

Helma recognized him at once as the same man she'd seen in Saul's Deli with Sunny.

"Hi, Helma," he said without recognition. He wore a flannel shirt over a black T-shirt that showed his athletic upper body, on his face a slightly bewildered air.

On the table in front of him sat a small pile of brochures that exhorted, "Keep Bellehaven Green!"

"I told Julius about your Local Authors club and how you'd *love* to include Tanja's work in your collection," Ruth said.

"Actually," Helma began, "Tanja only lived in Bellehaven for . . ." when she felt the blunt end of Ruth's shoe against her shin.

Julius didn't notice. He nodded and shoved a copy of *Women in Jeopardy* across the table toward Helma, then patted a box the size of a paper ream. "I brought both books. Here's the published book and a manuscript of her new book. It's the only copy," he said, his hand resting protectively on the box.

"Surely Tanja made other copies," Helma said.

He shook his head. "Tanja said she destroyed the earlier drafts when she moved here. Oh, it was all on her computer, but her computer was stolen during the move. I know that once she set up her office, she began reentering the whole thing, but she hadn't got very far."

"When did you clean out her office?" Helma asked.

"Yesterday morning," he told her.

"Yesterday?" Ruth repeated. "The morning after she died? You're jonny-on-the-spot, aren't you?"

"I can't let the library take responsibility for the only copy of her manuscript," Helma explained. "If you photocopy it first, we'd consider it."

"It's a big manuscript," Julius said. "I don't like using that much paper. It's a waste of trees."

"Then use recycled paper," Ruth snapped.

A sheepish looked crossed Julius's face. "It costs a

lot to copy that many pages. If the library made a copy and gave it to me, I could send it to a publisher."

Ruth sniffed and said to Julius, "Consider it an investment against royalties or advances or whatever they call it."

"None of that goes to me," Julius said stiffly. "It all goes to some charity for women. Besides, there *isn't* a publisher."

"But Sunny called it Tanja's new book," Helma said.

Julius nodded. "Yeah, the publisher who did the first book intended to publish it, but Tanja refused to do the edits they wanted." He shrugged. "Their exchanges escalated and they parted ways. She hadn't found another publisher yet when she . . . died."

"Her first book was a bestseller," Helma told him. "There shouldn't be any problem finding a new publisher."

"Maybe."

Ruth picked up *Women in Jeopardy*, Tanja's glossy published book. "Is it okay if I take this one home to read before it goes to the library?"

Helma nodded, refraining from explaining it was unlikely that either book, published or unpublished, would end up in the Local Authors collection.

Helma identified the odor emitting from Julius's clothes: woodsmoke. She pictured him living in a wood-heated house built of reused materials and chopping wood; a vegetable garden and alternative magazines; writing letters to the editor about clean water and urban growth. What didn't fit was that he was married to Tanja Frost, who'd appeared to be the epitome of glossy-magazine fine living. Helma couldn't imagine Tanja weeding radishes and stirring vegetable soup over a woodstove.

"Whadda ya say, Helma?" Ruth asked, turning to Helma so Julius couldn't see her face and gritting her teeth. "This is why we're here, to accept the manuscript and gather details for Tanja's display."

"The library could photocopy the manuscript for you," Helma conceded.

"Great." He shoved the box closer to Helma.

"I'm sorry about your wife," Helma said. "She impressed me as a talented woman."

"Oh, she was, all right," Julius said. "We were separated," he added as if he needed to explain the sharpness even he must have heard in his voice.

"So you and Tanja didn't move here together?" she asked.

"I moved here first," he told her, "a year ago. I had a job offer at the community college. Part-time. I wanted to live where the environment still mattered."

"And she followed you," Helma said, trying not to make her question sound like a question.

"Not exactly," Julius said stiffly, watching the bartender carry a tray of beer to a table of college-age men. "We had different life philosophies."

"But you're still married?"

"Legally, yes."

"Just packed with all kinds of helpful information, aren't you?" Ruth asked while Helma wondered if because Tanja had been technically married to a man with legitimate residency in Bellehaven, that might make her a local author the same way foreign citizenship worked for married couples. No, she decided, it didn't.

"Am I on trial here?" he asked, glancing from Helma to Ruth. "I thought we were meeting so I could give you Tanja's manuscript and share a few facts about her."

"Any confusion is my fault," Helma quickly assured him. "I saw you and Sunny in Saul's Deli yesterday. I know Sunny through her counseling career and I was aware that the two of you . . ." She paused, letting the words hang in the air so Julius could hear any implications he wanted.

Ruth stared at Helma, mouth open. Julius stared, too, his face flushing angrily.

"You and *Sunny*?" Ruth asked Julius. "The two of you were—"

"Sunny and Tanja were friends," Julius cut off Ruth. "I'd never do that to her."

"That a fact?" Ruth asked. "Just who *would* you do it to?"

"I don't need this," Julius said, rising from the seat.

"Oh, come on," Ruth cajoled. She laughed huskily and touched Julius's arm. "Just teasing. You made yourself too good a target." Then she picked up one of the "Keep Bellehaven Green!" brochures. "Helma, if you have to go back to work, I'd love to buy Julius another drink and talk about a contribution to his cause."

Helma left them in their darkened corner. Whatever Ruth was up to, it was wiser not to witness it.

"I couldn't shake anything salacious out of Julius," Ruth said as they walked a six-block grid, sidewalk and alley, between Helma's apartment building and Joker's bar. "Even after buying the guy two drinks and giving him twenty bucks to save the city. At least not about Tanja. Here, kitty, kitty. And he was too cagey about

Sunny—lots of 'just friends' stuff. Why'd you imply he and Sunny were a duo, anyway?"

"It was a sense I had, the way they were talking in the deli."

Ruth made a rude noise. "You're not running on all your senses right now, anyway."

It was an unkind comment but Helma knew it was true. Her normally keen perceptiveness was dimmed, as if wrapped in thin cotton. Add that to the mysterious weight that had grown so burdensome, she unconsciously kept straightening her spine. The *kugelis* hadn't worked.

"How did Julius and Tanja end up together?" Ruth asked. "Eco-boy and Society Babe. Like night and day."

"Obviously they didn't," Helma clarified. "They were separated. They were likely more compatible when they were younger."

"Nothing in common," Ruth said, half to herself, and Helma knew Ruth's thoughts had wandered away from Julius and Tanja to Minnesota.

"Check that box," Helma said.

"He can't figure it out and neither can I," Ruth said glumly. "How can you want somebody so much but you shrivel up and die when you live with him?"

"I don't know," Helma told her honestly as she checked the box herself. "Perhaps it's a matter of making a choice."

Ruth rolled her eyes. "I did, remember? I went to Minnesota, paintbrushes and all. It just didn't work. It's impossible. Goodbye, Columbus. Sayonara. That's all, folks. Hasta la vista, baby."

Helma thought the world would be far simpler if people were able to slice their life into segments bounded by their own decisions.

A light rain fell, more of a mist that clung to hair and clothes and instead of impeding any outdoor activities, only dampened them.

"I need a drink," Ruth said. "Want one?"

Helma shook her head. "I have to drive tonight."

"You're not really going to Commitment Issues tonight, are you?" Ruth asked after Helma told her of her conversation with Ms. Moon. "The game's off. I mean, she changed the rules midstream: exploiting murder victims for the sake of library visibility. And butting into your private life. What have you got to lose by skipping the last two group whines?"

"I'm curious about something," Helma told her.

"I guess I'll go with you, then, to watch your back. Murder and all that."

It was 5:30 and in a half hour Helma was scheduled to meet Boyd Bishop, the writer, at Echo's. Whatever had she been thinking to agree to meet a library patron, let alone someone whose phone number she didn't even possess?

"What do you know about this guy?" Ruth asked.

"I'm meeting him in a well-lit public establishment," Helma told her.

"That's not like you at all. Want me to come? Just sit in the background and watch?"

"No, thank you."

"Well, I'll check up on him for you, then."

"Don't, please," Helma said.

"Subtle. I'll be subtle, just ask around a tiny bit."

Subtle was not a word that fit within a mile of Ruth's name.

"If . . . I mean, *when* we find him, don't you think we

should start calling Boy Cat Zukas, BCZ?" Ruth asked
as she peeped over a bamboo fence into a lush yard.

"Why?" Helma asked. "Watch out for those black-
berries."

"It's shorter, like a nickname. BCZ, see? Only three
syllables instead of five."

"Boy Cat Zukas doesn't have five syllables; it has
four."

"Five," Ruth said, slowly, holding up her fingers one
by one and counting off, "Bo-y Cat Zu-kas."

"The word *boy* is a single syllable noun."

"Not in my book. Bo-y," she repeated.

"The *oy* serves as a diphthong," Helma explained.
"The *y* operates as an *i* and the sound change stays
within a single syllable. Boi."

"It's probably an error in the dictionary, like pneu-
monia. And once it was in holy print, wham-o—we're
stuck with it for eternity. Oh, look!" Ruth pointed at the
black head peering over the rim of an open garbage can.

Ruth's voice startled the animal and it jumped from
the can to a stack of mossy firewood—just a plain black
cat. "Sorry," Ruth told Helma, shrugging in apology.

Chapter 12

A Shocking Vision

Boyd Bishop sat at a window table in Echo's facing the entrance, one long leg stretched straight beneath the table. As Helma stepped through the doorway at exactly six o'clock, entering her second alcoholic establishment that day, Boyd stood and nodded his head, almost a bow, his smile wide. The lines around his mouth and eyes deepened into wrinkles.

"Helma," he said, pulling out the caned chair opposite him, "glad you could make it."

"Hello, Boyd," Helma said as she sat in the armed chair and felt, for just an instant, his hand brush her shoulder, then seeing his name—Boyd—in the air above his head like a dictionary entry: one single syllable.

"I was afraid maybe you'd change your mind."

"I might have if I'd had your telephone number," she told him honestly.

"That's why I didn't give it to you," he said and she couldn't tell whether he was teasing or not.

Helma considered Boyd more closely than she had in the library. No, he truly wasn't handsome; his features were rough and worn, his nose large and jaw broad. Until he smiled and his face mysteriously changed in all its creases. His hair still held a touch of brown although it had receded and grayed to pewter silver. His legs seemed inordinately long for a man, and his hips excessively slender.

"Do you read westerns?" he asked Helma, surprising her with his directness, skipping the weather and how-was-your-day chitchat. "That's what I write."

"When I was a child," Helma confessed, "but I'm afraid not since then."

He laughed. "Don't apologize. A lot of people don't, and if they do, won't admit it—afraid they'll look stupid. Lots of closet readers of mysteries, romances, and westerns are lurking out there."

Helma knew that for a fact. Since the Bellehaven Public Library had begun self-checkouts, and patrons no longer had to show library staff the books they were borrowing, the circulation of genre books had skyrocketed.

"When did you write your first western?" Helma asked.

"About twelve years ago. I got laid up with a smashed leg and ran out of things to do. Books and puzzles can't keep you going very long. So, heck, I wrote a book."

"I see," Helma said. If Boyd wanted to dangle details in front of her but withhold the facts, such as book titles and the pseudonym he wrote his books under, he was being too, too coy for her to encourage.

He dropped the lime perched on his beer bottle into the frosty glass and took a swig straight from the bottle, then asked, "Do you write as well? Is that why you're putting together this Local Authors collection?"

"I don't," Helma told him. "Letters only, but like all librarians, I'm an appreciator."

"What do you make of these murders? I read the story in today's paper. Do *you* believe a serial killer is out there stalking local authors?"

She felt his intense gaze and chose her words carefully. "The two victims both wrote, that's true, but Molly Bittern was the author of unpublished poetry, while Tanja Frost's subjects were women's issues and psychology. Their connection to one another—or to writing—was coincidental."

"Except," Boyd said, raising his bottle of beer toward her, "they were both at your local authors meeting on Monday night."

"They were?" Helma asked, surprised. "They were *both* there? I remember Molly, but Tanja as well? How do you know?"

"I recognized her from the photograph in the paper. Very professional-looking woman. When I first got to the library she was blocking the coffee, and I was stuck behind her by the crowd—great attendance by the way. She and another woman were discussing one-on-one counseling versus group sessions. Lots of what I guess you'd call psych lingo."

"Do you remember what the other woman looked like?" Helma asked.

He shrugged. "Not really. Dark-haired. Maybe a little . . . plump. Those folks must hear the stuff of life,"

he went on. "You know that Tolstoy quote about unhappy families?"

"'Happy families are all alike; every unhappy family is unhappy in its own way,'" Helma quoted, then
gave the proper credit. "That's the first line of Leo Tolstoy's *Anna Karenina.*"

He nodded. "That's where all the interesting stories
are—in our unhappiness." They paused while the waitress set Helma's iced tea in front of her.

"So you enjoy hearing the strife and sorrows of people?" she asked him. "Their tragedies?"

"Ah, interesting doesn't necessarily mean enjoyable."

"But for a writer, I'm sure those stories mean material."

He laughed, a laugh that emitted from deep in his
chest, and a woman at the next table looked over at him
and smiled. "You're exactly right. Writers, good writers anyway, are cannibals, parasites, and experience
junkies, a disgusting bunch of folks. I once heard a
writer say, 'Pity the family that has a novelist born into
it.'" He turned his piercing eyes on her. "But *you* lead
the life envied by every writer on earth."

"Me?" Helma Zukas was not a woman who appreciated over-extravagant familiarity or praise, always
aware that behind it lurked the hard sell, the inferior
product, or worst of all—the request for special favors.

"You have all that information at your fingertips
every single day. An arsenal, and you know how to use
it. Some guy wanders in looking for the number of
square feet in a hectare or grandma wants to know how
to cook a goose, and you've got the answer. We, the
public, have to throw ourselves on your mercy."

"The Internet has made it easier for people to find that information on their own," Helma told him. "Our own library's statistics indicate that reference questions have declined since the Internet became available."

She didn't mention that not long ago, when a patron approached the reference desk, it was in the quest for specialized knowledge. Now, it was more often "the printer's out of paper," "my computer's frozen," or worse yet, "it's my turn and he won't get off the computer."

"But for the *real* stuff, you can't beat a librarian."

Helma nodded. Even if he *was* being overly extravagant, he was correct in his assessment. Still, she thought it wise to deflect his interest. "Where were you born?" she asked. Through the window she saw a young girl pass the restaurant, check her reflection in the window, and pull in her stomach.

Boyd hesitated. "New Mexico," he told her. Another hesitation, then he said, "My family has a ranch in the southern part of the state. It came about due to the Mexican War."

"The Mexican War?" Helma asked. "In the 1840s?"

"That's right. Through what was called bounty land warrants. My great-great grandfather served in the infantry and afterward the U.S. government said he could have a hundred dollars or a hundred sixty acres anywhere in the United States. He was from Missouri so it's curious he chose land in New Mexico."

"Maybe he wanted to strike out on his own," Helma said, thinking of her own departure from Michigan.

"Could be," Boyd agreed. "Each generation of my family built on those hundred sixty acres until now it's a few sections of land. That's not as big as it sounds. It takes a lot of acres to feed a cow in that kind of country."

That explained the twang in his speech. Also the deep lines of his face. Sun and wind. For a split second she imagined him home on the range, riding a horse, seeing the illustrations she'd found for a middle school student doing a report on cattle roundups. It fit.

He set his hand flat on the table and she noticed calluses along his fingers. "Did you know either of the murdered women?" he asked, bringing the conversation back to the deaths of the two women.

"Molly was a library patron," Helma said, feeling Boyd's intense gaze. "I spoke to her often."

"Did she ever talk about the source of her poetry?"

Helma frowned. Boyd leaned across the table toward her, so attentive she expected his nose to twitch like a bird dog's. "I didn't know her on a personal basis," she told him.

"Sometimes people spill secrets to a person sitting behind a desk," he persisted.

Helma found the moment extremely uncomfortable. "Molly didn't divulge any secrets," she told Boyd firmly. "How long have you lived in Bellehaven?"

"Two years in November," he said, leaning back.

Long enough to qualify for the Local Authors collection, Helma thought.

For the next fifteen minutes, they chatted about inconsequentialities: Bellehaven's growth, the local theater, local politics. Helma glanced at her watch, surprised to see it was time to leave for her Commitment Issues group session.

As she raised her head from her watch, her attention

was caught by the flash of a black cat streaking across the street from the sidewalk in front of Echo's.

"Are you involved with someone?" Boyd was asking her.

The black cat had a white tip on its tail but it was not Boy Cat Zukas. She watched it safely reach the opposite sidewalk and dash in front of a couple walking toward the bay.

She gasped and Boyd said, following her gaze out the window, "Don't worry. He made it."

But that was not why Helma had gasped. The couple the black cat had crossed in front of was Chief of Police Wayne Gallant and, strolling beside him, gazing up at his face as if mesmerized by the stars and moon, was Gloria "Call me Glory" Shandy.

Helma drove, with her windshield wipers on intermittent, toward the Public Market building where the Commitment Issues group session would be held, eyes sweeping toward each cross street in readiness for inattentive drivers, vigilant for children who might run in front of her car, or loose dogs likely to bolt away from their owners, an ear toward the familiar purrings of her car's engine, aware of her posture and hand position on the steering wheel, calculating the shortest route, feeling her foot steady on the gas pedal. So diligently and attentively driving, she left no room in her head to speculate about anything—or anyone—else.

Chapter 13

Dangerous Women

Helma entered the market building, following two women into a meeting room and sitting in a wooden chair for five minutes, not realizing until women began removing colorful projects from tote bags that she was sitting in the Crochet It! meeting, not the Commitment Issues group session.

"Excuse me," she said to no one as she rose from her chair and began to fold it up to put away, "but I'm not where I'm supposed to be."

An older woman set down a small piece of mint green crocheting and touched Helma's arm. "It's all right dear," she said in a gentle voice. "Leave it. You do what you need to."

Helma nodded and left the room. She stood in the hallway until she finally noticed a hand-lettered sign on a piece of computer paper pointing to the Salmon Room, saying, "Join us for Commitment Issues."

Inside the Salmon Room, less than a dozen women were seated waiting for the meeting to begin. Helma sat in the first empty chair she came to, a seat in the back row. It only vaguely registered when another woman rose from a chair at the front and came back to sit beside her, scraping chair legs on the floor.

"Hi, Helma. Well, here we are again."

It was Pepper Breckenridge, who Ruth and Helma had watched ride away on her bicycle the night before, hoping she'd reach home safely.

"Hello," Helma responded, cool enough to discourage most people from conversation. The familiar black heaviness surrounded her: LaBrea tar pits, abandoned lead mines, deep sea caverns, closet floors.

"At least nobody died last night," Pepper chattered on, rooting inside her pack until she found a tube of lip balm, which she rubbed on her lips. "I stayed up to watch the eleven o'clock news just to be sure. I couldn't have slept otherwise." She continued on but Helma didn't hear her, nodding or shaking her head now and then according to the tone of Pepper's voice. What was there to say about the deaths, anyway? They'd happened.

Suddenly, as the group leader moved to the front chair, Ruth flopped down on the chair to the left of Helma. "You forgot me," she accused Helma. "Hi, Pepper. You here again?" and then she went on, "You were supposed to pick me up, remember? Must have been a hot date with Mr. Cowboy John Wayne, huh?" and she wiggled her eyebrows.

"I don't know why you're attending these sessions," Helma said. "They're useless."

"They're only useless to you because you're not getting into the spirit. Clipping your toenails is useful if you can get into the spirit."

"Personal hygiene is not an act that requires spirit, it's a utilitarian necessity," Helma told her.

"That's right," Pepper chimed in. "I always feel better after a pedicure, even if I'm wearing closed shoes."

Ruth blinked at Pepper, then sat back so Helma blocked Pepper's view of her. "What is with this woman?" she asked under her breath, then went on, "Did he turn out to be a perv?"

"I don't know why he was with her," Helma said. And when Ruth only grunted, Helma turned to look into Ruth's frowning face.

"Uh-oh," Ruth said. "I don't think we're on the same wavelength about the same man. I meant Mr. Cowboy. You don't know why *who* was with her-who?"

Now was not the time to discuss Wayne Gallant and Glory Shandy. "Mr. Cowboy's name is Boyd Bishop," Helma told her.

"I know," Ruth said. "Aren't you going to ask *me* about the phone call?"

"Did someone call about Boy Cat Zukas?"

"I meant about my phone call with Paul, but yeah, there were a couple of cat phone calls. Neither one had the right cat. Sorry."

The leader raised her hand to signal silence and Ruth whispered, "He'll come home, Helma. I know he will. I can feel it in my bones."

"He can see whomever he wants," Helma said. "We don't have an official commitment, not even a stated one."

Ruth blew out her lips as the leader of the group passed out a packet of articles, surveys, and self-tests.

Voices droned. Words like *trust, enablers,* and *cheating* flew about the room. Ruth contributed something about "distance defining dedication," the words all beginning with *D* reminding Helma of an ancient Chinese poem a former classmate had liked: "So dim so dank so dull so damp so dark so dead."

She closed her eyes and tried to bring the image of Wayne Gallant and Glory Shandy into her mind. Had they been arm in arm, laughing? Had he been gazing down at Glory in the same dazed manner she had been gazing up at him?

"That wasn't so bad," Ruth said. "Let's go."

"Why?" Helma asked.

"Because it's over."

And indeed, the session *had* ended. Women were picking up their purses and donning coats, glows of satisfaction and resolve on their faces.

"See you later, Pepper," Ruth said as they exited the building into the moonless night. "Now," she told Helma, "let's swing by Joker's for any cat news before we go home," overloud, Helma thought.

Once they were in her car, Ruth said in a lower voice, "Okay, follow her."

"Follow who?"

"You are driving me mad. What is wrong with you? Follow Pepper Condiment, or whatever her name is. See her right there on her shiny red bicycle? Well, follow her. I know all about her being new in town and wanting to meet new little friends, but this is ridiculous. Nobody goes to this many self-help groups without something being funny. Well, unless they were coerced like you, of course."

"Ruth . . ."

"Hurry up, don't lose her."

Helma slowly pulled out of the dark parking lot, following Ruth's orders to "slow down," "turn here," "hold on a second." Ruth leaned forward against the dashboard, her face close to the windshield. It took too much effort to tell her to fasten her seat belt.

A mere exercise, meaningless, even ridiculous, driving through the dark streets of Bellehaven following a bicycle. She simply did as Ruth instructed, her thoughts settling darkly elsewhere.

"Pay attention, would you," Ruth said, "you're going to run over the damn bike."

In only three days, just three twenty-four-hour days: her cat had disappeared; the man she'd believed to be, if not close then approaching close, had abandoned her without a clue; the project she'd been fostering in the library had become connected to murder and threatened to be removed from her purview; she'd been forced to attend group-counseling sessions; and she had turned forty-two years old.

She'd read that there was no one so dangerous as a person who believed they'd lost the most important aspects of their life. That person became reckless and unpredictable, an avenger who threw caution and control to the winds. No longer caring about consequences, wildly leaping without looking, jumping from frying pans. A person who abandoned good judgment and prudent thought. Who knew what that person might do? Every other being that person came in contact with was in jeopardy.

If all was lost, then there was nothing left to risk.

Somewhere after passing the Ducky Ice Cream Parlor and before the Promise Mission for homeless men, Helma felt a strange sensation at the back of her neck, similar to the beginning of a headache, but instead of the feeling rising to her head, it spread like a hot pinprick of light to the pit of her stomach and diffused throughout her body, each cell warming, her muscles loosening as if she'd just entered an 85-degree room after standing in a frigid hallway.

Her eyes opened, suddenly taking in a wider view, her spine straightened; she turned her head from side to side, noticing for the first time in days how the rain glistened on the sidewalks, how early the autumn darkness was falling.

Helma took a deep breath—the deepest breath she'd taken in a week—and stretched out her hands on the steering wheel, admiring the tendons between her fingers, feeling the power of her Buick beneath her.

Pepper careened around a corner on her bicycle, heading away from the bay. Helma blinked, once, twice, suddenly clearly seeing Pepper, the way she hunched over her handlebars, head up, legs pumping.

"There she goes," she said, leaning forward to peer through her windshield, confidently applying the brakes, slowing down so her turn wouldn't be so obvious.

Ruth shifted on her seat toward Helma, silently considering her, and for no reason, laughed in such delight that Helma couldn't help join in. "Oh, the thrill of the chase," Ruth said.

Even the air inside Helma's Buick felt more distinct, lighter. She eased around the corner and for a moment thought they'd lost Pepper. There was no sign of her reflective vest or the red bicycle. She and Ruth looked out both windows, down driveways and alleys. Then Helma spotted her.

"There," she said. "Don't look." And drove past Pepper pushing her bicycle behind a line of shrubbery in front of a two-story office building.

"Funny," Ruth, who of course *had* looked, said, "to hide your bike in the bushes instead of parking it in the bike rack that's practically blocking the building's front door."

"Maybe she forgot her bike lock," Helma suggested.

Ruth held up her wrist and tapped the face of the man's watch she wore. "You wouldn't think an office building would be open at eight thirty at night, would you? What did she say she did for a living?"

"She didn't." Helma told her as she pulled against the curb two blocks up and did a policeman's U-turn, turning the wheel the way her father had taught her: back up, go forward. "She only said she was new to Bellehaven."

Helma drove slowly back and stopped across the street from the office building. It was plain, brick fronted. No lights shone in the front offices, although Helma thought she saw a stream of light reflecting off bushes at the side of the building.

There was no sign of Pepper or her bicycle. Not even the shrubbery shuddered as if it had been recently disturbed. If Helma hadn't seen Pepper enter the shrubs with her own eyes, she'd never have known.

Helma switched off her headlights and turned off the engine. "We'll wait here a few minutes," she told Ruth.

"The woman's up to some nefarious deed," Ruth said with certainty.

"She *is* exhibiting curious behavior," Helma agreed,

studying the shrubbery. The colonial-style sign in front of the building read, HOPEWELL BUILDING.

"Do you know what kind of offices are in the Hopewell Building?" she asked Ruth.

"Not a clue. Can't be commercial or there'd be business signs outside."

"That's a very good observation, Ruth."

"Thank you." Ruth drummed her fingernails on the dashboard. "So tell me what had you so upset you forgot to pick me up tonight?"

Surprisingly, Helma was able to simply say it in a calm and steady voice, without a clutch at her heart. "I saw Wayne Gallant and Glory Shandy."

"Together?"

Helma nodded, her eyes on the quiet office building.

"Where? What were they doing? All snuggled up somewhere?"

"They were walking down the street near Echo's," Helma told her. Had someone passed in front of the Hopewell Building? No, it was the reflection from a passing car a street over.

Ruth leaned back. "Oh, hell, seeing them together doesn't mean a thing. Well, hardly. They could have just run into each other. Or," she mused, "maybe they were on their way to that new Italian restaurant for a cozy little dinner, I heard it's primo." She vigorously shook her head. "No, definitely not. It was a coincidence, guaranteed."

"All I observed is that they were together," Helma said, continuing to watch the Hopewell Building. "Glory looked quite satisfied."

Ruth grunted. "I bet she did. Do you think Pepper saw us and rode off?"

"You're assuming she's trying to hide her movements," Helma said.

When, after ten minutes, no one appeared and no lights were switched on in the office building, Ruth said, "Well, I guess that was a bust. Let's go."

Helma reached toward the car ignition, then pulled away her hand and instead placed it on the door handle. "I'm curious. I'm going to take a look."

"Wait," Ruth said. "Take a look at what? So what if Pepper's sneaking around? Besides, it's dark out there."

"There are streetlights. You can wait here. I'll be back when I discover where she went."

Chapter 14

A Formless Shadow

Helma stepped from her car onto the street and closed the driver's door, holding in the handle button so it wouldn't click, then stood motionless and soundless beside her Buick contemplating the dark Hopewell Building. Had Pepper actually gone inside? She might live nearby and prefer to hide her bicycle in the bushes, an idea Helma rejected as quickly as she considered it. Most bicycle owners she knew stored their bicycles in garages or even lugged them inside their homes when they weren't in use.

Behind Helma, as she took two deliberate steps forward to cross the street, the passenger door slammed and Ruth whispered, sotto voce, "Hey, wait up."

Helma turned and placed her finger to her lips.

"Oh yeah, right. Shhh," Ruth whispered in slightly lower tones, stepping up beside Helma, her boot heels clicking on asphalt. "You're going to check the bike, right? See if it's still there?"

"First," Helma said as she glanced both ways—no cars currently traveled the side street. A darkened auto body shop and a vitamin store with pale suffused light in its window shared the block with the Hopewell. Further down the street the flicker of a television emitted from a small house set back in a stand of cedar trees.

When she reached the opposite sidewalk, Helma headed toward the shrubbery where Pepper and her bicycle had disappeared. She identified the leaves glistening in the wan light of the streetlamps as photinia, a popular Bellehaven shrubbery with a tendency to flourish beyond reason. Behind her she caught the musky fragrance of Ruth's perfume. The Bellehaven evening was Thursday-night quiet. No more rain fell.

She longed to stop and relish the sharpness of her surroundings, the way the world had shifted back to its proper tilt, as if a mesh curtain had been raised from before her eyes. She touched a leathery leaf, feeling the cool moisture of recent rain, and stepped behind the six-foot-high photinia.

Against the wall of the Hopewell Building leaned Pepper's bicycle, a U-shaped lock uselessly attached to the seat post, a definite sign that Pepper had chosen to conceal her transportation, not simply stow it because she'd forgotten a lock. "She didn't take her bicycle helmet," Helma whispered, touching the smooth basketball-sized head gear with smily face reflectors adhered to it

"So where'd she go?" Ruth whispered as she brushed at her face to dislodge a string of spider web that clearly hung too high to interfere with either Helma or Pepper's passage.

"Inside," Helma guessed.

"Okay, then she's inside. Let's go home."

Helma emerged from the shrubbery and tried the plateglass front door. It was locked. Through the glass she made out a Danish modern waiting area—an off-sided square of stiff-looking sofas and a broad coffee table holding a clutter of magazines. A directory of office numbers and names hung on the wall behind a reception desk, but she couldn't read any of the names. To the left of the desk, a wide set of stairs led to the second floor.

She tried the door once more, hearing Ruth mutter, "Locked," behind her. "Hey! Where are you going?"

A sidewalk led to the dark side of the building where the stream of light had penetrated the night—and still did: a single shaft from a second-story window. It could be nothing: a janitor's closet, a restroom light left on, someone working late. The column of light did nothing to illuminate the sidewalk beside the building. In fact, if anything, it made the sidewalk blacker by comparison.

"There has to be another door," Helma whispered. "It's city code." She held her arms in front of her, one hand on the building's rough bricks, feeling her way along the narrow cement walkway that hugged the building, and stepped into complete darkness.

A thump sounded behind her. "Ouch, damnit."

"Move slowly," Helma advised Ruth. "Keep your hands in front of you."

"Right. I'll be sure to do that."

Helma halted directly beneath the lighted window,

waiting until Ruth stopped, too, then held her breath and listened. The window above her was closed, the type that was sealed shut to protect the artificial movement of air that in Helma's experience rarely circulated as planned.

"Shh," she whispered to Ruth, who brushed at her clothes, sounding like laundry flapping on a clothesline.

At that very moment, the beam of light disappeared and into Helma's mind sprung the phrase "plunged into darkness." She and Ruth froze, heads tipping upward toward the now-dark window. But no doors slammed, no voices called out demanding that they identify themselves, no bulk of an outline appeared at the window staring down at them.

"Do you think they saw us?" Ruth whispered.

There were only two directions to go: back to the front of the building or continue on. Helma Zukas rarely retraced her steps without having accomplished her objective, whether it was answering a complicated reference question involving a subject she was indifferent to, such as sports, or pursuing the perpetrator of sloppy automobile repair work. She pressed onward, feeling her way around the building, searching for what she knew by law had to exist.

She turned the corner into the alley behind the Hopewell Building and there it was, still in shadow but plainly visible by the light of a streetlamp: the rear entrance, a solid metal and windowless door mounted flush to the brick wall.

"Shouldn't that light over the door be on?" Ruth asked. "I mean, look, there's a fixture but no little lumens shining down. I'd say that's suspicious, wouldn't you?"

"It probably just burned out," Helma told her.

"That's exactly what I said. Suspicious. So what if Pepper's in there? I just thought a little chase would perk you up. I didn't mean we should actually hunt her down like a dog."

Helma was already turning the metal doorknob, positive that this door was locked just like the front entrance. Even in Bellehaven it wasn't sensible to leave windows cracked or doors unlocked. Helma locked her own dead bolt when she carried her garbage out to the dumpster beside her apartment building.

But the door soundlessly opened into a dark corridor. Helma stepped onto a carpeted floor, able to discern a stairway ten feet in front of her. A stale, spicy odor hung in the air. Helma tried to place the fragrance, reminded of St. Alphonse Catholic School back in Michigan. Then she recognized it: incense.

Ruth sighed, saying, "Oh, what the heck," and followed Helma along the short corridor to a set of stairs where Helma had already climbed the first five treads.

It was obviously the back, secondary, stairs since these were narrower than the more spacious staircase Helma had seen by the reception desk. She slid her hand upward on the metal railing with each cautious step, listening for furtive movements above them.

On the second-floor landing Helma halted, all senses alert, glancing at the cracks beneath the doors. The light had shown from an office on the south side of the building, which would be to her right, but now, except for the dimmest of bulbs marking the exit signs, all the offices were dark. Whoever had flicked off the light hadn't turned it on again. If they hadn't slipped out the rear entrance, they were still in the building.

"So now what, Sherlock?" Ruth whispered.

"We'll try each door," Helma whispered, taking a step forward.

Ruth grabbed her arm. "I don't think so. This is what those stupid girls do in teen horror flicks. You know, all alone in the house when the electricity goes off during the thunderstorm, so they start looking for funny noises. What if she's waiting behind one of those doors with a tire iron?"

"Bicycles don't have tire irons," Helma told her.

"That doesn't mean Pepper isn't packing one. Pepper could be packing a pipe." Ruth paused, then giggled a titter fringed with hysteria. "If Pepper packed a pipe, how many pipes could Pepper . . ."

"Shh," Helma whispered.

The exit light at the far end of the hall turned the doors into shadowy rectangles off each side of the corridor. Not enough light to read any names or office numbers but as their eyes adjusted, they might be able to. Helma had recently helped a student find that it took twenty minutes for most human eyes to completely adjust to a darkened environment. Although she was confident they'd be in the Hopewell Building less than the required twenty minutes.

"Something moved down there," Ruth hissed, pointing toward the end of the hall.

"I didn't see anything," Helma told her.

"That's because you weren't looking."

Two things happened so close together it was impossible to say which one occurred first: a crack reverberated through the corridor to the accompaniment of shattering glass, and the lighted exit sign at the far end of the hallway was extinguished. Ruth yelped, a flurry of motion swirled around them, and Helma gasped as someone—not Ruth—gripped her arm with abrupt fierceness.

"Follow me," a woman's frantic voice said. "Hurry! Somebody's in here."

And indeed, Helma heard the rush of movement at the end of the hallway, where the darkness was blackest.

She was swept along, her feet skimming the stairs as they clambered back down the treads toward the rear of the building, balance askew and grabbing at the metal railing to keep from tumbling in a heap to the landing.

"Move along now, move along," Ruth repeated behind her. "Move along."

In seconds they stumbled out the door and into the darkness outside the building: Helma, Ruth, and—Helma was not surprised to see—Pepper Breckenridge. Pepper's eyes were wide and her short hair stuck out in spikes. She still held Helma's arm and was half running, pulling her down the alley away from the office building, her pack hanging off one shoulder.

"Stop," Helma said, prying Pepper's fingers from her arm. "We're not accomplishing anything useful by running."

Pepper panted, wheezing as she tried to catch her breath. "There was a man after me, I swear to god. He carried something, a gun maybe. I was scared to death." She tugged on both Ruth and Helma's sleeves, pulling them into the shadows of a morning glory–covered fence that bordered the alley. "In here. We have to see who it is. For the police. He might come out the back door."

"Are you nuts?" Ruth, jerked her arm out of Pepper's grasp. "Let go of me."

"What were you doing in the building?" Helma asked as she smoothed the wrinkles from her sleeve. "And why did you hide your bicycle in the shrubbery?"

Pepper turned from the building toward Helma and Ruth, her face in shadow. "What were *you* doing in the building?" she countered.

"Just trying to cheer up my friend Helma, here," Ruth said. "But you're lying. Nobody else was in there."

"Oh no. It's true," Pepper insisted, pointing to the Hopewell Building as if a criminal was about to step into the alley and wave his arms in surrender. "You heard him, didn't you?"

"I heard *something*," Helma said, "and Ruth thought she saw a movement."

"And now, what I think *I* saw was *you*," Ruth added.

Pepper vigorously shook her head, still panting, still pointing back at the office building. "It was a man. Before I even turned on the light I heard somebody trying office doors in the dark so I hid, and then I heard you two come in and go up the back stairs." She looked at them accusingly. "You weren't very quiet. I tried to warn you. He must have come up the front stairway and broken the exit light. I didn't have time to call the police."

"Listen," Ruth said, tipping her head. "Somebody did."

Growing louder was the wavering wail of a siren, approaching from the central section of Bellehaven. At the same time, Helma saw a shadow slip across the front lawn of the Hopewell Building, but when she narrowed her eyes, the lawn was empty.

Helma expected the police car to pass in the distance, but within seconds she caught the eerie red flash of rotating color approaching them, bouncing between houses and trees and power poles. The siren cut off midwail as a police car screeched to a stop in front of the building.

"I might have somehow tripped an alarm," Pepper said. "I saw a little red light blinking." She backed further down the alley into the darkness. "We have to get out of here."

"No." Helma stood her ground. "We don't."

Pepper frantically shook her head. "What if he followed me from the group session? We can't let him see our faces. Let the police catch him first."

"Sounds unlikely but marginally reasonable, Helma," Ruth commented. "What'll it hurt if we wait a couple of extra minutes?" She loomed over Pepper. "She ain't goin' nowhere."

"That's completely unreasonable," Helma told her. "The police are here to assist us, and we will assist them by explaining what happened. I'm going out to talk to them."

"Don't," Pepper begged, but when Helma removed Pepper's arm from her sleeve, she shrugged and hoisted her pack higher on her shoulder, stepping further into the shadows. "I'm sorry but *I'm* a coward. I'll wait here to see what happens."

"Me too," Ruth said, stepping back beside Pepper. "I make too good a target. Can't you just sit tight until the guy's in the clutches of our boys in blue? And then we can pop out of the bushes and tell all. Be heroines."

"Time is of the essence," Helma told them.

"I'm staying here," Ruth said stubbornly. "I'll keep an eye on our peppy little friend." She nodded toward Pepper.

"I didn't do anything," Pepper protested.

"Says you."

Pepper peered into the darkness and looked left and right up the alley, even parting the vines that sheltered them. "Stay out of the bright light until you're safely with the police," she told Helma. Unnecessarily.

Helma stepped away from Pepper and Ruth and across a small puddle. The building blocked her view of the police car that had pulled up in front. A second police car approached from the opposite direction.

She was still obscured by the shadows of the alley, only three feet from becoming visible. A plain car screeched to a stop beside the building and Wayne Gallant jumped out of the driver's side. The dark form of a second person sat on the passenger side, whether man or woman, Helma couldn't tell.

She hesitated, her heel just touching the earth mid-step. Another police car pulled in and its lights shone on the passenger in Wayne's car. Perkiness was apparent even in the garishness of headlights. His passenger was Glory Shandy.

Exposing oneself to potentially humiliating situations held no appeal for Helma. She pivoted on her right foot, intending to return to Ruth's side.

And stopped, again midstride.

"Helm?" Ruth asked softly from the darkness.

The stars shone down on Helma Zukas, enveloping her in icy crystalline light. The situation was absurd, ridiculous, and . . . childish. She wanted an explanation for his behavior. She deserved it; she demanded it. Anything less was unacceptable, cowardly, and cruel on his part. Helma's chin raised, her back straightened, and her hands formed loose, but confident, fists.

In an instant, she'd spun back to face the Hopewell Building and begun striding toward Wayne Gallant's unmarked cruiser, purpose in every step, jaw jutted toward her objective. She had nothing to lose, and nothing was going to stop her.

"You are *not* doing this."

"Remove your hands."

"I will not." Ruth's voice dropped. "Listen to me, Helm. You have to save this battle for another day, do you hear me? This Pepper person is our bird in the hand. If we don't discover what she's up to now, we'll lose the chance forever, I can feel it."

"At this moment, what Pepper knows is immaterial."

Ruth sighed, but she didn't release her grip. "*He's* in the Hopewell Building looking for a crime, and I'm betting my new boots we've got the criminal right here."

Helma wavered.

Ruth lowered her voice. "You'll know what's going on before he does."

"I'm not involved in a game of one-upmanship with the chief of police," Helma told Ruth. She looked once more at the unmarked car. "But you're correct: we *should* pursue an unexpected opportunity like this."

"Good. Let's go."

"What happened?" Pepper asked when they rejoined her in the morning glories. "Why'd you change your mind? You saw the killer, didn't you? Did he see you? Do you think he knows we're hiding here?"

"Nah," Ruth told her. "We were just talking about the three of us surrendering. We probably scattered microscopic fibers all over the building. With all the gizmos the police buy, they'll have our bust sizes in fifteen minutes. What do you say we just go over there and . . ."

"No!" Pepper interrupted. "Come with me. I only live a block away." Her voice sagged. "It's time to tell you everything."

Chapter 15

Revelation of Reality

Pepper scurried ahead of Helma and Ruth along the darkened alley, her backpack bumping against her back, away from the Hopewell office building. Behind them, Helma heard voices, the incomprehensible garble of radios and still another siren in the distance. The red and yellow lights bloomed and faded, filling the night with emergency.

Helma skirted a garbage container left carelessly far out in the alley, following a virtual stranger with who-knew-what motives down a dark alley to who-knew-where while behind her a contingent of law-upholding public servants—local heroes paid to protect people just like her—created a safety zone around the Hopewell Building.

She'd hear Pepper's promised "everything." Then, if warranted, as Ruth claimed it would be, she'd inform the police and share all the details she'd learned. Of course she would. For the briefest instant she imagined the expression on the chief's face. No, it was definitely her duty as a Bellehaven citizen and public employee, that was all.

Ruth hummed an off-key and incomprehensible tune as they turned off the alley and onto a sidewalk, moving single file away from the police lights: Pepper, Helma, and lastly Ruth.

"Almost there," Pepper called out, sounding like an exhausted mother encouraging young children on a grueling road trip.

They entered a neighborhood that had reached its zenith when Bellehaven was a new port city in the late 1800s. Large ornate houses gently decaying side by side with small single-story clapboard homes of early mill and dockworkers.

"Don't let her out of your sight," Ruth murmured behind Helma, another bit of unnecessary advice.

Pepper led them up the cracked and root-raised sidewalk of a large house with a covered porch stretching across its front. Four mailboxes hung beside the front door. In the shine of the street and porch lights the house's gothic lines were exposed: a round tower on the top floor rose above the roof line; tiny eyebrow windows in the house's peak glowed in the night.

"I was lucky to find this place," Pepper told them as she opened the front door. "Rents are sky high in this town."

"Yes," Ruth said, sighing, "but it still doesn't keep people out."

Pepper turned, her eyes narrowing. "You already have your little corner, right?"

Ruth raised her hands. "Hey, I moved to Minnesota, you moved here. Even Steven, okay?"

A door stood off each side of the foyer and a wide staircase with scarred but still elegant banisters led above. Helma saw one door off the landing and one more at the top of the stairs. A nameplate like that on an old-fashioned card catalog drawer was affixed to each door.

Pepper unlocked the wooden door to the right of the foyer. The nameplate held only the initials P.B.

"Come on in," Pepper told them as she held the door. "Can I get you something to drink?" she asked as if this were a planned social event.

"Got anything alcoholic?" Ruth asked, stepping inside and peering curiously around Pepper's apartment.

Helma declined, deeming it wiser to keep her wits about her.

Pepper's apartment had once been the dining room of the grand old house. An ornate built-in credenza took up a portion of one wall and the division of kitchen and bedroom had been added later, plasterboard and hollow-core doors clashing with the fine old oak and fir woodwork. A dusty brass and glass chandelier hung from the center of the room, one electric taper burned out.

Comfortable, but nothing expensive or unusual. Ruth stood in front of an oil painting depicting a lone willow on a high hill.

"My mother painted that," Pepper said, carrying two glasses of red wine from the kitchen. She'd recombed her hair smooth. "Her claim to becoming legendary in our family history was that she studied for one year with Norman Rockwell."

"I thought it had a familiar ring," Ruth said, bending close and scrutinizing the willow. "Romantically realistic."

Helma noticed what looked like cat hair on Pepper's sofa, and chose a wooden rocker. "You said you could explain everything," she reminded Pepper. "Why were you in the Hopewell Building?"

Pepper sat on the pillowed end of the cat-haired sofa, pulling her legs under her and taking a swallow of wine before she began. "I lied," she said, shrugging.

"Please be more specific," Helma told her, gratefully observing that Ruth didn't drink any wine until Pepper had swallowed her own. The rocking chair creaked and she balanced herself with feet flat on the floor to keep it stable.

"Well, not everything has been a lie, only some things. Everybody lies."

"I do occasionally," Ruth agreed as she sat on the other end of the sofa. "When it's convenient, or to save my . . ." she glanced at Helma, "skin."

When Ruth looked at Helma with eyebrows raised and an expectant nod, Helma could see that the conversation threatened to veer off onto a new course and that focus was necessary.

"We'll begin at the beginning and go on," Helma said, addressing Pepper. "Are you new to Bellehaven, as you claimed?"

"Yes, I am," Pepper said, holding up her right hand as if she were taking an oath. "That's the truth. I moved here three weeks ago."

"Then your presence at the Local Authors meeting and the group counseling sessions," she continued, "was that actually to make friends?"

Pepper shifted, agilely rearranging her legs in a lotus position. Helma briefly wondered if cat hair was sticking to Pepper's pants. Boy Cat Zukas was not allowed on her furniture. She cast the image of the missing cat from her mind.

"I already told you how I ended up at the authors' meeting. I just followed the crowd," Pepper said.

"And the group sessions?" Helma prompted. "Please use a coaster," she added when she saw Pepper set her wineglass on top of a book from the Bellehaven Public Library: *Birds of Washington.*

"I really do want to make more friends," Pepper continued, moving the glass. "But actually," she held out her hands like a surrendering fugitive, "I was scoping out the competition."

Ruth snorted. "Competition for what, the Bellehaven male population?" She'd already emptied her glass and was moving toward the wine bottle Pepper had left on the kitchen counter.

"The counseling field has its cycles of popularity," Pepper explained, ignoring Ruth. She shifted two of the pillows so she could sit deeper in the sofa corner. "Like everything else, you need an angle: repressed memories, behavioral, transactional, cognitive, confrontational, Dr. Phil. There's very little straightforward 'listen and comment' counseling anymore."

From the kitchen, Ruth sang out, "You gotta have a gimmick."

Helma leaned forward in the creaky rocker, suddenly understanding. "*You're* a counselor, too?"

Pepper nodded. "I wanted to get the lay of the land first, so to speak. Maybe it *does* seem a little sneaky to some people, but can you blame me?"

"And your office is in the Hopewell Building?" Helma guessed, "where we followed you tonight?"

"I rented an office a couple of days ago, after my license transferred." Pepper told her and pulled a brass key on a silver key ring from her pocket. "I biked there after tonight's session to measure a wall. I hadn't even reached my office when the light in the hallway went out and I heard someone behind me." She shivered. "Do you think it was the murderer following me after all?"

"Where's the tape measure?" Ruth asked, reentering the room with her wineglass filled to the rim.

"What?"

"The tape measure. You said you were going to measure a wall."

Pepper patted her pants pockets. She frowned. "Oh. I didn't have a chance to measure. It's still in my pack." She stood and retrieved her blue nylon pack from a hook by the door. "Here it is," she said, pulling a worn yellow metal tape measure from a small zippered pocket. "I have a sofa in storage I plan to move in." She gazed at the battered tape measure. "This was my dad's. He was a carpenter. He was killed and it's all I . . ." She stopped, turned the tape measure in her hand and put it back in her pack, an expression of reverence on her face.

Ruth sat back, clearly disappointed.

"Is Pepper Breckenridge your actual name?" Helma asked.

Pepper blushed. "Pepper is, but Breckenridge isn't. Some of the women in the group sessions might become clients so I used Breckenridge, the name of an aunt."

"Your Aunt Myra?" Ruth asked.

Pepper looked at her blankly. Ruth shrugged and said, "Sorry. Literary joke."

"What's your true surname?" Helma asked her.

"Goodwin."

"You can't believe people wouldn't recognize you just because you changed your last name, not after they'd sat in a group session with you," Helma said.

"People don't notice as much as you believe they do," Pepper said. "When I'm in my professional guise . . ."

Ruth waved toward Pepper's gray pants, grommeted in the crotch area. "Yeah, lose the Gramiccis. A nice suit and good pumps, add a professional manicure and a stylish haircut. Makeup. It would fool me." She didn't look the least bit convinced.

"I only show up once or twice at these sessions," Pepper told them, turning defensively from Helma to Ruth. "People forget. They're involved in their own issues. They don't notice somebody like me who maintains a low profile."

Helma had to agree that Pepper wasn't the type of person who made heads turn. She blended in. Athletic, like most Bellehaven women. Nondescript, without makeup or attention-catching clothes, even forgettable.

"But you didn't actually *see* the person in the office building?" Helma asked, bringing the subject back to the incident at the Hopewell Building.

"Not really."

"Then why do you believe it was a man?"

Pepper gazed at her wall, remembering. "I think he was tall. I must have seen his outline. And aftershave." Her forehead creased as if it had just hit her. "I could smell his aftershave. One of those traditional spicy fragrances, you know, like our fathers wore, been around awhile."

"So an older man?" Ruth asked.

"Maybe. I don't know. He smoked, too. I could smell smoke. Like a cigar or something." Pepper stood up. "You're grilling me like I'm a criminal. I offered to tell you the truth and I have. I didn't hurt anybody; I'm just trying to make a living and it's a competitive world."

"You're right," Helma said, standing, too. "We *are* grilling you, and I apologize if it's misguided, but your behavior this evening was suspicious. Even you must admit that."

"Yeah," Pepper said. "From the outside, I guess." She frowned at Helma. "You seem . . . different."

Ruth sloshed more wine into her glass and gulped it down. "Same old Helma," she said. "That's the beauty of it."

"Do you believe all that crock about a big bad man chasing her through the building?" Ruth asked as they walked along the shadowy sidewalk toward the Hopewell Building.

"We'll soon find out," Helma said. "Pepper's story is based on deception."

"I know," Ruth said glumly. "Just deceitful enough to be true. Not much of a crime, I guess. Hang on a sec. I've got something in my shoe."

Helma waited while Ruth climbed off her shoes and shook them out. "What do you mean by 'We'll soon find out'?"

"You're going to talk to the police," Helma told her.

"About what? You want me to tell them we were in the building, jiggling office doors in the dark?"

"No. Not yet."

Police cars were still parked in front of the Hopewell

Building. The major excitement had obviously ended.
No lights flashed. There was no yellow crime tape,
only three officers talking outside the front entrance.
"I'll wait in my car," Helma explained. "You go find
out what exactly the police are investigating."

"And how am I supposed to do that?"

"Just stand close to them. See if they're questioning
anyone or if a man's been arrested. Stand there until
you know as much as possible, if any windows were
broken, anything stolen or destroyed."

"You do it."

"I would be too noticeable," Helma told her.

"You? I'm the one who stands out in a crowd, remember?"

"That's true," Helma explained reasonably, "but de-
pending on who's there, I might attract attention that
would deflect our discovering any new information."

"Oh. You mean if Glory saw you she'd squeal like a
trapped mouse, and the big brave policemen would be
so busy calming her down, criminal details wouldn't
get spilled?"

"I'm only interested in the intruder at the Hopewell
Building."

"Okay, seeing as how you've taken me in during my
moment of need, and this may be one small step in returning the favor, I'll do it."

They had nearly reached Helma's Buick. A small
group of curious citizens had gathered on the sidewalk
to watch the police. "Just walk over there, blend in
with the crowd and listen for the details, that's all you
have to do," Helma told Ruth.

"I don't 'blend,' " Ruth argued.

"You will in the dark. I'll wait here."

Lights blazed in the building, upstairs and down. Either Wayne Gallant had left in his unmarked car or he'd pulled it around the other side of the building, out of sight.

Helma sat behind the steering wheel and watched Ruth saunter casually to the office building. For a moment she disappeared behind two tall men and then reappeared.

She shouldn't have been surprised when Ruth simply walked up to the three policemen and began speaking.

One of the policemen she recognized as Sidney Lehman, who Ruth claimed she'd once slept with when he was younger, in appreciation for information that had ultimately saved a life. Helma believed her, at least about the sleeping part.

Ruth gesticulated as she spoke, which was normal, but then she extended her arm like a specter and pointed toward Helma's car. All three policemen turned and gazed her way.

Helma did not move. She ignored a moment's urge to lean down and straighten her floor carpet and sat totally upright, returning the policemen's curious gazes.

Ruth squeezed Sidney Lehman's arm, waved her hand to include all three men, and walked back to Helma's car, a wide smile on her face.

The first thing she said when she climbed in the car was, "Sidney's filled out nicely, don't you think?" and she made cigar-tapping motions.

"Did the police find anyone in the building?" Helma asked.

"Oh, that. No, but somebody *was* inside. Besides us, I mean. One of the office doors was jimmied open and papers messed up a little, but nothing was taken. The second-floor exit light was broken just like we heard." Ruth held up her hand. "Don't worry. I didn't tell them we already knew that. No perps in sight."

"Why did the police investigate? Did someone call?"

Ruth shook her head. "I couldn't get that out of them, but I bet the building's alarm is connected to the police station. So, they show up and no one's here. Do you think Pepper Breckenridge-Goodwin-Who's-it broke in?"

"She has a key. And besides, we all saw someone else or at least heard someone when they broke the exit light. She couldn't have done that."

"Yeah. Curious. Something's squirreled up about that place. Let's go home until more is revealed."

As Helma pulled away from the curb, Ruth said quietly, "And about that other subject."

"What other subject?"

"Mr. Wayne Knight-in-Tarnished-Armor Gallant. He *was* there, and she *was* with him."

Chapter 16

The Longest Night

Ten o'clock had come and gone but after they left Pepper and the Hopewell Building, Helma and Ruth drove slowly through the dark alleys of south Bellehaven, up and down, back and forth.

"He's probably out there watching us search all over town for him," Ruth said, staring out her window. "Playing a cat-and-mouse game with us." Her laugh was cut off by a yawn.

"I thought I'd hear of at least one sighting by now," Helma told her as she expertly steered around an unpruned shrub.

"He's a professional alley cat, Helma. This is what they do."

Between alleys, they passed a police car parked against the curb, its lights off, but Helma could see the outline of a policeman sitting behind the wheel. He might have been watching them, she couldn't tell, but he made no move to follow.

"I *will* find Boy Cat Zukas," she told Ruth, tightening her jaw. "Unless someone has taken him into their home and he can't escape."

"You don't mean, like someone saw him and *wanted* him, do you?" Ruth asked.

"What are you implying?" Helma asked, slowing at a glare of eyes that turned out to be a small dog at the end of a large woman's leash. Boy Cat Zukas had *chosen* to take up residence on her balcony; Helma had never encouraged him, in fact the opposite. What if now, for some unfathomable feline reason, he'd decided it was time to take up residence somewhere else?

"Nothing. Tell me, what happened between you and our chief of police just before your birthday? Did you have a little set-to? Insult the city's finest? Go on a date with a rival?"

Helma seriously considered Ruth's questions one by one, unable to come up with a single reason—not even a hint—for Wayne Gallant's sudden coolness. "Besides reminding me of the police department's superior professional skills, he's not said anything personal," Helma said. "And now I've seen him twice with . . ."

"About Glory Shandy." Ruth paused to squint at a clump of bamboo rustling in the breezes. "George Melville waxes poetic over her. He's usually a pretty astute guy, but if she's a paragon I'm missing it. Or else she's one exceptionally sly woman, neither attribute a plus in my book. Which is it?"

Helma Zukas always tried to avoid judgmentalism. "No one is a paragon," she said now. "Perfection is not to be found in humanity."

"I see." Ruth nodded, and nodded again. "Then what does she have to do with these two deaths?"

"Nothing," Helma answered, stepping on the brake in surprise.

"Careful," Ruth told her, placing a hand on the dashboard. "Think about it for a minute. What does little Glory gain if Molly the Poet is dead?"

Helma took her foot from the brake and continued up the alley. "Not a thing."

"There's at least the removal of Molly's presence. Maybe Molly was continually bothering Glory with her poetry. Like kids: 'Look what I did, Mom!' " Ruth held up one finger. "That's a reason, pathetic as it is. But what does Glory gain from the death of Victim number two, Tanja Frost?"

"I doubt they were aware each other existed."

"You don't know that. There could be a hidden connection: long-lost sister after the inheritance or something."

"These are farfetched suggestions, Ruth." She slowed next to a stand of garbage cans.

Ruth shrugged. "I just thought Wayne Gallant's new love interest could be removed from the picture completely. You know: Murderer goes to jail; man is abandoned; former love triumphs."

But Helma was still caught by Ruth's first sentence. "Seeing Wayne with Glory twice doesn't designate her as his new love interest."

"So what *does* it make her?"

When Helma pictured Wayne and Glory, a curious feeling of . . . red flowed through her, like touching a hot stove, or . . . lightning. Despite its twisty sharpness, the sensation was decidedly preferable to her earlier muddiness.

"Maybe what we're really dealing with here is a Local Author writing a mystery, manufacturing a plot for realism," Ruth said.

There was no sign of Boy Cat Zukas. He'd now been alone on the streets of Bellehaven for fifty-one hours.

Helma dismissed Ruth's more outlandish conjectures and mulled over Ms. Moon's demands that Helma not do what she'd referred to as Helma's "sleuthing," that she let the murders play themselves out unaided—all in the hopes the attention would help the library budget. And her request for displays of the murder victims, displays linking Molly and Tanja's homicides to the library, and to Helma's Local Authors project. Poetry and Death. Once the displays were erected, there would be an indelible connection in the minds of the public. The Library and Murder, Murder and the Library.

The displays could *not* be erected, they simply couldn't be. It was up to Helma to assure that they weren't. "I need to return to the library for a minute," Helma told Ruth. "I can drop you off at my apartment."

Ruth tapped the yellowish green face of Helma's dashboard clock. "Look, Helm, it's almost eleven P.M. Last time I noticed, your library closed at nine P.M. on Thursday nights. We just had our little after-hours adventure in a closed building, remember? Let's go home. I bet this time Boy Cat Zukas really is sitting quietly on your deck waiting for you."

"This will only take a minute. I'll drop you off."

Ruth slouched in her seat. "Never mind. Count me

in. We already broke and entered once tonight. What's one more?"

"We *didn't* break into the Hopewell Building; the door was unlocked. I possess an official key to the library. I'm fully and legally entitled to enter."

"Yeah, yeah. So just tell me *why*, okay?"

"After the publicity in this morning's newspaper," she explained to Ruth. "Ms. Moon said she'd given Glory Shandy a collection of Molly Bittern's poetry for the display. I don't know who donated it to the library and it doesn't qualify for the Local Authors collection. It may still be on Glory's desk. Possibly there's a clue in her poetry to who wanted her dead."

"Why'd she give it to Glory instead of you, the rightful leader of the project?"

"Glory's more sympathetic," Helma conceded.

"Got it. Those poems will be torturous to read. You're going to swipe it off Glory's desk?"

"The manuscript comes under the auspices of the Local Authors collection. I intend to restore it to its proper place."

She turned into the library's empty parking lot and pulled into her parking place, lining up her Buick's hood ornament with the flag pole in front of her. "Lock your door," she told Ruth as she turned off the engine.

"If you bought a new car you could get one of those clicker things so you wouldn't have to go through all this folderol every time you got in or out of your car."

"My car has operated perfectly since high school graduation. Why should I buy a new one?"

"That's precisely why." Ruth slammed her door, then blanched at the sound in the quiet evening. "Looks dark in there."

"It should be." Helma had her keys at the ready. After eighteen years at the Bellehaven Public Library, she could have unerringly found her way through the workroom or the public area in the inkiest of darkness without a single misstep, but luckily for Ruth, at night the library grounds and entrances were well lit.

Still, it was unusual to be inside the normally bustling library without there being a single man—or woman-made sound. It reminded Helma of the empty school. They unconsciously lowered their voices until Helma switched on the lights and the workroom brightened, appearing pitifully and hopelessly jumbled in the cold florescent glare, with all the books and carts and boxes in various stages of processing.

"You sure it's okay to be in here?" Ruth asked, turning in a circle and peering in all directions.

"Technically." She glanced toward the open door of Ms. Moon's office, imagining the director's face if she stumbled on Helma and Ruth.

"I heard," Ruth said, flicking the head of a bobble hula girl on George Melville's desk, "that if you're being attacked and shout 'Fire!' instead of 'Help!' everybody comes running because nobody can resist a fire. But 'Help!' is too mundane to be noticed. Do you think that's true?"

"You might try it if you ever have the opportunity," Helma suggested.

"Where's Molly's manuscript supposed to be again?" Ruth asked.

"Ms. Moon said she gave it to Glory. That's her cubicle."

"Well, I hope Molly's name's on it," Ruth said, gazing around Glory's cubicle at haphazard piles of books and papers.

"I expect it'll be stapled plain paper. Try not to disturb anything."

"So we *shouldn't* be doing this after all," Ruth said smugly.

Helma began carefully examining the papers on the left side of Glory's desk: memos, catalogs, Internet printouts, city bulletins. At the bottom of the pile a colorful glossy circular with a woman in a thong smiling over her shoulder. "Join our Great Buns! class."

Ruth held up a photo in a silver frame. "Who's this with her?"

Helma glanced at the photo, one of Glory's prize possessions. "Stephen King. She met him at a signing."

"Big guy. Look at her adoring eyes. She looks like somebody rolled away the rock."

Nothing on Glory's desk appeared to be poems. Helma searched Glory's bookshelves, carefully repositioning items exactly as they'd been before she examined them. Ruth moved randomly and unsystematically through the workroom, poking here and there, mostly at the staff's personal possessions.

Molly's poems were not in Glory's cubicle. Helma next entered her own in case Glory had appropriately passed the collection on for Helma's appraisal.

She sighed at the sheer volume of submitted materials for the Local Authors collection. There were still all the decisions to be made, the letters of rejection and acceptance to be written. She'd think about all that tomorrow. She turned in her small cubicle, removing one plain no-peanut M&M from the Chinese enamel box on her desk and biting it cleanly in two while she contemplated the missing poetry.

Just then, Ruth's voice rang out. "Found 'em!" and Ruth banged through the door to the workroom from the public area, holding up a set of stapled pages.

"Where were they?" Helma asked.

"On a table just outside the door."

"Show me." Helma took the poems and flipped through them. One poem to a page, centered, printed from a computer. Scraps of paper were stuck to staples near the center as if a sheet had been torn out. The pages weren't numbered, but as she scanned through the sheets again she noticed with approval that Molly's poems were in alphabetical order by title, beginning with "Absolute Grief" and ending with "Wishful Thinking." The torn shreds of paper clung to the staples between poems titled "Black Eyes" and "Ending."

"Right here, big as life," Ruth said, showing Helma a table close to the workroom door at the back of the public area. The table was clean, the chairs pushed in.

"Were the pages open?" Helma asked.

Ruth frowned. "Maybe. I don't know. Damn. I grabbed them up so fast I can't remember. Sorry." She turned in a circle. "Where is it you're erecting the cemetery for dead authors?"

"If you mean the display Ms. Moon requested, she's planned for it in the case near the front doors."

"But you're not going to let it happen, are you?"

Helma looked up from Molly's poetry. "No," she said simply.

"Good. Don't read those poems aloud, okay?"

The interior library lights blazed, an unusual spectacle at eleven o'clock on a week night, so Helma wasn't surprised to hear tapping on the plateglass front doors of the library.

Ruth yelped and darted behind a bookshelf as if a shot had been fired at her. "Now what? The guy from the Hopewell Building? Get down!"

"I'll see who it is," Helma told her.

"And be the sitting duck? Why don't you sink back into your blue funk and stop doing all this crazy stuff?"

Helma picked up an oversized and hefty volume of the *Oxford English Dictionary* and slowly approached the door, the book held firmly at her side. A lean policeman she didn't recognize stood outside on the front step, seemingly relaxed, but Helma knew that was his trained professional demeanor, that he was a vigilant public servant, prepared to apprehend her if she proved to be an unmanageable criminal.

"May I see identification?" she asked through the glass doors.

He narrowed his eyes, but when he opened a wallet and showed her proper ID—Officer Mark Young—she unlocked the door and explained who she was.

"Drop the globe, ma'am," he said over Helma's shoulder and moved his hand to his belt.

"Don't shoot," Ruth said, dropping the library's newest, most brightly colored world globe to the floor, where it pivoted around its base like a toy top.

"Weren't the two of you just driving through the alleys on the south side of town?" Officer Young asked.

"Caught," Ruth said.

"We were searching for my cat," Helma explained. "There's a record of his gone missing at the police department, although no one there has informed me of any sightings."

"And you thought your cat might be here in the library?" he asked pleasantly.

"No, I'd forgotten some work-related papers." She held up Molly's poetry. "Now that I have them, we'll be returning home."

"It's late, ma'am," he said smoothly. "I'll escort you to your car."

Helma would have liked more time to investigate the table where Ruth had discovered Molly's poems, but that would have to wait. There was no mistaking the firmness behind the policeman's courteous manner.

He followed close on their heels through the public area, reminding her of a herding collie, waiting and watching as she closed doors and switched off lights. With the poems in her hand and a last glance around the workroom, she and Ruth exited the library, with Officer Young right behind them.

"Have a nice evening," the policeman said as she and Ruth climbed into Helma's car. He stood in the parking lot until they pulled onto the street and turned the corner.

"Could you do me a favor before we go home?" Ruth asked as Helma drove through Bellehaven's core where only a few cars traveled the streets,

"If I can," Helma told her.

"Drive by my old house."

Before she moved to Minnesota, Ruth had lived for years in a converted carriage house off Spruce Street on what was referred to as "the slope," the older side of town with well-kept Victorian and Craftsman homes that had never deteriorated into rentals. Huge trees, sloping landscaped lawns, views of Washington Bay.

Ruth's former house faced the alley and when Helma pulled in front of it, Ruth said, "Just stop for a few, okay?"

Whoever lived there now mowed the lawn and kept up a garden. A white fence bordered the alley and a new carport had replaced the garage. A kayak hung from the ceiling above a white Volvo.

Ruth looked and looked at the dark house, sitting stone still. Finally she heaved a deep breath. "Okay, back to the real world."

Again, Boy Cat Zukas was not on the deck waiting for his kibbles, although a bouquet of six yellow roses arranged among heather stood in a vase beside Helma's apartment door.

"Well, it's about time," Ruth whooped when she spotted the bouquet. "A plea for forgiveness."

Helma carried the roses inside and set them on her kitchen counter. The subtlest of fragrance wafted through the room. She removed the card from its plastic-forked prong among the roses and opened it. "They're not from him," she said aloud.

"What?" Ruth grabbed the card out of Helma's hand and read it. "Boyd? Who's Boyd? Oh. The cowboy you had a drink with tonight?"

Helma nodded. Why on earth would Boyd send her flowers?

"Chin up. This counts," she said, watching Helma place the vase of roses in the very center of her dining room table and turn away from them.

Helma believed that beds should be used only for pleasant activities, so after Ruth said good night, even though she was tired, Helma removed Molly's poems from her bag and sat on her sofa to read them, looking for clues as to why she had met her death on Belle-haven's streets.

She was no critic, but the best she could say for Molly Bittern's poems was that they were heartfelt. Paeans of loss and sorrow, several in what could only be called jingle format. As she read a poem called "Ending," she rubbed her finger along the fuzzed and torn paper that still clung to the staples, wondering why a page had been removed from Molly's collection.

Ending

> *Remember how you pulled my hair?*
> *I asked, how did you dare*
> *We were lovers*
> *You wanted others*
> *I wanted you out of my bed*
> *I wanted to see you dead*
> *Why oh why did you leave me?*

At one A.M., when Helma had finally stopped toss-ing and dozed off, her telephone rang. She grabbed for it, instantly awake, unaccountably expecting to hear a man's voice.

"Yes?" she said, glancing around her bedroom. All was normal in her apartment, she could sense that, even in the darkness. A low hum emitted from her re-frigerator, a car hissed past on the wet street.

Silence.

"May I help you?" she asked.

She heard the faint movement of breath, then a squeak like a squeezed rubber duck.

"Excuse me?"

The crescendoing yowl of a meow sounded in her ear. She pulled the phone away and stared at the receiver, flicking on her bedside lamp with her free hand.

"Who is this?" she demanded.

The voice was gravelly and at the same time a monotone, something mechanically disguised. She couldn't tell if it was a man or a woman.

"I have your cat," the voice growled.

"What do you want?" Helma asked.

"Mind your own business. Give it up or the cat dies."

"You *don't* have my cat," Helma said. The telephone receiver was suddenly slippery in her hand and she switched it to her other hand, which was actually more slippery, so she grabbed the hem of her sheet and wrapped it around the receiver, pressing it so close to her ear that the flesh was pinned painfully to her skull.

"That's not my cat," she said, trying to simulate her silver dime voice.

"It is too" the disguised voice asserted. "Black, bent tail, a few white patches. Scrappy looking."

"A torn right ear?" Helma asked.

"Yes. Mind your own business or you'll never see your cat again."

"Could you make him yowl again, please?" Helma asked.

Silence. Then, "Hurt him again? What are you, a monster?"

"I'm sorry," Helma explained, "but I do not negotiate with terrorists."

"You're right. You *will* be sorry. Say bye-bye to kitty-kitty." And the connection was broken.

Helma sat on the edge of her bed, the sheet-wrapped receiver in her hand, her knuckles white, and a whooshing in her ears like the inside of a giant seashell.

"What's all the shouting about?" Ruth stood in the doorway, still in her clothes, swabbing a paintbrush in one of Helma's best juice glasses.

Helma replaced the receiver and pointed to it. She cleared her throat. "It was a crank call."

"About Boy Cat Zukas?"

Helma nodded.

"I heard you say he had a torn right ear. I've been describing him to every Tom, Dick, and Harry since I got here, and it's his left ear that's torn, not his right."

Helma nodded again, fervently hoping the caller was adept at knowing left from right and was therefore truly bluffing, and that Boy Cat Zukas at this very moment was safely tucked beneath a bush somewhere, dourly viewing the passing world through slitted eyes.

Chapter 17

A New Day

On Friday morning, instead of awakening to the music of her clock radio, Helma opened her eyes to Ruth's raised voice. She sat up in her dark bedroom, waiting for a response. It was still dark, the middle of the night. Had someone come to the door to return Boy Cat Zukas and was now arguing with Ruth about the size of the reward?

But no, there was only silence and then Ruth's voice again, even louder. "No, I need to be alone a few more days and then we can discuss it."

Helma lay back down and pulled the comforter up to her chin. Ruth was on the telephone, and she guessed Paul was on the other end of the line. It wasn't the middle of the night after all; it was two hours later in Minnesota, almost seven o'clock there, 4:51 in Washington. She could sleep another hour.

But that was not to be. The instant Helma

closed her eyes, the world intruded, not with the muzzy, muddy confusion of the last few days but with laser keenness. The heaviness was gone, totally dissipated. She caught her breath at the wonder of it, as if her body were lighter, the air clearer. Breath effortlessly filled her lungs.

Aunt Em had been right. So had TNT. And even her mother.

Each of the week's tragedies materialized before her: Molly and the murdered Tanja; Molly's poems; Glory Shandy and Wayne Gallant; Pepper and the stranger in the Hopewell Building; Ms. Moon's misdirected scheme for connecting murder and the library. But most of all, Boy Cat Zukas and the mechanical voice claiming he'd been kidnapped.

She switched on her bedside light, and reached for the pad of paper and pencil that always sat on her bed table for middle-of-the-night ideas. Luxuriating in her old familiar resolve, she listed her order of attack for the day, all to the accompaniment of Ruth's rising and falling voice at the opposite end of her apartment.

"I'm locking myself inside and painting today," Ruth said fiercely when Helma, now showered and dressed, stepped into the kitchen.

"You can't actually lock yourself inside," Helma explained. "That's no longer a feature of modern doors, due to disastrous consequences years ago."

"Yeah, well you know what I mean. I have to do this while I can—as long as I can."

A puddle of coffee formed a half-moon shape on the counter next to the coffee maker, coagulating around the edges. Helma didn't drink coffee. Ruth had brought home a battered coffee maker from a second-hand store—probably where she'd bought her new wardrobe—missing its lid.

"Were there any phone calls while I was in the shower?" Helma asked her as she wiped up the coffee spill with a damp paper towel.

"You mean from cat-nappers?" Ruth asked. "Nope. You really should tell the police about that one, Helma. Kidnapping is a federal crime. Cat-napping has to at least be a misdemeanor."

"Whoever called was bluffing," Helma told her, remembering the left/right ear discrepancy. "So many people in Bellehaven know he's missing, it was a prank."

"They're *not* bluffing; they don't want you poking around," Ruth pointed out. "The caller's guilty of *some* crime and thinks you're on to something, whether it's murder or cat-thieving."

"I'll wait. If they contact me again, I *will* call the police," Helma assured her as she removed a carton of orange juice from the refrigerator.

"Oh," Ruth suddenly said. "I forgot to tell you, I did a little sleuthing on my own last night."

"When?" Helma asked in surprise.

"After you went to bed." She nodded toward the roses on the table. "Your Boyd guy. I asked around, made a few calls." Ruth filled a glass with orange juice, drank it and filled it again.

"Who were your sources?" Helma asked.

"It doesn't really matter since I couldn't find out much." She frowned. "In fact, it was damn odd. He's lived right here in bonnie Bellehaven for a couple of years but keeps a *very* low profile, more like *no* profile.

No job that anybody's aware of. A few people know who he is but that's it."

"He says he's a writer," Helma explained. "Writers are solitary."

"Around here, if there's a whiff of creativity going on, even behind closed doors, *somebody* knows."

"He may not know the people you know," Helma pointed out. "I don't."

"Hmmph," Ruth snorted. "That doesn't mean they don't know you. Just something fishy about him, that's all."

"I don't intend to see him again, anyway," Helma told Ruth and changed the subject. "Now that you're painting, do you think you'll be able to paint in Minneapolis?" she asked cautiously.

Ruth touched her index finger to her chin. "Hmm, what a euphemistic question. Are you asking if I've permanently moved from Minnesota back to Bellehaven? Or if I've left Paul? Or if I can only paint here in the great Northwest?"

"All of the above," Helma told her.

"That's exactly what I'm trying to figure out before I lose my mind. How can a person want—desperately— every impossible opposing thing on this little green earth?"

"Human nature, I suppose. Sometimes we have to decide what we *won't* do rather than all we want to do."

"Ah, wisdom of the ages," Ruth said lightly, almost flippantly, but Helma observed the dark-rimmed eyes that no makeup could hide; the way she was tearing the magazine drop card into ever tinier scraps.

"I'm serious, dead-on serious," Ruth said, suddenly

appearing smaller, even fragile. "What kind of hope is there for two people who share absolutely *nothing*, who'd argue over whether movies need plots or if water needs fluoride? Who can't even stand the same climate?"

"Maybe," Helma said, considering Ruth's question just as seriously, "if two people agree on *everything*, one of them isn't necessary."

Glory Shandy stood in front of the staff bulletin board shoving a red push pin into a 5-×-8 piece of pink construction paper that read, "Library Party! Come as your favorite book character! Bring your favorite book-related food! Games! Prizes! A totally Library-themed party!"

Helma was not a woman to ignore people or "cut them dead," as her mother would say, whether they deserved it or she wanted to. "A well-bred lady never stoops to give her enemy the satisfaction," Aunt Em liked to say.

In Helma's bag, between the pages of a book on figure painting, which Ruth had rejected as "plebian," rested the stapled sheets of Molly's poetry.

"Hello, Glory," Helma said now, stopping beside the photocopier that Glory was partially blocking.

Gloria jumped, her eyes darting left, then right, as if searching for a quick means of escape.

"Excuse me," Helma continued politely. "I removed Molly Bittern's poems from you desk and I'd like to photocopy them."

"What?" Glory squeaked. "Poems? Molly's poems?" She didn't meet Helma's eyes.

"Yes, Molly's poems. If you'll just move so I can

copy a set for you. You seem to have stabbed a pushpin into your thumb."

"Oh." Glory wildly shook her hand and the pushpin came loose and flew across the room. She stuck her bleeding thumb into her mouth.

"Are you planning a party?" Helma asked as the copier whirred.

"Oh, yes," Glory said. "A party. We are." She glanced sideways at Helma and, sensing she was safe, began to gush. "A gigantic get-together for the staff. We thought it might help promote respect and teamwork."

There was no mistaking Glory's emphasis on the word "we," so Helma obligingly asked, "Is it being planned by the marketing committee?"

The Library Marketing Committee had once promoted a "Behind the Scenes in Library Book Cataloging!" tour for the public, complete with exhaustively detailed signs that explained each step, balloons, punch and cookies, and free pencils stamped with 613.96: DO IT BY THE BOOK. The event had been attended by Aunt Em, Helma's mother, and four giggling teenagers who'd angered the committee by signing in, grabbing their free pencils, and skipping out.

Helma had been impressed that the teens were knowledgeable enough of the Dewey decimal system to appreciate what 613.96 referred to.

Glory laughed her shiny little laugh, still avoiding Helma's eyes. "Oh no, not this time. I'm helping May Apple . . . I mean, Ms. Moon. She didn't have time to plan all the games and themes, but I found a lot of really great ideas on the Internet. It'll be so much fun."

If Glory hadn't been acting so jumpy, Helma would

have expected her to dance a few happy steps. "I'm sure the staff will be surprised," Helma said and began her way to her cubicle.

"Oh," Glory called after her. "Guests are invited, too. Family members, significant others. It doesn't have to be just library staff. We can all invite anybody we want. *Anybody.*"

In her cubicle, Helma slipped off her coat and hung it on her coat hook. On the other side of the low bookcase, Harley Woodworth sat in his cubicle, hunched over his desk.

"Good morning, Harley," Helma said.

In a hurry and a flurry, Harley dropped a magnifying mirror and a pair of tweezers in his middle desk drawer. "Morning," he said, vigorously rubbing his nose.

"Was it busy last night?" Helma asked. It had been Harley's night to work until the library closed at nine.

Harley nodded. "It was. I could barely keep up with it all. When it gets that busy, I question whether we're providing adequate service to the public."

No task passed Harley's notice without comment on its difficulty, its toll, its impossibility. He eagerly and morosely shared every aggravation apparent on his watch.

"Did any patron ask you for a copy of Molly Bittern's poetry?" Helma asked. "A stapled sheaf of papers?"

"Molly?" Harley asked, his eyes shadowing for a moment. "Poor Molly. No, nobody asked me. Why?"

"Someone read them at the table by the workroom door. The poems were still on the table after the library closed."

"I didn't see them," he said defensively. "And I'm the last one to check when *I* work nights. Windows were closed, computers were off, chairs pushed in."

"Thank you," Helma told him.

"Do you think any more writers will be murdered?" Harley asked. "Ms. Moon said they're all in danger, that everyone in the library is at risk. She didn't mean librarians, too, did she?"

"Certainly not," Helma assured him, seeing Harley's face fall in disappointment. "But," she added, "we should all behave prudently during this dangerous time," and he brightened considerably.

Harley hesitated. He cleared his throat. "I've taken up cigar smoking," he said.

"You have?" she asked, plainly surprised since she'd never met anyone as obsessed with bodily health as Harley.

He nodded solemnly. "Outdoors. Could you tell your friend Ruth that?"

Helma was confused—Ruth?—until Harley touched his reading glasses, which no longer hung around his neck on a silver chain but were tucked into his shirt pocket, beside a thin cigar box sticking out that read, *GARCIA Y VEGA MINIATURES*.

Then she remembered Ruth teasing Harley about keeping his glasses on a "leash," maybe even impugning his manliness.

"They have all-natural leaf wrappers," he explained to her, touching the box of cigars.

First, Helma flexed her fingers over her keyboard and performed a fast and efficient Internet search using the keywords, telephone, voice, and disguise. In 2.43 seconds she was rewarded with 1,310,000 hits. A few more clicks of her mouse and there they were arrayed across her screen: "Telephone Voice Changers." Available to anyone who possessed $21.95 to $498.99. They even came in colors. She'd had no idea.

Next, she walked carefully around the table where Ruth discovered Molly's poetry, and found nothing unusual, no note or dropped library card. Helma pondered the connection between Julius, Tanja's husband and Sunny, Tanja's friend. She'd thrown away Sunny's handout from the Age of Certain Years session, so she no longer had Sunny's last name.

She folded her hands on her desk and closed her eyes, allowing her mind to play with Sunny's image. According to well-documented memory studies, as well as a national poet laureate, names were the first to go. Accepting this deficiency, Helma had long ago devised mnemonic methods for all sorts of memory problems: names, shopping lists, streets, the states and their capitals. It was second nature; it just took a few seconds to recall the specific mnemonic aid.

Sunny wore scarves: no. She was plump: no. Her hair cupped her head in a close style. That was it: cup, peanut butter cup. Reese's peanut butter cup.

With a smile of satisfaction, Helma opened the telephone book to the yellow pages and under Counselors, ran her finger down the list of names until she reached *R*, and there it was: Sunny Reese, Compassionate Counseling, specializing in Women's Issues and Relationship Skills.

She should have looked sooner. Sunny's office was in the Hopewell Building.

She dialed Sunny Reese's office number twice but there was no answer, only an answering machine, and Helma Zukas did not speak into answering machines.

* * *

In the public area, the origami exhibit had been removed from the display case in preparation for the displays Ms. Moon had ordered for Molly Bittern and Tanja Frost. Brightly twisted paper birds, animals, stars, and clever packages made from dual-colored paper sat in a cardboard box at the end of the checkout counter.

"Glory said to put these in your office," Cheryl, one of the pages, said when she saw Helma standing in front of the box of jumbled origami.

"You may give the box to Ms. Moon," Helma told her. "I believe she has assumed control of the displays."

Dutch, who had worked at the circulation desk since his retirement from the military and had risen from part-time fill-in to the desk's full commander, surveyed Helma and Cheryl as they spoke, his thumb-shaped head erect, chin lifted as if sniffing the air for hidden devices.

Dutch shadowed the periphery of every library occurrence, his aloof—one could say disinterested—presence a discreet distance from the action. Dutch didn't gossip; Helma didn't gossip.

"Do you recall anyone delivering a sheaf of poetry yesterday for the Local Authors collection?" Helma asked him now. "Poetry by Molly Bittern?"

Dutch nodded and glanced at the wall clock behind the desk. "It was eleven fifteen. A woman brought it in."

"Do you know who she was?"

"She didn't identify herself," Dutch said briskly.

Helma waited. Dutch looked both ways before he said in a quieter voice, "She was older, a little . . . worn. My sense was that she was the dead woman's mother."

"Thank you," Helma told him. "That's very helpful."

"It's only the situation as observed," Dutch said stiffly, beckoning toward a page who had stopped reshelving to talk to a boy her own age. The page jumped guiltily and returned to shelving in the 100s.

Dutch turned back to Helma. "I don't believe displays of murdered women do any service to the library."

Helma nodded neutrally and returned to her cubicle, stopping once as she walked through the public area when her keen eyes caught that once again someone had pulled several books on women's rights from the 300s and tucked them into the 220.5s, in the midst of the library's various versions of the Bible. She reshelved them and continued on her way.

Back in her cubicle Helma reopened the Bellehaven telephone book, this time to the Bs. There were two Bitterns listed: M. Bittern, who she guessed was Molly, and D. Bittern, no address. Once thought to have been a way of disguising someone's sexual identity, now listings like these screamed out, "Woman Alone!"

The number for D. Bittern rang four times before a woman's voice briskly said, "Yes?"

"Mrs. Bittern," Helma said, taking her cue from the briskness of the woman's voice. "This is Miss Helma Zukas from the Bellehaven Public Library. I'm responsible for the Local Authors project and I'd like to discuss your daughter's poems that you delivered to the library yesterday."

D. Bittern was silent but Helma heard the woman breathing. She waited patiently.

Finally the woman said, "Stepdaughter. What's wrong with them?"

"Nothing. Nothing at all. Thank you for the donation. I wonder if we might discuss her motivation for writing them."

"No, I don't think so," D. Bittern told Helma. "Good—"

"The director of the library is erecting a display to honor your daughter . . . stepdaughter's poetic talent." Helma came to a full stop to allow the absorption of that information. Then she added. "I'd like to hear about Molly's life and poetic aspirations. Perhaps you have some photographs we might include in our display?"

"A display?"

"Yes. In the library foyer, facing the main entrance, where everyone entering the library will see it. The director would like one panel devoted to your stepdaughter."

"All right, then," she said, still sounding reluctant. "Come by around eleven this morning and I'll have something ready for you."

"I'll be there," Helma said, although she was scheduled to be on the reference desk at eleven. "Does the *D* stand for Diane?" she asked as she took down Molly's stepmother's address.

"Deeter," the woman told her.

"Helma," Ms. Moon called out as Helma walked past her office door. She stopped and entered Ms. Moon's office as far as the doorway, only her toes inside the room. Ms. Moon did not rise from her desk.

"I noticed no progress has been made on the displays," Ms. Moon said.

"I believe the origami display has been removed," Helma told her.

"Which *I* ordered."

"Displays of murder victims are not appropriate for the library," Helma began, "especially so soon after . . ."

Ms. Moon rapped her knuckle on her desk and said, "I'll remind you that we are a *public* library and these deaths concern both the public and the library."

"Our mission is to promote reading, literacy, and literature. If we . . ."

But shockingly, Ms. Moon had covered her ears with her hands. Her face went blank, and she shook her head at Helma as if her head were inside a vacuum.

Helma retreated from Ms. Moon's doorway and found George Melville, the cataloger, looking at Helma appraisingly. He stroked his beard and said, "It's nice to have you back, Helma."

"I beg your pardon?"

"You know, at full throttle, in the pink, rarin' to go, back in the groove. The spark has returned to your eye."

"Thank you," Helma told George, wondering if the "spark" had returned due to her association with murder. That was a disturbing thought. "I have an appointment at eleven. Would you be willing to trade desk hours with me?"

"I would, gladly, but I'm committed to participating in a deadly teleconference on catalog authority files. Give me the reference desk and troubled patrons any day. Sorry."

Helma asked Harley, who had a doctor's appointment, and Eve, who was meeting her boyfriend for an early lunch.

She sat at her desk, wondering if she dare ask Ms. Moon, when a voice sang out, "Knock, knock."

Helma turned to Glory's smiling, cheery, beaming, face.

"Oh, Helma. I just heard you were looking for someone to work your desk shift at eleven. I'd be happy to do that for you."

What choice did she have? "Thank you. We can trade shifts."

Glory shook her head, still smiling. "Oh no. I'm happy to do this. I've already gained so much from knowing you. I don't want you to repay me at all."

"Glory told me she's taking your hours at the reference desk for you," Ms. Moon said, raising her eyebrows.

"If you expect me to create displays for women we know very little about," Helma said, phrasing her words cautiously under Ms. Moon's suspicious eyes, "I need to be away from the library to collect material."

Ms. Moon's dress rippled. "Certainly, certainly. We'll manage here without you. I knew you'd finally agree that these displays can only benefit the library's budget, and the public, too, of course."

"Also," Helma said, "I have finished attending the group sessions."

Ms. Moon frowned. "There's still one more: Troubled Pets."

"No," Helma told her, shaking her head. "I have finished," and she left Ms. Moon gazing after her.

At 10:45, as the library door closed behind Helma, her mind on her appointment with Molly's stepmother, she looked up to see Chief of Police Wayne Gallant bounding up the library's front steps. They both stopped, facing each other across a gulf of four feet.

"Good morning," he said.

"Good morning," she said.

He placed a hand in his pocket. Jingle jangle, sounded his coins.

She lifted her purse on her shoulder.

He nodded.

She nodded back.

"Were you looking for me?" she asked.

"No . . ."

"Excuse me, then," Helma cut in, feeling her face flush.

"But . . ." he cut in. Jingle jangle.

"Have a pleasant day," she interrupted.

"You, too," he countered.

And they passed each other, traveling in opposite directions.

Chapter 18

Lost Images

Helma drove to the east side of Bellehaven; beside her on the seat, the collection of Molly's poems.

Deeter Bittern lived in a small one-story bungalow that Helma recognized from a recent reference question as a Sears & Roebuck house, kit houses that people were once able to order from the Sears & Roebuck catalog until the 1940s. The houses were shipped by train all over the nation as kits that contained every nail, shingle, and board numbered for "easy construction." Even the paint was included.

Wooden whirligigs hung every few feet from the eaves and on poles in the front yard. Helma could see more figures in the side yard. Fishermen, boats, and airplanes; skunks and little boys; Dutch children in blue. When the wind blew, the line was cast, the propellers turned, the oars rowed the air, the skunk raised his tail, the Dutch children kissed. Whirligigs were part of Helma's childhood in Michigan, made by hobbyists and the retired. She wondered if the whirligigs were a legacy from Molly Bittern's father.

She stepped onto the porch and pushed the doorbell which was set into the belly of a red-eyed wooden toad. No answer. She glanced at her watch and knocked on the door.

"She's out back," a woman pruning roses in the next yard called to Helma, waving her pruning shears toward the rear of Deeter Bittern's house. "Right where she always is."

"Thank you." Helma walked down the driveway lined with white painted rocks toward a tidy red garage.

Inside the garage, a woman in her late fifties stood in the midst of whirligigs in every possible state of construction. She held a paintbrush dripping with enamel red paint over the wooden cutout of a woodpecker. Old rock music played and the woman, dressed in jeans and an oversized sweatshirt, hummed along with it.

"Excuse me," Helma said, and the round-faced woman looked up, paintbrush poised. Her hair was platinum, the ageless color that younger women sometimes dyed their own, cut straight at the shoulders. A smudge of woodpecker green stained her chin.

"Are you the librarian?" she asked, setting her brush in a paint-spattered Campbell's soup can.

Helma nodded. "Helma Zukas. And you're Deeter? Molly's stepmother?

"That's right."

"I'm sorry about your stepdaughter's death."

Deeter nodded. "They're calling it a murder. Do you believe that?"

"I believe hit-and-run does qualify as murder," Helma told her.

"Keeping busy helps," Deeter continued. "Unfortunately Molly and I haven't been close the past few years. I feel bad about that. Guilt stays with you longer than grief."

"I have a friend who says that," Helma told her. "Do you mind talking about Molly's poetry?"

"Not at all." She wiped her hands on a paint-stained towel. "Come with me."

She led Helma through a glassed-in porch to a square kitchen. Sears houses were laid out with minimal hallways and little wasted space.

On the table sat a photo album and a stack of papers. Helma could see that they'd been taken from a cardboard box balanced on one of the wooden kitchen chairs. M. BITTERN was written on the side of the box in black marker.

"Do you mind if I don't offer you anything?" Deeter asked. She held up her paint-stained hands.

"Of course not," Helma said. "Perhaps you could just tell me about Molly while I look at these photos. May I?"

Deeter nodded. "They're from Molly's apartment. She didn't have much. She never did. Just one of those people who threw things away when she was finished, even her toys when she was a little girl. Not like me."

"Except for her poetry," Helma said, tapping the pile of papers. She opened the album, expecting the first pages to hold photographs of a young Molly, but instead there were a few poems from magazines: the light and happy from women's magazines, the self-indulgent from the *New Yorker*, the deadly dramatic from literary magazines.

"It would seem so."

"Have you read her poems?"

Deeter shook her head. "I've never cared for poetry. It's feels like cheating to me, not enough words, not like *real* writing. Da da, da da, da *dah*," she said, beating time in the air, unknowingly capturing the meter of Molly's poems.

"Yet you brought a collection of Molly's poetry to the library."

Deeter nodded. "She left a note to give the pages she had paper-clipped together to the library."

"A note *to* you?" Helma asked in surprise.

"No. It looked like a note to herself. So that's what I did. She hadn't asked me to do anything for her since she was eleven."

"She was independent?"

Deeter exhaled and rubbed her nose. "You could say that. I haven't . . . hadn't, spoken to her in two or three years. Her father—my husband—drowned eight years ago in a boating accident, and Molly blamed me." She ducked her head briefly. "I was the one who loved the water, not Pete. He couldn't swim."

"I'm sorry."

"No matter. What is, is. He left Molly enough money she'd never have to work again. And I've carried on his backyard hobby." She smiled. "And I'm better at it than he was. I have contracts with stores and catalogs and online, too. He just did it for fun."

"I'm sure he'd be pleased," Helma said, turning the album's pages past photos of vacations in San Francisco and somewhere tropically lush and warm. None of Molly, although she passed two, three, then four blank slots, as if the photos had been removed.

"So what do you need to know about Molly?"

"What drew her to write poetry?" Helma asked first.

"Beats me."

"She was sensitive?"

"Well," Deeter drawled. "I guess so. The birthmark on her cheek; she was sensitive about that. And she was gullible, too. She believed *everybody*, one of those women who'd smuggle contraband under her shirt on an airplane if a man asked her. She'd just do it because she was asked to. No discrimination."

"So she was likely to have her heart broken in a relationship?"

"You said it. Oversensitive, overeager. Not like me."

"I'm sure not. May I take this?" Helma asked, pointing to the only photograph of Molly in the album, wearing a sundress and holding a wide-brimmed straw hat, and smiling—a far different Molly than the precarious, nervous woman Helma had been familiar with in the library. Molly looked happy, and Helma wondered who was holding the camera that made her smile so eagerly.

Deeter hesitated and Helma said, "It would work well in the display. We could enlarge it."

"As long as I get the original back," Deeter told her.

"Did you make a copy of the poems you brought to the library?" Helma asked after leafing through the stack of papers on the table and not seeing the collection. "One of the poems didn't come through."

"Sure, right here." Deeter picked up a stapled set of papers from her counter. A round circle of coffee blotted its top page. A yellow sticky note was still attached to the cover that read: "copy for library—Zukas." "I thought I should save something of hers, something that didn't take up much room."

"I'll copy it and return it to you," Helma said, "along with the photo."

"Well, if you can't trust a librarian, who can you trust?"

"Was Molly ever married?"

"No."

"Did you know the man who left her in these po-ems?" Helma persisted. "You didn't run into her in town now and then? Perhaps see her with a man?"

Deeter Bittern frowned at her. "What's that got to do with a display in the library?"

Helma carefully removed the photo of happy Molly from its clear sleeve. "Nothing. I'm sorry. I've read some of her more . . . emotional, poetry and it was a personal question."

"Well, you sounded like those policemen, asking for the details I couldn't give them."

"Yes," Helma said. "The police even talked to those of us who knew her in the library." She spoke casually, without finality, giving Deeter the opportunity to add more details about the police.

Deeter shrugged. "She didn't date much, anyway. Like I said, Molly believed men too fast, even as a teenager, thinking they were in love with her, search-ing for happily-ever-after, then being devastated when they dropped her." She sighed. "Which they always did. Men took advantage of her. It made me so mad."

"At Molly?"

Deeter's face changed. The hard lines slipped away and her eyes softened. She shook her head. "Just the way the world works sometimes, I guess." She took a step toward the door. "Got what you need?"

"I do. Thank you very much."

"No problem," Deeter said and she walked out of her house ahead of Helma, neither looking back nor saying goodbye.

After carefully placing the photo and poetry manuscript in a manila folder she'd expressly brought for that purpose, labeled BITTERN, MOLLY, Helma drove to Poe's Point, a small park that sat above the water near the ferry terminal where she could park close to the bank that overlooked the rocky shore.

The tide was high and the wind had risen, churning the usually placid bay water against the rocks. Every little while, froth splashed above the shore and foam drifted through the air. On either side of her, other drivers sat in their cars, reading or simply gazing out at the water, contemplating their worlds.

She turned the pages of Molly's poetry and compared it to the copy from the library, balancing the two collections side by side against her steering wheel and flipping page by page, poem by poem, looking for a missing poem.

But the original collection also proceeded from a poem called "Black Eyes" to "Ending," without a page between that might have held another verse with a title situated between *B* and *E* in the alphabet—one that might have given her a clue as to why it had been torn out of the library's copy. She closed the pages in disappointment, watching a seagull hover over a car where the driver was eating lunch. Perhaps Deeter herself had made a mistake when she copied the original.

Maybe copying a page twice and then tearing out the duplicate.

As had become her habit in the past several days, Helma scanned the park for a black cat. Nothing. The kidnapper's phone call hung threateningly on the periphery. As she'd told Ruth, if she received another call, she would contact the police, no matter which policeman she ended up talking to.

She picked up the original poems again, leafing through them one by one: "Absence" to "Beauty Gone" to "Black Eyes" to "Ending" to "Flown Away," and on. She flipped to the last page, and there it was: the title began with a *C*, "Cast Away," alphabetically out of order in the original but probably put in its rightful place when Deeter stapled the collection together. And then it was removed.

She compared the original and copy one more time. No, the copy that had been delivered to the library did not contain the poem "Cast Away," only scraps of paper clinging to the staples where it rightfully should have resided between "Black Eyes" and "Ending." Helma lightly touched the tip of her index finger against the shred of paper. Where someone had definitely torn it out.

She held up the page and read:

Cast Away

> *You cantered past, a look in your eye,*
> *Lassoed my heart and lifted me high*
> *Oh dash, I did not expect the crash*
> *You were the world I gave you my best*
> *And you stole all the rest*

*When the cache is lean it's time to go
    downstream
When the larder is lost and the land is covered
    with frost
And the bed is cold
You know what you've been told.
Why oh why did you leave me?*

"Oh my," Helma said aloud, wincing a little.

Chapter 19

A Moment of Reflection

Since she'd already informed Ms. Moon she'd be absent from the library, Helma decided to show Ruth Molly's lost poem, that is, if Ruth was still actually inside painting, as she claimed she'd be. But first, she stopped at the Humane Society. The short-haired woman at the desk looked up as the bell dinged, face poised to welcome, her smile weakening as she recognized Helma.

"No sign of your cat yet, Miss Zukas," she said, shaking her head, fingers pausing over a computer keyboard.

"I'd like to look at the cats, anyway," Helma told her, as she had every other time.

"Go ahead."

"Thank you."

"But he isn't there."

Helma entered the cat room, feeling all the goldy-green feline eyes turning silently toward her: tiers of metal cat cages, each one implemented with clever water and food devices. Bright, clean, well tended, but yes, she admitted, clinical and some might say, sorrowful.

Helma was not by nature a cat fancier. Their ungovernable habits, their studied . . . sneakiness, reminded her of snakes. Boy Cat Zukas was bearable by default and long association.

After walking the length of the rows of cages and peering inside each one but not touching any of them, although she did leave a cat treat she found in the bottom of her coat pocket at the edge of the cage of an especially lean white kitten, Helma left the cat room.

"Please tell the drivers my cat is still missing," she reminded the receptionist.

"Will do," the woman told her. "But you might consider giving one of these cats a home."

"One cat is adequate," Helma told her.

"I mean, in case your cat doesn't . . ."

"One cat is adequate," Helma repeated and left the shelter.

TNT was maneuvering a man-sized metal apparatus with pulleys and springs out of his apartment door. "Damn spring stretched out of shape," he said when he saw Helma. "Luckily it's still under warranty, so I'm having the whole contraption redone." Sweat shone on his forehead. "Find your cat yet?"

"Not yet," Helma told him.

"Well," he said, "don't forget all those stories about cats coming back years after they disappear." He shrugged as if he didn't know what else to say, then went back to lugging the apparatus out his door. "Never buy this brand," he warned her. "Piece of junk."

"I won't," she assured him, still not knowing what kind of device it was that had stretched its spring and caused TNT such frustration.

When Helma stepped inside her apartment, she was greeted by a canvas the size of her coffee table leaning against her refrigerator. Streaks of blue, gray, and black, indefinable shapes growing out of indecipherable shapes. Ruth stood hands on hips six feet back into the living room, surveying the painting.

"I think it needs a touch of black right there," she said, stepping up to the canvas and leaning down to touch the lower right corner. "Don't you?"

Helma couldn't see why, but Ruth's question was obviously rhetorical. "I've brought a copy of Molly's poetry with the missing poem," she told Ruth, "and a photo, too."

"Oh, goody." A paintbrush behind Ruth's ear dripped blue paint into her hair. "And who does she name as the guilty lover?"

"She doesn't. Here. You can read it."

"Let's see the photo, first," Ruth said, wiping her hands on Helma's dish towel.

Helma gave her the photo of Molly in her sundress, and Ruth held it out at arm's length, squinting. "There's a man behind the camera," she said with certainty.

"Or someone who made her happy," Helma agreed.

"A man," Ruth repeated. "Where'd you get it?"

"From her own photo album," Helma explained. "Her stepmother had it. It was the only photograph of Molly in the album, although several photos had been removed."

"The guy who broke her heart was probably in those, the star of all her poetry. Nice dress," Ruth said, still examining Molly's photo. "This is exactly why I stopped taking photographs a few years ago. All they do is end up being objects to mourn over."

She gave the picture back to Helma and took the sheaf of poems, boosting herself to sit on Helma's counter. Helma had opened the collection to "Cast Away," the missing poem.

Ruth frowned, her lips moving as she read. Then she nodded. "Yep, this is the guy holding the camera, I'd bet my last paintbrush on it. A last name would have helped. How do we find some guy named Dash?"

"What are you talking about?" Helma asked, reaching for the pages.

Ruth pulled them closer to her body, turning the page toward Helma, one finger to the line, 'Oh dash, I didn't expect the crash.' "Dash," Ruth said. "The guy's name is Dash. It's perfectly clear. You didn't miss that, did you?"

"That's not a name, that's an expletive."

"An expletive? You mean like 'Oh damn' or 'Oh darn'? I don't think so."

"Molly didn't strike me as a person who would say 'damn.' 'Dash' is a euphemism that sounds very like the original word it replaces, but is less offensive."

"Like 'Oh Faulkner'?" Ruth asked, grinning at Helma.

"That's ridiculous. But I've never heard of the name Dash."

"It's a nickname."

"Then it would have been capitalized," Helma said. "A nickname is a proper noun."

Ruth shrugged. "So she didn't have an editor to correct all her grammar and doo-dads. It's a nickname."

"All right," Helma said, momentarily conceding to Ruth's assertions for the sake of discussion. "Let's assume Dash is a nickname and Molly failed to capitalize it. If you're correct, that might explain why someone tore the poem out of her collection, because they were afraid the nickname would be recognized. And that would associate them with Molly's death."

"Especially if they actually had something to do with her hit-and-run."

"Or if they had a reason to keep their association from becoming public," Helma added. "If the publicity would ruin a career . . . or a marriage."

"Makes sense to me. He was probably married and his wife tracked Molly down and nailed her with her car. And don't forget: she was rich, right?"

"At least able to live without working."

"That rhymes with rich to me." Ruth studied the poem again. "It definitely has a cowboy motif, doesn't it? All this cantering and lassoing. Plus, cowboys have nicknames." Ruth licked her lips. "You know, like Buck and Stud, Hoss, Tucker. Slim, maybe."

"But cowboys in Bellehaven?" Helma said, thinking of fashionable barn coats never intended to see the inside of a barn, brand-name jeans, pullover cashmere sweaters, and boat shoes.

Ruth raised her eyebrows and met Helma's eyes.

"Oh," Helma said, his name coming to her in a startled flash. "Boyd Bishop."

"He's the closest to a cowboy I've seen in this town. And he says he writes westerns under an assumed name, right?"

"And he sat next to Molly at the Local Authors launch meeting."

"Bingo. Call the cops."

"But I never would have known he was sitting next to Molly if he hadn't told me," Helma pointed out.

"He didn't know that. Call it a preemptive strike on his part. He believed you saw him sitting right there beside her laughing his head off while she bared her soul to a roomful of rioting authors."

"That's an exaggerated description."

"Call it what you want. He tried to allay your suspicions before you told the law about his bad behavior."

"I don't know . . ." Helma began, thinking of Wayne Gallant asking her if she'd seen anyone suspicious sitting near Molly, then of Boyd Bishop. Despite the fact that he hadn't divulged his pseudonym, an aura of . . . well, earnestness, hovered over him. Not that she hadn't been wrong before.

"You've been wrong about people before," Ruth said as if she'd been reading Helma's mind.

"I'm aware of that."

"So call the cops." Ruth still sat on the kitchen counter and she swung her legs, bumping her heels against a cabinet door, stopping mid-swing when she caught Helma's expression. "Sorry."

"I'll talk to Boyd first. There's no point in bringing in the police right now."

Ruth rolled her eyes. "You'd be singing a different song if that hoary Glory woman wasn't involved." When Helma didn't respond she asked, "You don't write poetry, keep a diary or anything like that, do you?"

"No."

"Did he ask you if you did?"

She tried to remember. "I believe I mentioned that I wasn't a local author, that I *didn't* write."

"Good. Then he might not believe it would be important to kill you. No lingering evidence in a sweet little Dear Diary entry."

"Ruth, that's absurd."

"Helm, here's a guy who hasn't exactly shared the truth with you. He claims to write novels under a pseudonym but he conveniently withholds the vital nom de plume. Now, if that isn't lying with a straight face, I don't know what is. Believe me, that man is being coy, and that rhymes with Boyd, another one of those pseudo-monosyllabic words, like 'Boy' in Boy Cat Zukas. Even his name is linguistically suspect."

Chapter 20

Shockingly Wrong

Boyd Bishop wasn't listed in the Bellehaven telephone book or with directory assistance.

"So that name's a lie, too," Ruth pointed out as she watched Helma return the phonebook to the drawer, stating exactly what Helma was thinking.

"He *did* give me a telephone number when we met at Echo's," she said, trying to remember what she'd done with it, an unusual plight engendered by the sighting of Wayne Gallant and Glory Shandy. "I left it in my coat pocket."

"And your coat is . . . ?" Ruth asked.

"At the library. I'll have to go back."

"If you decide to meet with him, make sure it's in a public place with lots of people around who look like they pay attention. Or call me."

Helma found the slip of paper with Boyd's telephone number in the pocket of her coat still hanging on the hook Jack, the janitor, had installed against the only real wall of her cubicle.

She smoothed the paper on her desk, took a deep breath, and dialed the number. The recording of an answering machine advised her to leave a message. It wasn't Boyd Bishop's twangy voice but the factory-installed inhuman voice reminding her again of the professed catnapper. Since Helma didn't leave messages on answering machines, she hung up.

"Hey, you're back," George said, passing Helma's cubicle as she sat considering her telephone. "I thought you'd already left for that session about pets."

The "Troubled Pets" group session. "I'm finished attending Ms. Moon's sessions," she told George.

"Bravo," he said. "But they might have had a segment on runaway cats. Any sign of him yet?"

Helma shook her head.

He gave her a thumbs up. "Keep looking."

Helma had learned long ago that Ruth ignored her telephone when she was painting, but like many artists, curiosity usually got the best of her. When Helma *really* wanted to speak to Ruth, if she redialed her phone number, sometimes even three or four times, Ruth was likely to answer.

She suspected the same might be true of Boyd Bishop, so she redialed his number and was rewarded just as the recorded message started by Boyd himself picking up the receiver and cutting off the machine. "Hello?" he said, sounding distracted.

"This is Helma Zukas, from the Bellehaven Public Library," Helma said in a businesslike fashion. "I'd—"

"Helma," he broke in, his voice warming. "How good to hear from you."

She doubted that was true. "Could we meet for a few minutes?"

"Today?"

"If possible."

"It so happens I'm ready to take a break right now. I can meet you at Sorenson's Coffees across from the library, say, in fifteen minutes?"

Normally, Helma wouldn't have assented to such a hasty meeting, but there were critical circumstances. The sooner she discovered any connections between Molly Bittern and Boyd Bishop, the sooner Molly's and maybe even Tanja's deaths would be resolved, the sooner the connection between the library and murder would evaporate from the public's minds, and the sooner the library could return to normal operations. Without displays.

She briefly considered Ms. Moon's warning that she refrain from involving herself in murder, and the caller who'd threatened to harm Boy Cat Zukas if she didn't "mind her own business." And finally, Chief of Police Wayne Gallant who might as well have called her a "meddling citizen."

And rejected them all.

"Fifteen minutes from now at Sorenson's Coffee sounds fine," Helma said firmly.

"I'm looking forward to this," Boyd said with such a show of pleasure Helma was resolved to complete the meeting as quickly as possible.

"Oh, Helma," Glory called out as Helma passed her cubicle. "Can we go over the display layout now? I've designed the cutest logo."

"Cute?" Helma asked, startled by the affiliation of "cute" with murdered women.

"May Apple helped me. Angel wings attached to books. All sparkly. Flying over Molly and Tanja's pictures."

"Ms. Moon's approval outweighs mine on this," Helma said with a touch of graciousness, because the display was never, ever going to happen. "Excuse me."

"Goody. Oh, and if you need any ideas for your costume for our . . . I mean, the library party, I can help," she said, holding up a library book titled, *Shakespeare's Shirts*.

Boyd and Helma reached the front door of Sorenson's Coffees at the same moment and Boyd held the door open for Helma, looking up at the sky and announcing, "It looks like the rain has stopped. Should be a beautiful day."

"I agree," Helma said, taking in his face and stance. Relaxed, loose. The belt buckle above his slim hips had a silver star stamped onto it. Did his gaze up at the sky, instead of meeting her eyes, denote guilt? Or wariness? Surely, he was suspicious or at least curious about her phone call.

Boyd ordered from the counter while Helma sat at a table that wasn't *in* the window but afforded a view of the sidewalk and the street. Boyd returned, carrying green tea for her and a cup of black coffee for himself.

His smile widened as he set the cup in front of Helma. "Thanks for calling me," he said. "I can't think of a more enjoyable way to take a break in my day."

"Were you writing?" she asked.

He raised his right hand and flexed his fingers as if they'd been gripping a pencil too long. "Rewriting. And rewriting and rewriting. My editor expects this

manuscript in her hands two weeks from yesterday."
He laughed. "She's a tiger if you're late."

"Is she unusual in your field?"

"Do you mean editor as tiger?" Boyd asked.

"No, I mean a woman editor of westerns."

For a moment Boyd's face went blank, then he
stirred his coffee, gazing into the dark liquid. He spoke
softly. "I wouldn't have expected you to be prejudiced."

Helma felt her cheeks pinken. "Never explain or
complain," her father had always counseled. "You're
right," she said. "That was unfair. Where are you setting this western?"

"In the vague west," he said vaguely.

"In the area where your family lives?" she persisted.

"I guess elements of New Mexico can't help but
creep in." He stirred and stirred his coffee.

"Do you still have relatives there?"

"Oh sure." He regarded her, his forehead creasing.
Helma could see he was debating something in his
mind, whether to speak it now, or later, or not at all.
She said nothing, waiting.

He spoke quietly and Helma truly and completely
believed every painful word he uttered. She would
have even if she couldn't see his eyes, which she could.
He gazed straight ahead, beyond her and the coffee
shop, then swallowed.

"A sister," he said slowly. "Some cousins still live in
New Mexico. I don't go back much." His body tensed
and then relaxed. "My wife died there, one of those
slow and ugly things." He met Helma's eyes. "She was
the finest person I've ever known, and the most fun,
too." He grinned. "And funny, real funny. I'll always
miss her."

"I'm sorry."

"Yeah," he said. "Thanks."

They both busily stirred and raised their hot drinks to their mouths.

"Cowboys have interesting nicknames," Helma finally said as she set down her cup, returning to the subject that had prompted her to phone him. "When I was little, I watched Roy Rogers."

She actually had, once, accidentally, when her brothers had tormented her by turning on the TV full blast while she was trying to read in "their spot" on the sofa, and she'd refused to move. "Gabby Hayes and Jingles," she said, pulling the names from some distant corner of her memory.

Boyd nodded. "Ah yes, Gabby Hayes. But I do believe that Jingles fellow was Wild Bill Hickock's sidekick, not Roy Rogers's. Andy Devine."

"Did you grow up with a nickname?" Helma asked.

He laughed. "Sure did. My grandfather started it. He called me Pasta."

"Pasta?" Helma repeated. "Like spaghetti and noodles?"

"That's right. Not too cowboyish, is it? I was crazy about any kind of pasta when I was a kid. Couldn't get enough of it: macaroni and cheese, spaghetti and meatballs, just plain old buttered noodles. Luckily, that didn't last or I wouldn't have been able to sit a horse."

"I knew someone who had a friend named Dash," Helma tried, but Boyd's face didn't register any emotion except interest. No shock of recognition or a guilty jump or even embarrassment.

"Like fifty-yard dash?" he asked. "There are some good ones out there. What was your nickname?"

"Helma is actually shortened from Wilhelmina, after my Lithuanian grandmother. Do you use a lot of nicknames in your books?"

Again that hesitancy. "Sometimes," he said.

They were uncomfortably silent again for a few moments, then Boyd said cheerfully, "I had the feeling when you phoned that there was a serious subject you had a mind to chat over."

"The library director has asked me to create a display of the two women who were killed," Helma began. Boyd's eyebrows raised. "Despite they're not actually being local authors."

"They say death is the best career move an artist or writer can make," Boyd told her.

"I've heard that," Helma told him, "but you sat with Molly Bittern at the Local Authors launch—"

"Not with," he corrected, "next to."

"Next to," Helma amended. "And I wondered if you had any additional information suitable for our display."

He didn't believe her; she saw that in an instant. She wouldn't have either. His tone when he answered carried polite distance, distraction. He hadn't moved, but it felt as if he'd leaned further back in his chair, away from Helma.

"No. As I told you that day in the library, the only time she might have noticed me was when I let myself laugh at her poetry."

"I see," Helma said. They were speaking to each other so very politely, but each of them knew the other was not quite telling the truth. They avoided one another's eyes, spoke brightly. She asked him if he liked cats.

"I'm more of a dog person myself," he told her.

The awkwardness was unbearable. Helma glanced

at her watch. "I'd better return to the library. Thank you for the tea."

He rose. "Helma, I . . ." Then a small smile crossed his lined face. "You're welcome," he said and walked her out of the coffee shop, where they exchanged pleasantries and separated.

Helma felt a curious bleakness as she returned to the library, as if unspoken opportunities had slipped past them both, and it had been her doing.

Instead of the service entrance that led to the workroom, Helma entered the library through the main doors and stopped in front of the display case in the foyer.

The case stood empty. A few pushpins remained imbedded in the cork backing from the origami display, and a dead spider with curled legs lay on the bottom shelf. On a stand next to the display case, a placard read in a variety of fonts: "Coming soon: a tribute to deceased local authors. Read their words! View their faces!" And in yet another curlicue font reminiscent of Ms. Moon's loopy handwriting, "Are *you* in danger?"

As Helma stood gazing at the final words in dismay, a woman's voice said, "That reads like one of those tabloid covers at the grocery counter, doesn't it?"

Helma turned to see Pepper Goodwin, aka Breckenridge, her arms laden with library books: two novels and one of their "bestsellers," *Operating Your Own Business in Washington State*. A bicycle helmet hung from her arm by its chin strap and one pant leg was held tight at her ankle by a bicycle clip.

"It does imply a certain level of drama," Helma agreed. Pepper was clear-eyed and friendly, as if the events in the Hopewell Building had been wiped clean, as if she hadn't confessed to Helma and Ruth that she'd lied and misrepresented herself to all the women at the group sessions.

"Does this refer to Molly Bittern and Tanja Frost?" Pepper asked.

Helma nodded and before she could make any clarifications, Pepper said, "I didn't think they met your criteria."

"There's some debate. Are you here to check out library books?"

Pepper shifted her books so Helma couldn't see the titles. People did that; it was part of the circulation staff's training never to comment on what a patron checked out for their personal enjoyment. Some patrons felt it was an invasion of privacy, and Helma agreed, it was.

"I'm bringing them back," Pepper said. "I intend to become one of your best customers. As soon as I rented my apartment, the next thing I did was apply for my library card. After my Aunt Aggie left the convent, she became a librarian." She dropped her voice. "She had a baby."

"I've known librarians who've had babies," Helma told her.

"She had hers *while* she was a nun," Pepper clarified and went on brightly. "One of our family scandals. Every family has its skeletons, they say, the kind that make great stories, only much, much later, after everybody involved is dead. Doesn't yours?"

Helma thought of her overly loud, overly emotional, oversensitive—that is, sensitive to what was said to them but not to what *they* said—family. Uncles and aunts and cousins and brothers, clinging to the comfort of their Lithuanian heritage, resistant to being totally merged into the Great American Melting Pot. How many times had they looked at her in puzzlement and said, "You take after . . ." dwindling off in bewilderment.

"I'm sure every family does," she said to Pepper now.

"Well, I'd better turn these in; they're a day late." She hugged the books closer. "And thanks for being so understanding about, you know, last night. I didn't mean to trick people, at least I didn't think of it that way." She shrugged. "I just didn't process the implications."

"You said the man in the Hopewell Building smelled of smoke," Helma said. "Could you describe it?"

Pepper shrugged. "Just smoke. Cigars or cigarettes. Maybe a pipe. I don't know many smokers."

"Could it have been woodsmoke?"

"Like from a campfire?" She frowned, puckering her mouth to one side. "Maybe. I don't know. Why?"

"Just curious."

"Ruth and I are going cat hunting this afternoon," Pepper said and winked at Helma. "Beginning at Joker's bar, naturally. We'll find your cat, I just know it."

"Thank you," she told Pepper. "I appreciate it."

"No prob."

A boy of about eleven stood behind Pepper and as soon as she left, he looked up at Helma. "Are you a librarian? They sent me up here from the kids' room."

"I am," Helma told him. "How may I help you?" He was blond and thin and elongated, even his face.

"You know that guy Shakespeare?"

"Yes."

"When he said somebody got hoisted by his own petard, did he really mean a guy got blown up by his own farts?"

He was earnest, deadly serious.

"Let's look up the word petard," she said, leading him to the reference area and reaching for her favorite dictionary.

"Can't you just tell me?" he asked. "Do we have to look it up?"

"A person using unusual language needs to speak with authority," Helma told him and when he still appeared reluctant, she added, "When you say that to your friends and *you* know exactly what it means, they'll believe you. It will . . . knock their socks off."

"Okay," he said and contentedly leaned against the shelf, his shoulder against her arm so he could see inside the open dictionary.

Helma had barely reached her cubicle when her telephone rang.

"Helma, this is Boyd Bishop. I'm in your lobby. Can I talk to you for a minute?"

"I'm . . ." Helma began and stopped, wondering exactly how she'd intended to end that sentence.

"This will only take a minute," he promised. "I'll be waiting between the glass doors, clearly visible to all." And he hung up.

Helma could remain exactly where she sat, or leave and drive to the Hopewell Building as she'd planned, or begin making decisions on the cart load of Local Author offerings. She sat for another ten seconds, then rose and walked swiftly through the public area, not even stopping to caution two girls giggling over an anatomy book, before she approached the glass doors, averting her eyes from the gaping display case.

Boyd Bishop stood between the doors watching her approach, on his face a mixture of discomfort and determination. He held a paperback book in his hands.

"You wanted to talk to me?" Helma asked.

He nodded, waiting for a mother with identical twin boys to pass through the front door. "Hurry up, Lewis, pick up your feet, Clark," before he turned to Helma.

"I don't feel comfortable about the conversation we just had," Boyd said. "From your questions, I think you suspect me. I'd like to come clean."

Helma was disappointed, bitterly disappointed. "About Molly?" she asked with a heavy heart.

He frowned. "Molly Bittern? The dead poet?" He took a step back from Helma. "What about her?"

"Dash," Helma replied. "You're the Dash she referred to in her poem. The cowboy who broke her heart? I suspected it when you became agitated as I spoke of westerns and cowboys' nicknames. It's the police you should be talking to, not me."

"You don't think . . ." He rubbed his hands through his hair. "Uneasiness is right. But . . ." He stopped again as an elderly man stabbed the automatic door button with his cane and passed them out the door, then he leaned closer to her.

"I'd like to know you better, Helma. I've wanted to ever since I saw your determination at the Local Authors launch, how you genuinely care about authors and books, how you remained calm and polite in front of that rabble. I don't want to just let this pass." A slight smile warmed his face. "I may be a small fish in your world, but I'm a steady swimmer."

Boyd held up his hand as if to stop her from protesting. "Even if we never become more than friends, I would be honored." He looked down. "That's why I have to be honest with you, or I'm afraid even a friendship is doomed."

"I'm not expecting you to divulge personal secrets," Helma told him. A cautionary lump had risen at the back of her throat. She couldn't swallow it away.

Without another word he held out the paperback in his hand.

The cover was pink, embossed wings surrounding the cutout of an angelic woman's face, a virile bare-chested man gazing at the woman in adoration. *Love's Loss* was the book's title, by Angelique d'Boudier.

"That's one of our most popular paperback authors," Helma told him. "My mother and aunt can't read her books fast enough. We have multiple copies. If it's overdue, I'm sure it won't be much of a fine."

"This isn't a library copy," Boyd said. "It's mine."

"There's no need to be embarrassed," Helma assured him. "Many men read romances and this particular title has been on the *USA Today* bestseller list. I've heard the author actually lives in the Northwest."

Boyd gazed steadily into her eyes.

Helma, who believed hands that dealt with the public should never be placed near bodily orifices without a thorough washing, helplessly raised her hand to her mouth. "Oh," she said. Then, "Oh," again. "Oh my. You're . . ." and she pointed to the fluffy pink book.

He slowly nodded, watching her face.

"But the westerns," she argued with him, disbelieving. "You said you wrote westerns."

"I *do* write westerns. Good ones, I think, but so far no publisher's interested in them. So I write these to make my living. No one knows except my agent, not even the publisher." He paused. "And now you."

"No one?" she repeated, still trying to take in his words. Boyd Bishop was Angelique d'Boudier, one of the hottest romance authors in America?

"No one. I'm at your mercy. You know there's a saying that if you know another person's deepest darkest secret, you hold their life in the palm of your hand."

He grinned at her, obviously pleased by her shock. "And that's my deep dark lie to you," he finished.

"That's all? You're not Dash? You weren't involved with Molly Bittern?"

"No, ma'am. I only saw her that one time. Why would you believe that?"

"Because . . . well, you asked about her motivation for her poetry. I thought . . ."

He shrugged apologetically. "Just a writer's bad habit, I guess. Too curious by half."

"But this . . ." She nodded toward *Love's Loss*. "Any author would be proud to see a book he created on the bestseller list. It's an honor."

"And I am honored. But I prefer to keep it to myself."

"I understand," Helma told him.

"Now will you go out to dinner with me?"

Chapter 21

In the Hopewell Building

Helma stood in the lobby of the Hopewell Building and realized she'd been so distracted by Boyd Bishop's confession that she'd forgotten to phone Sunny's office. She searched the wall directory with its pushpin letters of names and office numbers for Sunny Reese. There she was: 209.

All the offices listed were only attached to personal names. No insurance, accounting, or legal firms, no medical offices. No one named Pepper, either.

Beneath the directory stood a receptionist's desk and counter, which appeared to have been vacated long ago. A few free, outdated events newspapers and mental health brochures sat in untidy piles on the desk. There was no chair, no computer or telephone, and two dead flies lay feet up in the midst of a thin layer of dust.

Someone *had* been replacing or editing names

on the directory, though. Black plastic letters lay scattered on the desk in random order. Helma fingered the letters, aligning them in a straight row of nonsense.
AAFTTONJRS

She gazed at the letters. They made no sense but sometimes, if she allowed information to simply "ease" into her mind as if it were inconsequential, it sorted itself out without any mental assistance. She let her eyes unfocus the way she'd read that hunters did when they stalked prey that was camouflaged by the hodgepodge of colors in an autumn woods.

"Can I assist you?" a man's voice interrupted.

Helma turned. A balding man descended the stairs from the second floor. He was her height and wore casual clothes with his blue shirt buttoned all the way to his neck, and lace-up leather shoes that shone seal-brown.

Helma stepped away from the muddle of plastic letters. "I was looking up an office number on the directory," she told him.

He looked at the directory, his mouth puckering. "Ever since we gave up the receptionist last spring, nobody's kept that thing up to date. We all pitched in for her salary, equally, and we all shared. There's always a maverick who decides he's paying too much for what he's getting, or somebody else has the receptionist picking up her kids after school. Gotta spoil it. And then it all goes downhill and this is what you get." He waved his hand toward the reception area, which held a potted ficus surrounded by a ring of dead leaves and couches out of alignment. A Starbuck's cup lay on its side on the floor.

"For want of a nail," Helma said.

He scratched at a red spot on his neck and Helma

politely looked away. "You said it. And what can we do but watch our kingdoms collapse?"

"I've noticed," Helma said, "that when one person with initiative begins to act, others will follow and soon—"

"That's what happened here, one after another, everybody let it collapse."

"I meant that when one person takes the lead—" Helma tried again.

"I need to look for a new office," he cut in, shaking his head. "It's obvious nothing's going to change here. And now the break-in last night."

"Do you know what happened?"

"No damage as far as I know. The police asked us to check our offices for anything missing. I didn't lose anything. Dumb kids probably, thinking counselors would have drugs just like a doctor. Hah."

"Are you a counselor?" Helma asked.

He nodded. "Me and everybody else in this building. Any neuroses you can think of, we've got it covered. My specialty is depression."

"I see," Helma said.

"Whose office did you say you were looking for?" he asked.

"I didn't, but do you know if Pepper Goodwin has an office in this building?"

"Like salt and pepper?" he asked, then shrugged. "Maybe. There are a few empty offices. I wouldn't know—unless her name was on the directory, natch. Used to know, when we had a receptionist. And there's the dead woman's office: that was just cleaned out, too, so it's empty. Maybe she's moving in there."

"Dead woman?" Helma asked and at the same time

she glanced down at the plastic letters on the desk and saw the name unravel itself from the jumbled alphabet as plain as day: Tanja Frost.

"Tanja Frost?" she asked at the same moment he said, "The murdered counselor, Tanja Frost." He glanced at his watch and gave Helma a quick wave. "Gotta go. Good luck."

"Thank you," she told him and again gazed at the letters. Tanja Frost had also had an office in the Hopewell Building. There weren't any numbers with the letters to indicate which office might have been hers. All three counselors she'd met were here: Sunny, Tanja, and Pepper.

From her fleeting exposure to Tanja Frost, Helma would have expected her to post her name as soon as she paid her first month's rent. Someone else had recently removed the information from the directory but hadn't put away the letters. Her husband, Julius? Sunny? Julius had said Tanja and Sunny had been friends, and Sunny had called her a "dear friend."

Helma left the plastic letters where they lay on the desk and peered once more around the lobby before heading for Sunny's office, peering left and right for signs of the night's disturbances.

Other than faint soothing music—Brahms, she thought—the building might have been deserted. No one waited in any of the Danish Modern chairs along the walls outside office doors, no phones rang. She caught the murmur of voices as she passed one door, crying as she passed another. All of it tucked discreetly away. The wall clock read fifteen past the hour, and she guessed she had entered the building between appointments.

Helma had never attended a session with a professional counselor. There were people who claimed the Catholic confessional was a near contender for baring the soul. Her cousin Ricky had once referred to the "catharsis of confession," and although she knew it wasn't an original thought of his, not many of his thoughts were, she liked the sound of it.

During the daylight hours, there weren't any features of the building that stood out as unusual. The second floor hallway was well-lit, innocuous. Someone had picked up the largest pieces of the broken exit sign, but several glittery shards lay close to the wall. The entire hallway would benefit from a thorough vacuuming, Helma thought. She walked its length peering down the back stairs at the closed exit door to the alley and then back again. It would have been simple for someone to slip up the front steps and attack them in the night. Tanja's office had been here. The intruder could have been after something of Tanja's. Had it been Pepper? But she remembered Pepper's hand on her arm as someone else smashed the exit light at the end of the hall.

No sound came from behind the door marked 209, but Helma knocked lightly and was surprised to hear the thump of a drawer closing and a voice call, "Come in."

Sunny's office was smaller than Helma's bedroom, a cubby with room for a desk and table, two chairs and a filing cabinet. Sunny sat at a desk piled with folders. A computer, its keyboard covered by more folders, occupied the table behind her desk. All Sunny had to do was swivel her chair to access all she possessed. Helma thought of a command center in those space movies her nephews liked.

Sunny gazed at Helma blankly. She wore a black scarf with trails of silver threads through it, and she twisted an end while she considered Helma. Finally, she smiled as she recognized her. "Helma, did we have an appointment?"

"No, I was just visiting the building. I hadn't realized Tanja Frost had an office in this building, too."

Sunny nodded. "She did. At the end of the hall. She didn't have time to completely set it up before . . ." She removed a pencil from a stack of folders and rolled it between her hands.

"You saw her fall?" Helma asked.

Sunny shuddered. Her eyes instantly teared up as she nodded. "Only the end of it. I didn't see whoever . . . It was horrible. I already talked about it with the police. They even tested the bowl I served chips in that night to see if it was the murder weapon."

"The oval shape," Helma said. "Tanja's wound." She gripped her hands together to squelch the urge to touch her left temple.

"Yes. Can we not . . ." and she made motions with her hands as if she were wiping away a stain.

"I'm sorry," Helma said, and changed the subject. "You gave a moving tribute to Molly Bittern at the session Tuesday night."

"Molly deserved a better life," Sunny said grimly.

"You knew her well? Beyond the group sessions, as a friend?" At the narrowing of Sunny's eyes, Helma hastily added, "I met Molly through the library and I've read her poetry," and Sunny relaxed.

"Not well," Sunny said. "She began attending the sessions about six weeks ago."

"She was in pain over her failed romance," Helma

said, watching Sunny closely as she added, "with Dash. Did you know him, too?"

There was no sign that Sunny recognized the name. "Molly was a private person and I'm the kind of person who respects that. All I know is she had the financial means to spend her life in self-exploration," Sunny said and firmly closed her mouth.

"You and Tanja came to the Local Authors launch Monday night—are you a writer, too?"

"Maybe someday, when I have the time. I only brought Tanja so she could get a sense of the local services."

"I met another counselor downstairs," Helma told her. "He said the building was broken into last night."

Sunny rubbed the fringe of her scarf against her upper lip. "No damage done. But then, the building's gone downhill. It used to be—"

Helma forestalled another lament over the missing receptionist by asking, "Does Pepper Goodwin have an office here as well?"

Sunny's face reddened. "So I discovered yesterday. It was dishonest of her to attend the group sessions under an assumed name. That's not a game professionals should play, and not one that will gain her any respect in this field, either. She'll be lucky if she has any clients at all." She stabbed her pencil into a brightly painted papier-mâché pencil holder. A touch of spittle moistened the corner of her mouth.

"My nephew sent me a very similar pencil holder," Helma told Sunny in a calm voice. "He made it in fourth grade." She nodded toward a framed photo of a preteen boy sitting on top of Sunny's computer. "Did your son make yours?"

"He did."

"Which school does he attend?" Helma asked.

Sunny didn't answer for a few seconds, still focused on the photo, absently unscrewing the lid of a silver thermos and pouring dark liquid into a white mug. The odor of coffee wafted through the small room. Helma didn't drink coffee but she appreciated its dark, roasty fragrance.

"He lives with his father in Oregon," Sunny said tersely.

"That must be difficult for you," Helma said noncommittally, and moved quickly on. "The library director—"

"May Apple," Sunny interjected.

"Yes . . . She plans to create a display honoring Tanja as a local author." Helma paused. Helma avoided direct lies. "I'm collecting information about Tanja. She moved to Bellehaven because of you?"

"It's complicated," Sunny told her.

Helma nodded. "That's what Julius said."

Sunny froze, coffee mug halfway to her mouth. She thumped down her cup, sloshing coffee onto a folder. "You spoke to Julius?"

"We had lunch yesterday." Helma concentrated on keeping her expression bland as Sunny scrutinized her face.

"That ended long ago," Sunny said, her voice rising. "He had no right to bring that up."

"He did attempt to deny it," Helma told her, remembering Julius saying, "I'd never do that to her." Which "her" was he talking about?

Sunny sat up straighter, her face now even redder. "Deny it! As if it were some trivial fling."

"But it wasn't," Helma said in the same voice she'd used to coax a toddler from behind the library photo-

copier: calm, firm, hoping not to scare him further into
the shadows.

"Of course not. Ostensibly, he left Tanja and moved
to Bellehaven for that job with the community college.
But it was really because I was here. Back then, I was
into a more natural lifestyle. I even used to make my
own biscotti, can you believe it? My marriage had
ended and Julius and I . . ."

"But I understood you and Tanja were friends,"
Helma said.

"Well, that had nothing to do with our *friendship*."

Helma felt dizzy. "And you and Tanja remained
friends?"

"It was easier after he subsequently left *me*," Sunny
explained in a perfectly reasonable voice. "It bound
Tanja and me together, don't you see? Shared experience."

Helma tried to put this startling information into
context. "Julius left Tanja for *you*, and then he left you
for *another* woman? And that gave you and Tanja a
common ground for friendship?"

"Correct. I phoned Tanja as soon as I saw him ride
away from my house. I knew it was over and our
friendship could safely be revitalized." Sunny looked
serene, sunny even.

"Ride away," Helma repeated, thinking it was a curious expression, and also remembering Molly's poem
with the cowboy references. "Julius rode away on a
horse?"

"On his bicycle," Sunny corrected. "He was between
cars at the time. He tried to be environmentally con-
scious, but it's more like he's environmentally ADD,
jumping from one cause to another."

"Why was seeing him ride away on his bicycle an indication your relationship was over?" Helma asked. "He could have been going to the store. The food co-op," she added.

"Because he had strapped his toolbox on the rear fender. A man leaving with his toolbox is as final as a woman leaving with all her jewelry."

"I didn't know that," Helma mused. "Who did he leave you for?"

Sunny squinted at Helma. "If Julius didn't tell you, then it's not my business to provide that information. It's part of my professional ethics to be discreet." She paused. "But I will tell you he left *her* as well."

Helma had learned far more than she'd expected already. So she smiled as if none of it was terribly important. "The counselor I met downstairs said his practice concentrated on people with depression. Do you have a specialty as well?"

"Yes, I do," Sunny told her. "I'm basically a marriage counselor," and at the look on Helma's face, added, "Who better than someone who's had a personal struggle with the institution?"

Chapter 22

Thickening Plots

"Call Julius and ask him to meet us at the Wild Hare again," Helma told Ruth over the telephone. "Right away."

"I'm painting."

"This won't take long. It's important."

"Does it involve dead writers? Unless he's the murderer, I don't have time."

"Call him, and then meet me there and I'll explain while we're waiting."

"Why me? What makes you think I know how to get ahold of him anyway?"

"You already tracked him down at least once," Helma said.

"What do you mean, 'at least'? Oh, never mind. What excuse do I give him for *this* get together?"

"I'll leave that up to you," Helma told her.

"In other words, you want me to concoct some ridiculous story to lure him to the Wild Hare."

"I don't condone lying."

"That's easy for you to say." She sighed. "All right. I'll do it, but I have to clean my brushes first."

"You could clean them while you call," Helma suggested.

"All right, all right. If you don't hear from me in ten minutes, meet me at the Wild Hare in fifteen. Hey, what about Cowboy Boyd? Did you talk to him?"

"He's innocent," Helma told her.

"Nobody is," Ruth said with certainty.

Helma had entered the library through the loading dock and proceeded directly to her cubicle to phone Ruth. She'd avoided Ms. Moon and Glory, and even George, intending to only use the phone and leave.

But now she had ten minutes to remain in the library, and Helma was not a person to sit idly marking time.

While she waited for Ruth's call, which she *didn't* expect because she knew that Ruth's curiosity would only heighten her persistence in tracking down Julius, she confronted the three carts of local authors' offerings, bending and moving around them, scanning the book trucks for romance novels by Angelique d'Boudier.

None were on the book trucks so she checked the library's online catalog from her desk computer and discovered the Bellehaven Public Library owned an even dozen titles by Ms. d'Boudier, and three to four copies of several of those. Nearly all were checked out, and twenty-three people were on the waiting list for Angelique's latest.

The trick to invisibility was to think insignificant, avoid eye contact, and move purposefully and silently.

So Helma took a moment to do just that. She entered the public area and pulled an Angelique d'Boudier title from the paperback shelf, touching a finger to the embossed lettering on the cover: *Hearts Afire*.

Inside the back cover, where the author's photo usually resided, there was no image, only a statement that Angelique led a quiet life of seclusion in the "beautiful Pacific Northwest."

On her way back to the workroom, she paused long enough to pick up a toy airplane, a metal Boeing 747 some child had dropped on the floor, and slipped it into the pocket of her sweater.

Ten minutes later, when her telephone hadn't rung, Helma left the library as discreetly as she'd entered. She gave George a quick and impersonal nod as she passed his desk and walked to the Wild Hare, where Ruth paced outside the front door waiting for her. The sun was no longer shining but the day felt light, as if the clouds comprised only a high thin layer.

Ruth wore a one-piece version of denim farmer's pants, the pant legs rolled up and the suspenders lengthened with oversized rubber bands so they'd fit her long torso. Beneath those, an orange sweater with the turtleneck unrolled so it cupped her chin.

A man in colorless clothing slumped against a parking meter further up the street eyeing Ruth. In a boarded doorway of a building in the next block, two men squatted, smoking. Soon, all these blocks would be renovated, pushing men like these closer to the railroad tracks below.

"What's going on?" Ruth asked before Helma was within normal speaking distance. Helma never shouted unnecessarily so she didn't answer until she stood directly in front of Ruth. "I just spoke to Sunny, the counselor who held the Age of Certain Years group. According to her, Julius was not only married to Tanja but he had an affair with Sunny."

"Whew," Ruth said. "So you guessed right. But I thought Sunny and Tanja were 'dear friends.' That gives co-counseling a new meaning. Sunny and Tanja *both*? At the same time? Like together?"

"I don't know, but he allegedly left Sunny for another, unidentified woman."

"But he's still married to Tanja. I mean, he got possession of the ashes, right?"

"Legally, yes."

"God bless the logic of the law," Ruth said.

The man at the parking meter straightened himself and wandered closer, watching Ruth with a sloppy, hungry expression on his face.

"So we're meeting Julius to . . ."

Helma nodded significantly toward the man who advanced in a rolling gait behind Ruth. When Ruth turned, he asked her in a blurred voice, "You know what time it is?"

"Time for you to buy a watch," Ruth said, casting him such a withering look of dismissal he wandered off mumbling curses.

"Julius smells of woodsmoke," Helma said when the man was gone.

"He does? And that's a crime? More criminal than banging best friends?"

"Remember Pepper saying the man in the Hopewell Building smelled of smoke?" Helma asked. "Not only do Sunny and Pepper have offices there, so did Tanja."

A buzzing sounded behind Helma and Ruth nudged her arm. "Would you look at *that*? It's the unsavory little fella himself."

Helma turned. On the street, Julius putted toward them, standing on a motorized scooter. Helma had owned a scooter as a girl, one she had to push with one foot.

"I know an eleven-year-old who'd die for one of those," Ruth said.

Julius's smile widened when he caught sight of Helma and Ruth, and he turned off the scooter's motor. He coasted to the side of the street between two parked cars and jumped onto the curb, lifting his scooter up to the sidewalk.

"Cute," Ruth told him. "You've given up your car to save the environment?"

"Not a bad idea," Julius said, "But my car's in the shop. Transmission problems."

Julius continued smiling, but Helma noticed the tense, slightly raised angle of his shoulders and wondered what excuse Ruth had used this time to lure him to the Wild Hare.

"Helma," Julius said as he leaned the scooter against the building, then flashed a meaningful white-toothed smile at Ruth, "Good to see you both again."

Ruth rose to her full height, neck stretched, shoulders back, a quick swipe of her fingers through her bushy hair to create a higher, wider nimbus above her head, exaggerating the affect of tallness.

Julius's smile faltered. "What's up?" he asked, leaning away from Ruth.

"You are a wretched, wretched man," Ruth pronounced, peering at him through the bottoms of her eyes.

"What?" Julius's question came out not only surprised, but downright scared. Ruth could do that, jumping in and knocking the messenger flat before he could deliver the news. Helma had to rescue what tatters of information she could.

She laughed lightly, as if Ruth was teasing and Julius looked from one woman to the other uncertainly. "Let's go inside," she said, nodding toward the shadowy interior of the Wild Hare.

"I don't know . . ." Julius said, gazing in longing at his scooter.

"Oh, come on," Ruth said, taking her cue from Helma. "Just kidding," sounding not at all like she was.

They sat at the same table at the rear of the Wild Hare, which was empty except for two men at the bar, deep in conversation, yellow paper and pens between them.

Julius was nervous and there was no sense wasting time, so Helma got right to the point. "Were you in the Hopewell Building last night?"

"Last night?" Julius repeated. "Yesterday, but not last night."

"Perhaps you'd forgotten to retrieve something from Tanja's office so you went back to get it last night?" Helma asked.

"I finished cleaning out Tanja's office in the morning, why? Why would I go back at night?"

"To destroy evidence," Ruth supplied in exasperation, "because Helma's getting too close to . . . What *are* you getting close to, Helma? Did you kidnap Helma's cat?"

"Cat?" Julius repeated. "I don't know anything about anybody's cat."

"Just thought I'd get that out of the way first," Ruth said. "What do you know about the murders?"

"Molly and Tanja?" he asked.

It was the way he said their names. What had Ruth said when they'd watched the report of Tanja's murder on the morning news? It was too late to ask her now. Helma thought furiously; it was when the photos of the two women were shown side by side on the screen, the professional publicity photo of Tanja and the youthful casual photograph of Molly, something about Molly and Tanja resembling each other.

Ruth glanced from Julius to Helma and back again. She raised a finger to her cheek as if she were pressing in a dimple. Helma recognized the glint in Ruth's eye and said to Julius before Ruth could, even as Ruth's mouth opened, "Are you Dash?"

"What?" He stiffened, sitting back, then laughed shortly. "Dash? I don't know what you mean. 'Dash like a bunny'?"

"I believed that's 'quick as a bunny,'" Helma clarified. "You're Molly's Dash, aren't you? The 'Dash' in her poem?"

Ruth snorted. "You. And *Molly,* too? *You're* the 'why-oh-why-did-you-leave-me' guy?"

Julius looked as if he were still about to deny the connection but then some aspect of Ruth or Helma's expressions altered his thinking.

"I don't know what you're talking about," he repeated, but weaker, a formality of denying until being caught out was too obvious, pulling down the ribbing of his sweatshirt, looking away from Ruth and Helma toward the open door, his lips moving as if he were reading the lettering on the side of a passing panel truck: Hill Top Café.

"It sounds like you two have already made up your minds I'm guilty," Julius said.

"Of what?" Ruth asked sweetly.

"Of Molly's—" He stopped.

"Don't give it all away at once," Ruth advised. "Save the juicy parts until I get my drink."

He sagged, shrinking, shoulders and head lowered, looking so miserable Helma could almost have felt sorry for him, if she hadn't been able to so clearly recall Molly's pained and earnest face as she ill-timedly read her poetry aloud. Or Tanja's genuine if effusive eagerness to help troubled women.

"You will go directly to the police," Helma told him. "And I shall accompany you."

"Let the man have the last drink of his life first," Ruth said.

Julius's eyes widened. He rocked so far back in his chair, the front legs came off the floor. "The police? The police already talked to me. I didn't have anything to do with Molly's death." Shaking his head so hard it made Helma's neck hurt. "Or Tanja's."

This was the moment to use caution, Helma knew. She didn't intend to be responsible for frightening a criminal to run. "You hold vital information about the two deceased women. That knowledge could assist the police in solving their deaths."

He slouched deeper into his chair, sulky. "I'm innocent," he said.

"Not quite," Ruth said. "You're responsible for Molly's poetry."

He rubbed his hands through his hair, front to back, and his face changed from sulky to surrender. "I didn't expect the poetry. I made a mistake I'll regret the rest of my life."

"Which one?" Helma asked.

He looked caught again. "More than one. Too many, too damn many."

"You left Tanja and followed Sunny to Bellehaven," Helma said, making it a statement, then waiting for Julius to answer.

He slowly nodded, eyes going distant before he considered his hands on the table in front of him, turning them palms up, then palms down. "Mistake number one. Tanja was on the whole professional track thing, and I wasn't. Sunny was more like me, an earth-mother type . . ."

"But in the end she didn't make your earth move?" Ruth asked.

"And Tanja wouldn't let me come back," he finished for Ruth.

"You were attracted to Molly's resemblance to Tanja so when Tanja rightfully rejected you, you began a relationship with Molly," Helma said as Ruth snapped her fingers and said, "That's right, they did look alike."

Julius raised his head, a dawning look on his face as if for the first time he realized the connection. "Molly was more fragile than I ever guessed. I just wanted to have a good time, but she thought we were getting married. She had this total vision of our future, this lacy, flowery fantasy world. I tried to tell her. I never meant to hurt her." He shook his head. "I never meant to hurt her," he repeated. "I'll regret it forever."

Tears filled Julius's eyes and Ruth gazed at him in what Helma recognized in horror was delight. "This is very refreshing," Ruth said and Helma nudged her beneath the table.

The waiter approached their table, stopped, and made a U-turn back to the bar.

"The hit-and-run?" Helma asked Julius. "Were you responsible?"

"No. I swear to god. After we split up, Molly would call and read her poetry over the phone. I stopped answering, so then she read it into my answering machine. It was so . . . black. I honestly believed she might have stepped in front of the car. But then, I guess the driver would have stopped if it had been an accident. Most drivers, anyway."

"When was the last time you saw Molly?" Helma asked him, thinking that two men, Julius and Boyd, feared their actions had influenced a woman to step in front of a moving car to her death.

"The afternoon she died. I teach English one-o-one part-time at the community college." He cringed at the memory. "There were students all around us, and I more or less brushed her off. But I never saw her again, I swear."

"Did she read you *all* her poems?" Ruth asked.

"I don't know, a lot of them. Most were about our breakup, all ending with that question."

" 'Why oh why did you leave me?' " Ruth said and Julius nodded.

"And she named you in one of the poems," Helma

said. "How did you tear that specific poem out of the library's copy?"

"After I read about the displays, I stopped by the library. Her collection was on the counter by a display case, and I asked a clerk if I could see it. She'd read that poem into my answering machine."

Julius tapped his glass and looked down into it, speaking quietly. "After Molly died, that poem was frankly an embarrassment and a possible complication." He took a deep breath. "So I tore it out and dropped the collection on a rear table and left when the clerk was busy."

That easy, Helma thought. If Ms. Moon had passed Molly's poems to her, as the manager of the Local Authors project, instead of to Glory, they never would have been left on the library counter.

"But *why*?" she asked Julius. "How would anyone have connected you with that poem? Do other people call you Dash? Do you have a horse?"

He shook his head, looking uncomfortable. "No, but I wasn't sure how much Molly shared with people."

"Hah!" Ruth leaned forward, her eyes bright. "So you're not a cowboy and you don't own a horse. This cowboy thing was maybe a *game*? Like 'Cowgirl Up'?"

Helma had no idea what Ruth was talking about, but obviously Julius did because his face flushed deepest red. He raised his head and looked directly into Ruth's eyes, then Helma's. "But I swear, I had nothing to do with Molly's death. Tanja's neither. I swear it."

"He's lying," Ruth said after the sound of Julius's scooter faded away. "His car's in the shop—hah. I bet it's the blue car the police are looking for and he stashed it in some dark alley."

Helma and Ruth remained sitting at the table in the Wild Hare. Ruth was finishing her second beer, an expensive draft that was nearly black and smelled of grain, served in an elongated glass, while Helma still sipped at her first glass of iced tea.

"And you let him go," Ruth continued. "We'll never see him again—well, until he sneaks up behind us some dark night, anyway."

Helma considered Julius and answered thoughtfully. "I believe he tore the poem out of Molly's collection so he couldn't be connected with her death and I believe he was involved with all three women."

"Yeah, the slimeball. Too bad we can't get him arrested for that."

Helma again considered Julius's demeanor and face. "But the murders were too complicated for him, although I don't believe he's completely ignorant of their deaths, either."

"And somebody was in the Hopewell Building besides you and me and Pepper. We need to find out what the cops know. What about Sunny? What's her story?"

"Sunny didn't appear romantically interested in Julius any longer. In fact, she seemed satisfied that her friendship with Tanja could be reestablished once Julius left *her*."

"Could have been a ploy to get you off her track. That's why Sunny was over-effusive when she read Molly's poem at that group, a nasty mix of guilt and glee that Molly was out of the picture—permanently. What about the tête-à-tête you saw Julius and Sunny having in Saul's Deli? What'd you call it . . . tense?"

"She said she confronted him over his history with Tanja."

"Conveniently leaving *herself* out of the equation? As if she hadn't wanted to chase after him when he rode away on his bicycle and clobber him with a tool out of that toolbox on his fender?" Ruth shook her head. "Un-uh, no woman can witness *that* without a teensy bit of resentment, trust me."

Helma drove Ruth back to her apartment and braked beside the stairs so Ruth could get out.

"Come in a minute and see my new painting," Ruth urged. "It's one you'll like."

Ruth knew her paintings were a mystery to Helma, that she never *really* expected an opinion from Helma, and in fact preferred that Helma not offer an opinion, so she was surprised by her request.

But she turned off her Buick's engine and followed Ruth up the steps, waving once to Walter David, the Bayside Arms manager and hearing the rhythmic bump-bumping of TNT pounding the punching bag that hung in the middle of his living room.

Ruth had a key to Helma's apartment and she opened the door, waving Helma inside. "Sit down there." She pointed to Helma's sofa. "This one requires fanfare."

Helma sat. Ruth strode back to the bedroom that she'd so casually turned into an art studio and nest, her one concession to Helma being that she kept the door closed.

After thirty seconds, Ruth called out, "Hang on. I have to fix something. It'll only take a second."

Helma waited, gazing out at the balcony and up at the eaves where Boy Cat Zukas sometimes lurked. When Ruth still hadn't emerged, she idly picked up Tanja's glossy-covered book, *Women in Jeopardy*, from her coffee table and leafed through it.

Chapters with titles like, "Be Sassy for Yourself," "Waking Your Inner Devil," and "You Don't Have to Trust." There were self-scoring tests and assignments at the end of each chapter accompanied by drawn illustrations of happy, take-charge women. Tanja had been decidedly enthusiastic, Helma thought as she flipped to the end of the book, where there was an excerpt, a "teaser," for Tanja's next book, the one that now might never be published, the manuscript in Helma's cubicle at the Bellehaven Public Library.

"Winning Life," the ten-page excerpt was titled. "True tales from a counselor's case files." A tale of "Barbara," a woman who overcame stunning abuse followed by "Mary," who carried her dead father's tape measure everywhere with her, symbolically measuring the world against her memory of his perfection.

"Ta-da!" Ruth stood in front of her, smiling broadly, a canvas held out but turned toward her chest so Helma couldn't see it. "Ready?"

Helma steeled herself for one of Ruth's wildly colored incomprehensible paintings and nodded.

Ruth turned the canvas toward Helma. "What say you?"

Helma gasped. The painting was a perfectly rendered vision of Boy Cat Zukas. The torn ear, the patches where his hair had grown in white. He sat in the basket that was still positioned beside the sliding glass doors to her balcony, gazing unenthusiastically out of the canvas.

"Oh, Ruth," Helma said, then again, "Oh, Ruth. It looks exactly like Boy Cat Zukas, even the way he tips his head. And his fur, you even added the silvery tips."

"You like it, then?"

"Oh yes. It's . . . perfect. I didn't know you could paint so . . . representational."

Ruth snorted. "Of course I can. You have to learn all the rules before you can break all the rules. That's why they call it creativity." She turned the painting so she had a better view of it herself.

"Consider it a belated birthday present. Something to remember him by."

"Remember him?" Helma repeated. "We'll still find him."

"Oh, Helm," Ruth said, then after two heartbeats, she said, not looking at Helma. "Sure we will. I'm going to take this back to my room and add a few finishing touches."

"It really is beautiful, Ruth. Thank you."

"You're welcome. Seeya later."

Helma's finger still held its place in Tanja's book. She opened it, intending only to smooth the pages and set it on her coffee table, but her eyes caught the word, "tape measure" again.

Tape measure. The fictional Mary's father's tape measure. She frowned and read the remainder of the excerpt, sensing as she did that the ten-page excerpt was filled with mere teasers, not the actual text. It was put together before Tanja had completed the manuscript, obviously.

And Tanja's manuscript was at the library on a book truck in Helma's cubicle.

She closed Tanja's book and set it on the coffee

table, then stood outside the closed door of her guest bedroom and told Ruth, "I have to return to the library. I'll be back before dinner."

"Uh-huh," Ruth's voice came distractedly through the door.

Chapter 23

Questions Intensified

The manuscript of Tanja Frost's unfinished book, unopened since Julius had given it to Helma, resided in a box on the bottom shelf of the book truck, beneath a copy of a self-published book titled *Meditations on Road Work: The Musings of an Asphalt Repairman*.

Helma moved the box to her desk, lifted the lid, and removed the stack of pages. Tanja's manuscript was 326 pages long. She hadn't had time to create an index or table of contents so there was no shortcut into its contents. Helma began to turn over the pages, scanning the text for mention of a tape measure.

"Hey, Helma, you back again?" George Melville asked, stopping at her cubicle entrance.

"Just for a minute," she told him.

"Look at this. Glory gave it to me." He pointed

to the chain around his neck on which hung a six-inch-round plastic disk. "It's a fake Olympic gold medal. I'm going to the library party as a rabbit."

"I understood the party had a literary theme."

He nodded eagerly and fondled the medal. "I'm going as an Updike novel. Guess which one."

Helma didn't play guessing games so she waited, a finger holding her place in Tanja's manuscript, knowing George wouldn't be able to resist telling her.

"Rabbit Run!" he said triumphantly. "Get it?"

The only way she'd be able to concentrate on the manuscript was to take it with her somewhere private. Not back to her apartment where Ruth was painting, not to Saul's Deli where she was liable to run into another Bellehaven public employee or even someone from the library.

No, she needed complete silence and her undivided attention.

Helma packed the manuscript into an oversized envelope that had once held interlibrary loans and donned her coat.

"You really don't plan to attend your Troubled Pets session?" Ms. Moon asked, glancing up at the wall clock.

Helma hadn't seen her standing with Glory outside the restrooms. Glory ducked her head and moved a small step away, her face pinking as if she were the type of person who'd feel guilty if she was caught gossiping.

"No, I do not," Helma told her.

"I think . . ." Ms. Moon began.

"That's inadvisable," Helma told her. She held up the envelope containing Tanja's manuscript. "I'm searching Tanja Frost's manuscript for the significance of her life and death," she said truthfully, and left the library.

She drove to the north end of Bellehaven where there'd once been an exclusive subdivision overlooking Washington Bay but when the airport expanded, the houses directly beneath the runway approach had been condemned and removed, their foundations bulldozed. Here and there, stray perennials and a few exotic shrubs attested to their former presence.

The vacant land had been converted to a little-used park—an afterthought with minimal facilities yet a breathtaking wind-swept view that took in the length of Washington Bay to the southwest where the mountains of the Olympic Peninsula hung ghostly visible on a clear day.

No other cars were parked in the graveled lot. Helma removed the emergency blanket she kept in her trunk and carried it and Tanja's manuscript to the lone wooden picnic table that sat tipsily on a small rise. After she opened a prepackaged moist towelette and wiped off the table, she spread the blanket on the bench seat, removed the manuscript from the envelope, and began to methodically page through it, notebook and pencil in hand.

Within a few moments she realized that the chapters in Tanja's manuscript were titled with different, more blandly anonymous names than the teaser she'd read at the back of *Women in Jeopardy*: Bob, Mary, Catherine, Paula, Jim, Sally. Each chapter contained that person's story, as elicited, illuminated, and ultimately dissected, by the counselor, Tanja Frost.

In the excerpt at the back of *Women in Jeopardy*, it had been Mary who owned her father's tape measure, but when Helma read the chapter titled "Mary," she found no mention of a tape measure. Not in Catherine, Paula, or Sally's chapters, either. Had Tanja dropped the tale from her book?

Helma restacked the manuscript and rested her folded hands on it while she gazed out at the silvery blue water. The sun came out and shone on her face, and she closed her eyes, feeling its warmth on her eyelids and lips. There weren't many days left like this before the misty rainy days of winter closed in, blocking the sun for days at a time, sending library circulation statistics skyrocketing and plumping Bellehavenites' faces into dewy paleness.

She glanced down at her notebook, which listed Tanja's chapter headings in order of appearance. None of the women's chapters contained the information she was searching for. Would Tanja have disguised her subjects by changing their gender?

She reopened the manuscript, beginning with Bob, a schoolteacher with commitment issues. No tape measure. Nor Jim, who had murdered his father and conveniently found God in prison.

But John. Helma felt a prickle on her arms as Tanja launched into the tale of effeminate John who'd suffered from fear of abandonment his entire life. His story read like a novel, features Helma imagined a thriller would contain, the kind that would transmogrify neatly into a nine-part television series.

Born into a "fractured family," a carpenter father blown to pieces so completely in a gas explosion that only his tape measure was recovered, a mother who studied with a famous artist, then subsequently drank herself to death, a grandmother who was a former exotic dancer, an imprisoned brother.

And there. There it was: an aunt who'd been forced to leave her convent because she'd had a baby and then had become a librarian. Helma swallowed. Next was the sister who'd had an affair with a high government official.

Helma sat back and turned her face unseeing toward Washington Bay.

Pepper. Tanja was describing Pepper Breckenridge/ Goodwin.

Helma drove back toward downtown Bellehaven, her mind busily sifting through this new information. Pepper had been Tanja's patient, how else could Tanja have obtained Pepper's story? It was too coincidental.

Her speedometer passed the speed limit and she lifted her foot from the gas pedal, briefly considering informing the police, but instead decided to phone Ruth.

The payphone at the 7-Eleven was open and Helma dialed her own number, misdialing once and losing her quarter as "Good afternoon, Sherrie's Terriers" answered. She let the number ring ten times, for the first time ever wishing she *did* believe in the rudeness of answering machines. She dialed her apartment twice more, letting the phone ring eight and seven times respectively, then gave up. She'd talk to Pepper first.

Neither electronic nor live directory assistance had a listing for Pepper Goodwin or Pepper Breckenridge. Helma couldn't remember seeing a telephone in Pep-

per's apartment. So instead, she drove to the divided
old house where Pepper lived.

There was no response when she rapped on Pepper's
wooden door, which still held P.B. in the name holder,
and no sound from behind it, only the quiet sense of no
one home. She didn't see Pepper's bicycle, either.

Helma then drove to her own apartment and hurried
up the stairs to 3F, fumbling for her keys before she unlocked the door.

Her apartment was silent and she knew without
looking that Ruth wasn't there.

Facing her, propped on the kitchen counter, was the
lifelike painting of Boy Cat Zukas. Ruth had added a
faint golden halo above his head. The halo was tipped
very, very slightly, giving Boy Cat Zukas a beatific but
rakish demeanor.

A note sat beside the canvas. Helma snatched it
up. It was written on the back of a card reminding
Helma of her teeth-cleaning appointment with Dr.
Frier.

H: Off to give Tanja's book to Pepper. TTFN! R.

Ruth was with Pepper? Helma glanced at the coffee
table where she'd left Tanja's first published book,
Women in Jeopardy. It was gone. *Where* were Ruth and
Pepper? How had they gone? She stepped next door to
3E and knocked, grateful when it was immediately
opened. At least *someone* was home.

"Helma," TNT said. He wore his gray sweats as
usual. "Come on in."

"Thank you but I'm in a bit of a hurry. Did Ruth bor-
row your Jeep?"

He nodded. "Yup. She drove away not more than

five minutes ago. Didn't say where she was heading, though. Sorry."

After Helma stepped away to return to her apartment, TNT called after her, "It's damn good to see you back in fighting shape, Helma."

She could hear her phone ringing as she opened her door.

"Hello?" she said, expecting Ruth, her voice already dipping into relief.

"I meant it," the mechanical disembodied voice growled at her. "The cat will never get out of here alive—unless you butt out."

Helma swallowed. Boy Cat Zukas had disappeared three days ago from only two miles away. Sufficient time for him to return to her apartment—if he were able—and if he were so inclined. Either this caller actually had Boy Cat Zukas or . . . The haloed cat in Ruth's painting gazed at her. She simply couldn't consider any other possibility.

"Who are you?" she asked, distractedly glancing out at her empty balcony.

The caller responded to her question, but Helma's attention was caught by a flash of untidiness on the sisal mat in front of her sliding-glass doors. A leaf blown onto her balcony?

She stretched the telephone cord as far as it was able toward the glass door, trying to catch a better view of her mat. The cord wouldn't quite stretch far enough.

"Would you excuse me for a moment?" she said to the caller, and while still holding the receiver at arm's length with the cord stretched as long and taut as a well-hung electric line, and hearing the buzz of the anonymous voice, she was able to reach the door, unlock it, and slide it open.

There, squarely in the middle of her mat, lay the neatly severed head of a small brown mouse.

Never had a display of death left her so . . . satisfied. She couldn't help it; she actually smiled at the little bodiless head.

Helma quickly stepped back inside her apartment and spoke into the telephone. "This conversation is irrelevant. You do not have my cat."

"I do too." The peevishness was obvious through the mechanization.

"I assure you, you do not. Goodbye."

Helma hung up and returned to her deck, stepping over the mouse head to peer up at the roof. No sign of Boy Cat Zukas

She sighted both directions along the balcony railings of the adjoining apartments and spotted no cat. "Come, cat," she said to no avail.

Still, with a lighter heart, she wrapped the mouse head in a tissue and flushed it down the toilet before peering once more around her balcony and down into Boardwalk Park beneath the Bayside Arms, and then telephoning George Melville at the library. "Has Ruth been there?' she asked him.

"We have not been graced with the lady's presence," he said. "Want me to pass on a message should she appear?"

"Tell her not to. . . ." What, Helma thought—not to meet Pepper? Or to return to Helma's apartment and paint out Boy Cat Zukas's halo? "If you could ask her to call me," Helma said.

"Will do. You coming back in?"

"I don't believe I will."

"Smart. She's on the wild trying to squeeze every last ounce out of the Author Serial Killer. We're all laying low. Everybody but . . ." He paused. "Well, just about everybody."

Chapter 24

Questions Finally Answered

Helma didn't take the time to puzzle out which person George Melville meant who *wasn't* laying low while Ms. Moon went "on the wild."

If Tanja's "John" chapter and Pepper's life story were too similar to be coincidence, and if Pepper had been Tanja's patient, then was Pepper's story of being a counselor also a lie? Pepper had implied that she'd completed transferring her counselor's license from California to Washington.

Fortunately, inquiring into the credentials of a Bellehaven doctor, psychologist, or other professional such as a masseuse or an electrolysist, was a common question at the Bellehaven Public Library reference desk. In fact, as a professional, Helma had committed the telephone number of the Washington State Department of Health—and other vital phone numbers—to memory, a practice that, curiously, she found easier than remembering names.

"Health Professions Quality Assurance, please," she requested when she finally reached a living voice.

There was not a license in Pepper Goodwin's name. "Try Breckenridge, please," Helma asked, then wondering if the name Pepper could be a false name after all, she added, "Could you also check for counselors under either surname with a different first name?"

"There's a Ronald Breckenridge in Skagit County," the clerk told her.

"Would you possibly have her name on file if she'd *applied* but the license hadn't yet been granted?"

The woman hesitated but when Helma said, "I plan to see her this afternoon," her sense of civic responsibility won out.

"I can check the applications file. One moment, please."

While she waited, Helma hopefully reexamined the sisal mat on her balcony for other, suddenly appearing, small animal body parts, but her mat was clean.

"I'm sorry, ma'am," the clerk returned, "but there's nothing in our application file under either name."

"Thank you," Helma told her appreciatively. "I too am a civil servant and I'm proud to be your colleague."

So Pepper had fabricated the counselor story. But why go through all the pretense of attending counseling sessions and renting office space? Especially in the same building as Tanja? If Pepper had been Tanja's patient, a patient with such a dramatic and unforgettable story, Tanja would have recognized Pepper the first time they passed each other in the hallway.

After one last check of her balcony, Helma hastily left her apartment, and recalling Pepper's claim that she and Ruth were planning to search for Boy Cat Zukas, she drove first to Joker's bar. Ruth might have met Pepper at the bar. Only two cars were parked in front of Joker's and neither was TNT's Jeep. She stopped anyway and rushed inside.

"Excuse me," she asked Kipper the bartender, who was aimlessly wiping the bar and watching television, "have you seen Ruth?"

"Not today. Find your cat?"

"Not quite," she told him, turning from his puzzled face and running back to her Buick.

Red lights on the downtown streets were inordinately frequent, flipping to yellow from too far a distance to even accidentally drive through. Helma impatiently tapped her left foot against the carpeted floor, waiting for the green light to signal the go-ahead.

TNT's Jeep wasn't parked at the library nor the Hopewell Building. Helma swung around past the Victorian house that held Pepper's apartment and didn't spot it parked anywhere on the street, either.

She was about to turn the corner beyond Pepper's house when dull metal caught her eye. She braked and backed up. The rear of a Jeep was visible, pulled far into the driveway beside the converted Victorian, nose-in to one of the rickety moss-covered garages that dotted Bellehaven's alleys and side streets. She recognized the Jeep as TNT's by the peeling bumper sticker that read, BOXERS GO THE DISTANCE.

Helma parked her Buick against the curb so it wouldn't block the driveway, picked up the envelope containing Tanja Frost's manuscript, and climbed out, assuring that all her car doors were locked before she stepped away from the driver's side and approached TNT's Jeep, glancing warily at the garage.

The once-brown paint had mostly peeled off the garage walls. On its roof, more moss was visible than shingles. The odor of decaying wood tingled in her nostrils. A netless and rusted basketball hoop hung crookedly from the peak of the garage; there was always a melancholy air about basketball hoops, engendering the same feeling in Helma as bronzed baby shoes.

"Hello?" Helma called softly, squinting into the dark garage.

A red Honda with cat tracks leading up its dusty trunk to the car's roof was parked inside. A shiny black motorcycle stood in the lea of the ramshackle garage, a flame decal on the gas tank.

Helma wasn't the least surprised that Ruth had parked TNT's Jeep so it blocked the car in the garage, or that she'd left it unlocked. She opened and locked the driver's door, although she supposed if anyone *really* wanted to break into it, all they needed to do was slash through the canvas back.

Ruth and Pepper had to be inside Pepper's apartment. The day was quiet, the afternoon soft-aired, the street peaceful. Deceptive, Helma thought. She placed her car keys inside her knuckles the way she'd learned in self-defense class and approached the house, her every sense alert to the anomalies of sight and sound.

Just-audible music filtered through Pepper's apartment door. Folk music, so it definitely had to be Pepper's choice, not Ruth's. Helma listened, breath held, until she heard Ruth's big laugh. Then she knocked.

Immediately, Pepper opened the door a foot and peered into the hallway, her face questioning. At the sight of Helma she smiled and opened the door wide. "Come on in. Ruth's here." Pepper was dressed, as she'd been every time Helma had seen her, in gusseted pants and a cotton T-shirt, wearing sneakers, as if in a moment she'd hop a bicycle or jog out the door and down the street.

Ruth sat on the arm of Pepper's corduroy sofa, waving time to a song that had a rollicking line that went, "A wicky sticky wicki-up," a nearly empty wineglass in one hand. "You got my message. Good. Join us."

"I'll get you a glass," Pepper offered, but Helma stopped her. "No, thank you." She turned to Ruth, "How long have you been here?"

"Ten minutes maybe. Did you like what I did to the painting?" She turned to Pepper. "I did a fabulous rendition of the missing cat and gave him a goldy gossamer halo, because, well, you know, kitty heaven and all that."

"You may be able to remove the halo," Helma said, closely watching Pepper whose head snapped around toward her.

"No!" Ruth jumped up from the sofa, the wineglass tipping precariously. "You found the little devil?"

"There are signs he's reentered the area."

"That's good news," Pepper said. "You must be thrilled."

"It's always safer for animals to live in a permanent home," Helma replied. Pepper's eyes went to the envelope Helma carried, frowning slightly. Helma sat in the wooden rocking chair and tucked the envelope tightly between her side and the chair arm.

"Were you looking for me?" Pepper asked.

"For Ruth," Helma told her. From outside, from the direction of the garage, Helma heard the revving of a motorcycle engine, then the roar of it passing the house and fading down the street. Unaccountably, she wished the motorcyclist hadn't left.

"Well, here I am," Ruth said. "What's up?"

Over the years, despite their differences and, yes, clear frustrations with one another, certain mannerisms of Ruth's or Helma's had served as signals to the other, so when Helma now hesitated before answering, Ruth slapped her forehead and said, "Right. I forgot about that. Sorry," endeavoring to at least alert Helma she was aware of *something* Helma didn't want to say in Pepper's presence.

"Pepper called and asked to see Tanja's book and silly me, I brought her the wrong book," Ruth said, pointing to *Women in Jeopardy* sitting on the sofa seat.

"I believe Tanja only had one published book," Helma said.

"Really?" Ruth asked. "Maybe you didn't know that, Pepper?"

Pepper had remained standing, casually leaning against the wall closest to Helma. "I knew the second book was about to go to her publisher," she said. "Sunny thought it would be even more groundbreaking than the first, a deeper insight into Tanja's methods."

"Had Sunny read it?" Helma asked.

Pepper shook her head. "She said Tanja was superstitious about letting anyone read her books before they were published."

"That's what her husband said," Helma remarked casually, closely watching Pepper's face, but no unusual emotions registered there.

"You mean Julius?" Ruth asked helpfully.

Still nothing in Pepper's face showed she was interested in Julius or his opinions.

"So you wanted to read Tanja's book *before* it was published?" Helma asked. The envelope containing Tanja's manuscript burned against her leg.

"Sure. It's eagerly anticipated by counselors."

"Anticipation," Ruth said, "is the sauciest sauce on earth."

"We always want to be the first, don't we?" Pepper explained. "Look at the Harry Potter books. Bestsellers before they're even in print. Can you imagine what a bootleg copy would bring before its publication?"

"Geesh," Ruth said, frowning at Pepper in surprise. "You were going to *sell* Tanja's book? Is she so popular that an unpublished manuscript would make you much money? Where? On the shrink black market?"

"Not to mention breaking copyright law," Helma added.

"I *didn't* want to sell it," Pepper stated emphatically, standing up straighter from the wall. "Tanja was a heroine of mine. Emulating her experiences would make me a better counselor."

"Is your counseling office ready to open yet?" Helma asked.

"Nearly," Pepper told her. "There are still a few details to work out."

"Did the sofa fit?"

Pepper looked at her blankly and Helma said, "The sofa you were measuring for your office."

"Oh. Yes. I just need to hire movers to lug it inside for me."

"Was it complicated to switch your counseling license

from California to Washington?" Helma continued. "Are the standards between the states quite different?"

"Not very. It . . ." Pepper's voice trailed off. Her expression changed in an indefinable way. She shrugged, appearing almost mischievous. "Actually," she said, "You've caught me. I lied again. I *don't* have my license. The application isn't tough, just a ton of paperwork and on top of moving and everything . . ." She sighed and held out her hands as if she were surrendering. "That's my goal for this weekend, though: to finish it and mail it off. I can still get my office ready while I'm waiting."

Noting how easily Pepper had sidestepped her suspicions, Helma wished she'd taken her research further and telephoned the California Department of Health.

Pepper stepped away from the wall. "I think I'll make a cup of tea. Would you like one?"

"Yes, please."

As soon as Pepper entered the kitchen that had been carved out of the parlor in the old house, Ruth raised her eyebrows and began waving her hands at Helma. "What's going on?" she mouthed silently and in exaggeration.

Helma did not engage in pantomime, but she did discreetly tap the envelope beside her that held Tanja's manuscript.

"Any phone calls for me?" Ruth asked, loud enough for Pepper to hear, at the same time she pointed to the manuscript, then mouthed silently, "Tanja's?"

Helma nodded and answered Ruth's other question aloud. "No, there weren't." She'd had quite enough of double conversations and calmly gazed at Ruth as Ruth frowned and gestured and contorted her mouth in exaggerated and incomprehensible questions.

Even if Pepper's explanation as to why she didn't have her counselor's license was true, there was no clue why her family tales matched Tanja's written "John" chapter. Pepper had asked Ruth to bring her Tanja's manuscript; and her reasons for requesting it, now that Helma had read the chapter, were too thin to believe.

Suddenly a crash and clatter sounded from the kitchen and Pepper screamed. Both Helma and Ruth jumped up.

Pepper stood back from the stove, her arms raised in the air and the water kettle rolling across the floor, water splashing and streaming over the kitchen linoleum.

"Did you burn yourself?" Helma asked, already turning on the faucet so Pepper could plunge her hands into a stream of cold water.

Pepper didn't answer but stood with her hands still raised, eyes wide, paralyzed.

Ruth leaped for the fallen kettle and Helma grabbed a towel from the refrigerator door handle and threw it on the spreading water. "Be careful," Helma warned Ruth.

Ruth hefted the kettle, holding it away from her body, a quizzical expression on her face. "It's not even hot," she said, just as the door of Pepper's apartment slammed.

"Uh-oh," Ruth said, looking out into the living room.

Chapter 25

Crash of Titans

Not only had Pepper disappeared out her apart-ment door, but so had Tanja's manuscript. The rocking chair still gently swayed forward, back-ward. Empty.

"What's going on?" Ruth asked. She shook the kettle still in her hand and water sloshed back and forth. "Is *Pepper* the criminal?"

"She lied," Helma told her, adding, "allegedly."

"I can catch her," Ruth said, racing for the door, dropping the kettle to the living room floor where it rolled beneath an end table, again spewing wa-ter from its spout. Helma cast one glance at it and ran after Ruth.

"Her bike's still here," Ruth said in the hallway, pointing to Pepper's bicycle. "She's on foot."

Pepper's bicycle helmet hung from the handle-bars. Helma stopped. The helmet . . .

"Hurry up!"

They dashed into the yard, to the driveway where TNT's Jeep sat in front of the garage, then to the end of the gravel drive, peering up and down the street.

"She couldn't have got away that fast," Ruth said, catching her breath.

"She's hiding," Helma told her. "You check the alley and I'll circle the house."

"What if she has a gun?"

"She doesn't," Helma told her, already hurrying toward the side of the house.

"How do you know?" Ruth demanded.

"I didn't see one when she left the apartment," Helma said even as she checked behind the old overgrown shrubbery beside the house.

"That doesn't mean she didn't have one stashed out here somewhere," Ruth called over her shoulder. "Stay low."

Helma quickly circled the house, finding no sign of Pepper, not even a rustling bush.

Ruth met her on the front sidewalk, her hands out and empty. "She's not in the alley. She got away, damn it. Now what do we do?"

"We'd better call the police," Helma conceded.

"Why's she running?" Ruth asked, wiping the sheen of perspiration on her forehead. "And why the manuscript? I don't get it."

Before Helma could answer, a noise sounded behind them. Helma turned to catch sight of Pepper, body hunched and partially blocked by the Jeep, trying to wrench open the driver's door.

"I didn't lock it," Ruth shouted, running toward

the Jeep, tripping over a crumbling rock wall and sprawling flat on the weedy lawn. "Hurry! She'll get away."

"I locked it," Helma said, as she helped Ruth up.

"You did? Of course you did," Ruth said at the same instant that Pepper abandoned the Jeep and ran into the dark garage.

"She's trapped herself in there," Ruth said. "The idiot."

But Helma recalled the rotten boards in the building. There might even be a door in the back wall.

"I'll watch the back," she told Ruth. "You call the . . ."

Suddenly, the red Honda in the dilapidated garage roared to life, as much as a Honda was able. The rear taillights flashed, then the white backup lights, indicating the car had been thrown into reverse.

The Honda inched part way out of the garage; there wasn't enough turning room between it and TNT's Jeep. Pepper had nowhere to go, but she slowly backed up until her car's bumper touched the Jeep's bumper. Helma could see Pepper's outline behind the wheel, head twisted to see out the rear window.

"We've got her now," Ruth said as she brushed a smear of grass from her knee. "All we have to do is nab her when she gets out of the car."

The outline of Pepper turned forward again and Pepper pulled the Honda back into the garage.

Instead of the engine being switched off as Helma had expected, it growled two, three times, as the gas pedal was tapped. Then she realized that Pepper hadn't pulled the car back into the garage to turn it off and quietly surrender but to get a running start. She slammed her foot down on the gas pedal. Exhaust billowed. Tires spun.

"Don't do it!" Ruth shouted, "that's not my Jeep!"

But the car kept coming. Dust and gravel flew. Burning oil smoked the scene.

"Wait!" Ruth called. "I'll move it." She took a step toward the Jeep but Helma grabbed her arm.

It was absurd. Honda against Jeep. Small, aging foreign car against a vehicle designed for war. An act of a desperate woman who'd lost everything, who had nothing left to lose. Helma stood stock still and watched the car, spellbound. She knew that feeling.

Ruth shouted, "Stop," one last time and covered her eyes.

With the sickening sound of metal meeting metal, the Honda smashed into the Jeep, its rear crumpling. The Jeep stood like a rock, immobile and unscathed. The crash echoed between the houses.

"If she's not dead, I'm going to kill her," Ruth said, uncovering her eyes.

Far from being dead, Pepper sat in the driver's seat, pounding her fists against the steering wheel. Blood dribbled down her cheek, but she looked more enraged than hurt. The envelope containing Tanja's manuscript had slid to the floor on the passenger side.

"You get that," Helma told Ruth, pointing to the envelope, "and I'll help Pepper."

Pepper glared as Helma opened the driver's door. Oh for a weapon. Helma put her hand purposefully to her sweater pocket, hoping Pepper might be addled enough to be fooled. And there she discovered, still in her pocket, the toy Boeing 747 she'd picked up from the library floor.

"We can phone the police now, she told Pepper, holding the Boeing by a wing inside her pocket so its nose bulged menacingly against the fabric of her sweater, "or you can come back inside to discuss this situation."

"Great, a gun," Ruth said. "That's a relief. So you *did* suspect Pepper, after all."

Pepper touched her bloody cheek. "You could show some concern for my injuries, maybe offer to call an ambulance."

"That doesn't appear necessary," Helma told her, deciding not to point out the incongruity of requesting one public emergency service when the threat to hopefully get Pepper moving was to call another public emergency service.

Pepper wobbled as she climbed from her car but righted herself by grabbing the top of the door and straightening her spine. "This is ridiculous," she said, hissing her *S*s. "Just because I want to read a colleague's book. What about your commitment to reading? What kind of librarian does this make *you*?"

"No librarian in good standing would advocate the circulation of unpublished copyrighted material."

"Yikes! What are you doing?" Pepper demanded when Helma, instead of guiding her back to her apartment, jabbed her Boeing 747 into Pepper's side and ushered her around the front of the Honda.

The right front fender of Pepper's car wasn't red like the rest of the car; it was blue. "You have a blue fender," Helma said.

"It's a repair a friend did; I just haven't had it painted yet."

"It never pays to scrimp on repairs," Helma said as she bent and examined the blue fender. "You also have a dent," Helma said, pointing to the depression behind the right headlight as Pepper jerked her head away, refusing to look.

"I bumped a parking meter."

"I've done that," Ruth offered. "Expensive as heck to fix. You wouldn't think so but it is. I have a five-hundred-dollar deductible. What's yours?"

"I'd like you to leave," Pepper told them, one hand to her cheek.

"I believe we're beyond that," Helma said, hand gripping the metal airplane. "As I suggested, we can all three go inside your apartment now or request the police come and sort it out. Ruth and I will explain to them the facts we have, about Molly and Tanja"—she paused to be sure Pepper was listening, uncertain of the significance but guessing it was substantial—"and give them Tanja's manuscript."

Pepper's shoulders sagged. She longingly eyed the manuscript in Ruth's hands, biting her lip.

Ruth wagged the envelope at Pepper. "Here it is," she taunted, "the blood and guts of this mess."

Helma had expected witnesses to run from their houses at the sound of the crash and the spectacle of three women shouting and arguing in the middle of the driveway, perhaps a small whispering-and-pointing crowd congregating on the sidewalk, sirens screaming in the distance. But the neighborhood was still. A car passed, the driver gazing straight ahead. Two young boys on bicycles raced down the sidewalk without glancing their way, both of them standing on their pedals for extra power.

"Okay, let's go," Ruth said as she raised her arm and pointed toward Pepper's apartment like an avenger leading her troops.

Chapter 26

Desperate Truths

Inside her apartment, Pepper sullenly dropped into the rocking chair where Helma had sat earlier. Ruth took a seat on the sofa opposite Pepper, watching her as if she were a newly materialized and incomprehensibly fascinating creature. After Helma picked up the kettle from the floor and returned it to the kitchen counter, she handed Pepper a damp paper towel for her cut chin.

"I probably loosened a tooth," Pepper said accusingly, grabbing the towel from Helma.

"Whose fault is that?" Ruth asked, rhetorically, of course.

Helma pulled an afghan from the back of the sofa and laid it on the seat to protect her clothes from cat hair, then sat down beside Pepper. Ruth handed her the envelope and Helma slid Tanja's manuscript onto her lap.

She tapped the stack of pages with her finger and faced Pepper. "You're John in Tanja's manuscript."

"I am?" Pepper asked, her face bland.

"She is?" Ruth chimed in.

"The gender's changed but it's your life story: the tape measure, the pregnant nun, the artist mother and the sister who had the affair with the high-ranking public official. You were one of Tanja's patients, weren't you?"

"No," she said emphatically. "What do you want from me? I haven't done anything. You came charging in here threatening me."

"You just smashed into a Jeep that I only borrowed," Ruth pointed out.

"I hurt *my* car, not yours. I'm leaving." But she didn't make any move to rise from the rocker, darting a glance toward Helma's hand, which was back in her pocket fingering her Boeing.

"The details between your story and Tanja's chapter are too similar," Helma persisted. "It's *not* a coincidence."

Pepper's mouth closed into a tight line. She began to rock the chair back and forth. The wooden rockers creaked irritatingly loud.

"You and Tanja were acquainted prior to your move to Bellehaven," Helma continued. It wasn't a question and Pepper's eyes dropped in uncertainty.

Ruth clapped her hands together once. "You weren't sucked in by Julius, too, were you?"

"Julius?" Pepper asked. Her forehead wrinkled. "Oh. Tanja's husband. I've never met him." She said it so easily, with just a touch of surprise.

"Why did you want this manuscript?" Helma asked as she straightened the stack of pages, evening the edges. "Enough to break the law to steal it."

"I already told you, to read it."

"You attended the Local Authors launch," Helma went on, "as did Tanja and Molly."

"Who *did* know Julius," Ruth added, still trying to follow the Julius line. "Both of them."

"I told you"—Pepper's words were measured, as if Ruth and Helma had the combined intelligence of a fence post, and she raised her chin—"that was accidental. I followed the crowd to see what was going on. And when I discovered it was just a bunch of people talking about books, I didn't stay very long."

"Did you know Molly?" Helma asked Pepper.

"No. I did not. Please leave my apartment," Pepper said, this time with more authority, as if she realized Helma didn't have any incriminating facts, that she was only fishing. Or maybe she'd finally recognized that the toy Boeing 747 didn't actually resemble a gun.

Helma stood, holding the manuscript tightly to her body like a schoolbook, and began to walk around Pepper's small apartment as if she were casually observing Pepper's furnishings. She felt Pepper's eyes following her.

Helma was an observant woman and as she crossed the room toward the door that obviously led to Pepper's bedroom, she noticed Pepper stiffen.

She stopped, turned, and walked back toward Ruth and Pepper, and Pepper relaxed. Helma remembered a game her cousins had played, where they all searched for an object while one person guided them by calling out, "You're getting hot" or "You're getting colder" or "You're freezing!" which her cousin Ricky always amended to, "You're freezing your cahooties."

Standing to the left and slightly behind Pepper, Helma studied the area where she'd been standing when Pepper stiffened. All Helma could see through the open doorway was a neatly made futon bed and the corner of a white dresser.

On the living room side of the door sat a small bookcase, tilted off the level by the carpet thickness, and next to it a wooden table that Pepper had turned into a desk. A black computer and matching printer stood on the table and a set of three wire baskets beside it, the top one empty and the other two filled with paper.

Stacks of paper—8½-by-11 inch sheets of white paper in fairly even piles, two and three inches tall—not like brand-new reams waiting to be inserted in the printer but pages that had been used and then stacked. A project. A big project.

"This is a silly mistake," Pepper said and laughed lightly, brushing a lock of her short hair behind her ear. "I feel like I've been kidnapped. Should I call my lawyer?" The rocking chair moved faster, clunking on the forward motion.

"You don't call the lawyer until *after* the police arrest you," Ruth pointed out.

Helma walked back to Pepper's desk and stood in front of it. Not touching anything, just observing. There was nothing personal on the desk, just Pepper's computer, a pencil holder, and the paper.

"I have confidential files there," Pepper warned her, her voice rising. "The interchanges between counselor and client are privileged information. Legally."

"As are the interchanges between librarian and patron," Helma told her as she reached into the second wire basket and pulled out the largest stack of paper. She lifted the blank top sheet of paper to read the few words centered on the page beneath.

"The Crooked Little Path," the heading read. "A novel by Pepper Siper' "

"Don't touch that!" Pepper leaped out of the rocker and charged Helma, who held tight to the pages even as Pepper rammed into her shoulder and knocked her sprawling to the floor, flailing and grabbing for the sheets Helma held.

As with all librarians, Helma had spent her career touching, holding, and perusing books of all sizes: lifting heavy encyclopedias from low bookcases; replacing misfiled books on high shelves; detaching expensive volumes from small grimy hands—these activities had developed the lumbricals of Helma's hands, the book-gripping muscles.

Pepper struggled, but she was no match for Helma: it was impossible for her to rip the pages from Helma's hands, or even to loosen one single sheet from her firm grasp without tearing it. She jerked and twisted at the pages, grunting, her face reddening as she tugged. But Helma did not budge.

Thwarted, Pepper released her hold on the pages and grabbed a letter opener from the pencil holder beside her computer. She planted her feet wide apart, her arms out like a wrestler angling for the first throw, her face red and hair wild, brandishing the stiletto shape first toward Helma, then Ruth, who'd jumped up to assist Helma, but not fast enough.

"Oh, come on, Pepper," Ruth said, coming to a full

stop. "Think about this a second. You don't want to use that on anybody."

"Just drop everything and leave," Pepper told them, the pointed end of the letter opener facing Helma.

And that's when Helma realized that although Pepper had pulled the opener from her pencil holder, that wasn't what it was. The letter opener was actually a small dagger, its slender blade gleaming wickedly as the light glanced off its razor edges.

"Show me what's in your pocket," Pepper demanded. "Now. That's no gun."

Reluctantly, Helman pulled out the toy airplane. "It's a Boeing 747," she said, and Pepper shook her head derisively.

"Swell," Ruth said as Helma set the airplane on the desk. "Just swell. I was afraid it was a Cessna."

"You wrote a novel," Helma said evenly, holding up "The Crooked Little Path" manuscript as she eyed the dagger and shifted her weight, balancing for quick action. "What does that have to do with Tanja's book?"

"God, Pepper," Ruth said, taking one slow step toward Pepper, halting when Pepper waved her weapon at her. "Put it down. You're just turning what might be a little mess into a Godzilla disaster."

Pepper shook her head and waved the dagger back and forth between the two women, in her eyes a frightening gleam. Helma continued calmly speaking, deliberately looking away from the sharp object and studying the printed pages in her hands.

But she was acutely aware every second of the dagger's location. "This can all be resolved," she heard herself say. "Many people find themselves . . ." She stopped listening to her own words, focusing on the lines of print on the first page of "The Crooked Little Path," thinking simultaneously in the unaccountable way the mind did during moments of high stress that there was a children's book with the same title.

But Pepper's manuscript wasn't a children's book. Helma had never needed a speed-reading class; she scanned the first few lines in an instant.

Chapter one was titled, not very originally, "I Am Born," and began with the line: "On a cold February morning of the day I was born, my father was blown to pieces as he tried to save a small stray puppy who'd wandered too close to a broken gas line he was repairing. My mother enshrined his scarred yellow tape measure on our fireplace mantel."

That was all Helma needed to read.

She took a breath and began softly speaking. "The night of the Age of Certain Years group session, you left the room just after Sunny introduced Tanja. You kept your face averted and said you were going to the restroom, but actually you were terrified that Tanja would see you in the group. She'd have recognized you immediately."

Pepper's eyes bored into Helma.

"You somehow stole Tanja's files and created a novel from the records of her sessions, plagiarizing other peoples' lives."

Ruth slapped her forehead and said, "You never went back to the session, did you? Helma and I left, so we wouldn't know, but I'll bet *you* hung the out-of-order sign on the elevator earlier, and waited for Tanja. Then you whacked her and shoved her down the steps, thinking her book would die with her. Yep. Because if *her* book was published it would expose you as a cheap thief too lazy to write her own book. What a rotten trick."

This wasn't how Helma would have confronted Pepper, and suddenly another realization interrupted her thoughts.

"Your bicycle helmet," she said, realizing why Pepper's helmet hanging on the bicycle in the foyer had caught her attention. "You hit Tanja with the edge of your bicycle helmet before you pushed her/down the steps."

"Aha," Ruth joined in, touching her left temple. "The oval-edged injury that my favorite cop described."

Pepper crouched lower, like an animal about to spring, her neck muscles tightening in unattractive cords. She spat out her words. "I didn't steal a word from Tanja Frost, not one damn word. That bitch stole from *me*."

"But how?" Helma asked. She raised Pepper's manuscript pages. "This is *your* novel which I can already see bears remarkable resemblance to Tanja's chapter titled 'John,' which also appears to be your complicated life story. Who stole from whom?"

"And what?" Ruth asked frowning.

"It was *my* story," Pepper wailed, sobs very close to the surface. Her hands shook. "Not my personal story but one I've been writing for thirteen years. That," and she pointed the dagger toward the pages Helma held. "That's the fourteenth draft of my novel. Fourteen! Can you understand how much work that is? *Years*."

"This *isn't* your personal story?" Helma asked, trying to sort conjecture from fact. "You *invented* your family? Your aunt who was a nun, the sister who had a political affair?"

Ruth pointed to the painting that hung over the sofa. "Even your mother who studied with Normal Rockwell? That's an original, who painted it?"

"Garage sale," Pepper said curtly.

"But the tape measure you showed us," Helma said. "Is it actually your father's?"

A change came over Pepper's face, half anger, half sorrow. "It's all he left behind when he took off with some tramp and left my mother, brother, and me."

"Another toolbox tale," Ruth muttered.

"But how did Tanja obtain your manuscript?" Helma asked hurriedly before Ruth's words registered with Pepper. "Why would she include a fictional tale in her book of cases?"

Pepper swiped her free hand across her eyes and Ruth moved her foot forward. Pepper raised the dagger more threateningly toward Helma's heart.

"Okay, okay," Ruth said, stepping back.

"Tanja read this manuscript?" Helma encouraged, raising the pages and drawing Pepper's attention to them. "Was Tanja a friend?"

"No matter what I did, my characters weren't right," Pepper said. "Finally, I realized I had to discover more psychological motivation for their actions."

"So you took your characters to a counselor," Helma guessed.

"To Tanja," Ruth added.

Pepper nodded. "When we both lived in California. But I didn't tell her I created the characters; I pretended they were members of my family and I was trying to understand them. I just wanted her insight, that's all."

Ruth picked up a sheaf of pages from the bottom wire

basket on Pepper's desk. She whistled. "They *are* a little excessive, aren't they?" she said, even though Helma could see Ruth hadn't read a single word. "So this wasn't a case of you picking the scabs of your life?"

"Tanja *took* them from me," Pepper wailed, "from our counseling sessions."

"But you must have granted her permission," Helma said, "to have your account included in her book."

Pepper vigorously shook her head. "I did not. She never asked."

"Then how did you know she was using your story?"

"One morning at a session in her office, Tanja stepped out for an emergency phone call." She shrugged. "I took a peek at my file, looking for her notes, and there was the 'John' chapter, already written." She turned pleading eyes to Ruth. "Don't you see, *her* book would probably be a bestseller. How could I publish *my* book after hers? It would be considered plagiarism, that I'd stolen from *her* book. Nobody would believe it was originally *my* story. My own book, *my* people."

"But if Tanja *didn't* have your permission you could have sued her," Helma pointed out. "At the very least, it's a violation of patient/counselor confidentiality."

"It wouldn't have mattered. Lawsuits, money. It would still be too late for me and my book, don't you understand?"

"Yeah," Ruth said, "simpler to kill her. Didn't you ever think of just asking Tanja to remove the stuff about you?"

"Bad publicity isn't always bad," Helma said, paraphrasing Ms. Moon's "There's no such thing as bad publicity."

When Pepper didn't respond, Helma asked, "But why Molly?"

Pepper shook her head, the way people do about mistakes they can't bear to think about. "It was an accident. I thought she was Tanja."

Helma remembered how the two women had resembled one another. Poor Molly; her resemblance to Tanja had brought her ill-fated love, then death.

" 'There are mistakes too monstrous for remorse to tamper or to dally with,' " Ruth suddenly quoted.

Pepper straightened, her face going cold and still. Helma felt a tremor at the back of her neck, sensing a change had taken place. Desperation had been replaced by icy resolve.

"Step back," Pepper said in a deadly calm voice, "both of you." It was her voice more than her simple weapon that made both Helma and Ruth obey.

And when they were a step further away from her, Pepper casually reached behind her computer and pulled out a small black handgun, neatly reinserting the dagger in her pencil holder with her other hand.

"Not good," Ruth said, eyes wide as Pepper pointed the gun toward her.

Chapter 27

Fire!

As Helma found herself staring down the barrel of Pepper's gun, she realized that Pepper had premeditatedly set the stage for a confrontation. And with a reawakened awareness, she scanned Pepper's small apartment and spotted the evidence: a baseball bat leaned against the wall beside the front door, a butcher knife lay on the breadboard on the counter, a single barbell by her bedroom door, a rectangular can she could see by the sink, marked with a red Warning! label. And of course the letter opener that wasn't really a letter opener. All of it subtle but deadly. How could she have missed it?

Pepper wouldn't have simply smiled sweetly and thanked Ruth for innocently delivering Tanja's manuscript, then waved goodbye to her at her apartment door. No, Pepper's arsenal proved otherwise. Pepper had already murdered trying to get the manuscript; Helma and Ruth were minor impediments.

Pepper backed into her kitchen, the gun pointed at Ruth, who stood closest to her. "I'm leaving. Put the pages together and set my manuscript on the counter. Tanja's, too."

"Other people know about this manuscript," Helma tried.

"I doubt it," Pepper said confidently. "*You* only figured it out with *my* help."

Pepper was right. Helma hadn't even copied the manuscript. No one else had read it.

"I bet you don't have a publisher for your novel," Ruth said as she added her pages to Helma's stack under Pepper's watchful eyes.

Just like Ruth, Pepper couldn't resist responding to a comment about her art. Her voice was full of certainty. "I've paid an agent to shop it around. He believes in it. He swears it'll be a success. Bigger than Danielle Steel and Joyce Carol Oates."

"Now *there's* an interesting couple," Ruth commented.

"No reputable agent *charges* you before a manuscript is bought by a publisher," Helma advised her.

Ruth shook her head. "C'mon, Helm, anybody who commits murder hoping to get a book published wouldn't mind paying a few bucks to extend the fantasy."

It was the wrong thing to say. "Shut up and set the manuscripts on the counter," Pepper told them, her voice cold with fury.

Helma restacked the pages then tapped them on end against the countertop to even the pages.

"Now put Tanja's manuscript back in the envelope," Pepper said. "Hurry up."

"We did surprise you in the Hopewell Building, didn't we?" Helma asked. "You weren't measuring for a sofa, you were planning to break into Tanja's office and take the only copy of her manuscript, erasing all traces of her book. That's the *real* reason you rented an office in the same building."

"I would have only removed the relevant chapter," Pepper said primly. "It was mine," she said, as if her intent to leave the rest of Tanja's manuscript was more honorable than having already killed two women.

"You would've been too late, anyway," Ruth told her. "Eager Beaver Julius removed it from her office the morning after she died. Did you pretend to have Helma's cat, too?"

"That cat's lucky I *didn't* have him."

"But you're the person who phoned me," Helma said. She pointed to a round black phone coupler and small metal box that sat a few feet from Pepper's phone. "I wouldn't have recognized it if I hadn't researched telephone voice changers. You chose the least expensive model. It's despicable to threaten the life of an animal for personal gain."

"Yeah," Ruth added. "What if she'd been an old lady with a weak heart and that cat was her only—"

"Shut up." Pepper cut off Ruth's woeful tale. "Step back. Over there." With the gun, she motioned Ruth and Helma against the wall near her bedroom. "Palms flat to the wall," she ordered. Then she scooped up the two manuscripts and cradled them against her, a satisfied expression on her face.

"You," she said, pointing the gun at Helma, "use

your right hand and toss your car keys on the coffee table."

"It makes more sense to make your getaway in the Jeep," Helma suggested reasonably, keeping her palms to the wall. "You'll want to cut through forests and climb steep terrain to elude the law. The Jeep is a much better choice."

Pepper waved the gun. "Your keys. Now!"

"Do you even know how to drive a manual shift?" Helma asked, still not moving her hands.

Pepper looked momentarily thwarted. She bit her lip, then said resolutely, "Okay, then you'll drive. We'll all go."

"We will?" Ruth asked in a small voice. And to Helma, "Thanks a lot."

At that moment, a voice called out, "This is the police. Lay down your weapons and come out with your hands up." The voice boomed, magnified by a loud speaker.

Pepper froze, the manuscripts clutched tight.

"Who called the cops?" Ruth asked.

So someone *had* heard the crash and phoned 911.

"I'm not going out there," Pepper told them, "and neither are you." She backed toward the kitchen door, still pointing the gun at them.

"If it's the Bellehaven Police," Helma told her, "they've already established a perimeter. They always completely surround their target before they announce their presence. Go out peacefully, that's your only option. They know all about you. You're the person they want, not us."

"All three of you," the voice said next, as if he'd heard Helma. "Come out with your arms raised."

"No," Pepper screamed. "You'll have to kill every one of us."

"Hey, wait a minute," Ruth said, but Pepper had set down the manuscripts and grabbed the can Helma had noted earlier, with the warning label on it. It was a can of charcoal lighter fluid. She flipped the top open with her thumb.

"Come and get us, coppers!" Pepper shouted as she spun in a circle splashing liquid across the tile and over the cupboards. "You're dead meat. We have weapons and we're ready to use them."

The gun wavered, thrown off by Pepper's wild actions with the charcoal lighter. Helma jumped away from the wall, holding out her arms, and ran toward Pepper. Before she'd taken two steps, Pepper pulled a red automatic long-nosed lighter off the counter and touched it against a wet puddle on the table. With a whoosh, flames ignited upward, leaping from spill to spill, driving Helma back.

"Fire," Ruth screamed. "Fire!"

Ruth and Helma edged toward the windows. Helma could see members of the Bellehaven SWAT team in formation on the sidewalk, shields raised, a myriad of weapons pointed toward the house, toward *them*. *Someone* had believed the toy airplane was a gun and they'd witnessed a hostage situation. Pepper's fire crackled and flames burst upward toward the ceiling, soaring, already unbearably hot.

Pepper continued screaming. "One step closer and we'll kill you all! We dare you."

"I think this is what they call 'suicide by police,'" Ruth screeched. "Cut this 'we' stuff! I'm not interested."

The window shattered inward as a projectile shot

through it, scattering glass. Helma felt shards land in her hair and pelt her shoulders. A metal cylinder rolled across the floor trailing greenish clouds. Acrid smoke billowed and filled the apartment. Fortunately, as was her usual habit, Helma had taken careful note of doors and windows, and now she closed her eyes tight, grabbing for Ruth.

"Raise your hands when I tell you," she told Ruth. "Keep your eyes closed."

Pepper's gun went off and Helma felt deadly movement whiz past her head. She ran forward, eyes tight, hand on Ruth's arm, as two more shots were fired.

"Get back here, you bitches," Pepper shouted behind them.

"I hate it when people use that word, you unimaginative . . . typist," Ruth shouted back at Pepper.

"Now," Helma told Ruth, "raise your hands!"

They burst outdoors into the October sunshine.

Then stopped, smoke pouring from behind them, facing men with guns. Pepper was still inside screeching incomprehensibly about taking everybody to hell with her.

"Drop," a voice of undeniable authority ordered.

Ruth tumbled to the ground, her hands covering her head. Helma dropped to a sitting position on the grass, her hands in plain sight but facing the action.

Pepper appeared at the broken window, coughing and choking, but still wildly waving her gun.

A SWAT member stood on the sidewalk and raised his weapon toward Pepper.

Pepper screamed and dropped from the window.

Even in the danger and confusion of the moment—as the SWAT team and firemen rushed forward, as

Helma heard a woman shout, "That's her, the short one. I saw her from my window. She pulled a gun on the woman who hit her Jeep"—Helma was still able to scan the surrounding officers through watering eyes and note that Chief of Police Wayne Gallant was not among them.

Chapter 28

Fresh Air

Ruth and Helma stood in the fresh, clear air near the open rear doors of an ambulance, each of them holding an open bottle of water. Occasionally they wiped the remaining sting from their eyes with damp towels an EMT had given them.

The cut on Helma's neck from flying glass had been bandaged, her hair combed of the remaining shards. Ruth was untouched.

"Where's Pepper?" Ruth asked, blinking rapidly and gazing around them at the activity that had devolved from frenzied to deliberate.

The SWAT members had laid down their shields and removed their Kevlar armor. Police cars lined the street, lights still flashing. A second fire truck lumbered to life and eased away between vehicles. As was Bellehaven's standard 911 response procedure, fire trucks were already on the way when Pepper started her fire and the flames had been extinguished before doing serious damage.

"She's still in the other ambulance," Helma told her, nodding toward the second ambulance parked in the driveway blocking TNT's Jeep.

"She's nutso," Ruth said, stopping to cough. "If I'd been the cop, I would have used a *real* gun, not a Taser."

The stun gun had momentarily rendered Pepper helpless, but it hadn't interrupted her invective. Once she'd recovered from the shock, the police had been forced to place her in restraints, and still Pepper shouted and screamed nonstop.

Bending over the blue front fender of Pepper's red Honda were two investigators, wearing white gloves, with cameras and swabs and plastic bags.

"Hey, Pete," Ruth called to a blond policeman, "has she confessed yet?"

He grinned at her. "You're not catching me this time, Ruth," he said and walked back toward his patrol car.

"Okay, then, I give up. Where's our brave chief?"

"He'll be here later," he said over his shoulder.

The crowd, gathered in the street beyond the yellow police tape, pointed and whispered and explained the events to each new person who joined them.

"So Boy Cat Zukas has returned?" Ruth asked Helma.

"I'm not sure," Helma told her, "but I found a mouse head on the deck mat, and I don't know of any other cat that has ever left animal parts on my balcony."

"Generous little beggar." Ruth wiped at her eyes. Mascara streaked to her chin. "So let me get this straight. Pepper hit Molly on the way home from the author's launch, thinking it was Tanja, then parked her red car in the garage to hide the damaged blue fender and took up the bicycle until she was able to literally bump off Tanja?"

Helma nodded. "Tanja's appearance at the meeting must have seemed like fate had intervened. Her only weapon was her bicycle helmet."

"Whew, excessive response to a little plagiarism," Ruth said, pausing to turn her left side, her "good" side to a reporter who was snapping photos.

"Pepper's novel had become her obsession," Helma said, turning her own face away from the camera. "*Nothing* was excessive to her anymore."

"If Pepper had destroyed Tanja's manuscript, there wouldn't have been any other record of Pepper's story. Do you really think that was her only copy?"

"Julius said so."

"Score one for the computer nerds who nag us to back up our files." Ruth nudged her. "Now this isn't the appropriate time, but I have something to tell you. I . . ." Suddenly she smiled, looking beyond Helma. "Hey, look who's here."

Helma wasn't *really* expecting Wayne Gallant—she'd heard the policeman named Pete say he'd be there later—but she turned to follow Ruth's gaze, thinking that it might be him, that he might have arrived earlier than originally predicted. He'd naturally rush to the scene of an incident in progress.

But instead of Wayne Gallant, Boyd Bishop walked up the sidewalk toward Ruth and Helma, his lanky figure slightly bowlegged, his leathery face creased in concern.

"Put a horse under that man and the birds would fall

out of the trees," Ruth said, her voice husky in admiration.

He crossed the police line with a brisk step, as if it only served as a pesky suggestion, and walked directly to Helma. Nobody stopped him.

"Are you all right?" he asked Helma, and Ruth stepped back as if a mighty wind had blown against her and nudged her out of its path. He leaned forward and lightly touched the bandage on Helma's neck.

Helma nodded, unable to speak for a moment. But he gazed at her intently, waiting for her to respond. "Fine," she said, her own voice husky, assuredly from the acrid fumes. "I'm fine. It's just a scratch."

"Where'd you come from?" Ruth asked.

He answered without looking at Ruth, only at Helma. "I live about three blocks from here." He waved in the direction of Washington Bay. "I heard the commotion and walked over to see what was going on. Then I saw you."

Ruth waved her hand. "I'm fine, too," she said.

"That's good," Boyd Bishop said. "Real good." And Ruth touched her heart and rolled her eyes, mimicking a swoon.

In one natural, easy, smooth movement, Boyd pulled off the denim shirt he wore over a navy turtleneck and draped it over Helma's shoulders. She caught the slightest, not unpleasant whiff of a cigar.

The denim shirt made Helma feel far warmer than its light fabric. "Thank you," she told him as a plain car braked in front of Pepper's apartment and Wayne Gallant stepped out, his eyes on the threesome standing at the back of the ambulance. He wore a suit and looked as if he'd just left a meeting.

Ruth's eyes gleamed. "This oughta be good," she muttered.

"Hello, chief," Boyd said as Wayne Gallant approached. The two men gestured to each other, seemingly tipping invisible hats, one a Stetson, the other a fedora.

Boyd held out his hand and they shook. "I'm Boyd Bishop."

Wayne Gallant nodded as if already aware of Boyd's identity.

"Were you present during any of this?" the chief asked him. His attention caught for a moment on the denim shirt over Helma's shoulders.

"No, sir. Just attracted by the noise, that's all. It sounded like a pretty dangerous situation for these two women." He grinned at Helma and Ruth. "Cool-headed, they are, I'd say. Bet they would have ended it successfully themselves if your boys hadn't shown up when they did."

"If the police had been aware of all the information," Wayne Gallant said, glancing at Helma but not meeting her eyes, "the situation might not have taken place at all."

Boyd's eyes passed between Helma and the chief, his expression confused but touched by amusement. "Somebody holding out on you, chief?"

The air grew curiously tight. Wayne regarded Boyd and Boyd regarded Wayne. They were the same height, close to the same age. Wayne was a bigger man, but Boyd was wirier, faster appearing. They stared at each other, eye to eye.

"*Do* something," Ruth whispered to Helma.

Helma had no idea what Ruth was talking about. Ruth

gave an exasperated sigh and stepped between the two men, facing the chief. "Boy-oh-boy, do we have things to tell you," she told him breathlessly. "You cops are gonna love it: murder and mayhem, cheating and stealing, breaking and entering. Helma nearly got herself killed."

"I was *never* in danger," Helma said firmly. "I was always prepared."

The air around the two men suddenly softened.

"I believe that," Boyd said. "It looks like I'm leaving you two in good hands. I'll be going now. Ruth. Helma."

Again, that quick tip of his head, and he lazily stepped across the yellow tape and walked down the street.

"Into the sunset," Ruth said, sighing.

Wayne Gallant turned and studied Ruth and Helma with neutral policeman's eyes. "You two all right?" he asked, rocking back on his heels as if it afforded him a better view of their faces.

"You bet," Ruth told him. "Except Helma took a direct hit from flying glass. If it had been a few inches higher or sharper or thicker, well, who knows?"

"It was only a scratch," Helma said, touching her bandaged neck.

"Good," he said.

Good? Helma had expected a few more words than *Good*.

"Sid briefed me in the car," the chief continued, "so after we've studied your testimony, we'll get back to you. Officer Young will drive you in your car back to your apartment."

"We met him," Ruth said, "in the library. He nearly shot me in the globe."

"I'm able to drive," Helma assured him.

"Just a precaution," he said so seriously Helma expected him to add, "ma'am."

"Why can't we take TNT's Jeep?" Ruth asked. "I'm not looking forward to explaining this to him."

"We'll keep it for now. I'll give him a call to inform him what happened."

He glanced again at the denim shirt still draped over Helma's shoulders and then said in a quick nod that took in both Helma and Ruth, neither one more than the other, "I'll be talking to you later."

Helma sat up front with Officer Young. "If you press the gas pedal twice before you turn the key, my car will start easier," she told him.

"Yes, ma'am."

"It doesn't like to go over thirty miles per hour the first few minutes. Have you had extensive experience with a manual shift?"

Chapter 29

The Reason Why

The first thing Helma did when she and Ruth entered her apartment was to peer through her sliding glass doors at the mat on her balcony. Arranged across it was another mouse head, an indecipherable inner body part, and the graceful open wing of a bird, *sans* bird.

Ruth looked over her shoulder. "He's in the area, all right. I'll paint out that halo in the morning."

As Helma cleaned up the remains, she glanced at all Boy Cat Zukas's favorite hiding places without spotting a sign of the black cat.

"A productive day, I'd say," Ruth said as she retrieved the portrait of Boy Cat Zukas from the kitchen counter, touched a finger lightly to the halo, and glanced at her fingertip. "That Boyd boy is obviously interested."

"He's a widower," Helma told her. "He misses her."

Ruth shrugged. "So? By this age, we'd all better be dragging around *some* baggage or we haven't been alive. Adds texture. Do you want to finally hear my good news? At least I think it's good."

"I do," Helma told her.

"Paul's moving to Bellehaven for a year. He's arranging some kind of *sabbatical* to study flash-frozen-fish techniques here. He's not moving in with me, natch, but we'll find two places close to each other for a trial run at it. I'll start looking tomorrow. Maybe if we start from scratch again: his, mine, no co-mingling this time, we won't botch it up so bad."

Helma envisioned her back bedroom returned to its normal uncluttered state, the paint stains eradicated, clothes no longer hanging over chairs, the bed made, counters clean, and her refrigerator containing only food she ate. And, yes, Ruth back in Bellehaven. She smiled. "That's very good news, Ruth. Congratulations."

On Saturday morning when Helma awoke, she had the sense she felt sometimes when the barometric pressure had changed during the night, her eyes opening in a flash, nose flaring to catch the smell of rain or the dryness of approaching sunshine. She arose from bed and, in her robe, proceeded to her living room.

Boy Cat Zukas was pressed against the glass of her sliding glass door, peering into her apartment, two more mouse heads on the mat beside him. When he saw Helma, he gazed directly into her eyes. Helma did not ascribe human emotions to animals, but beneath the impatience of his stare, she thought she glimpsed a touch, just a touch of satisfaction. He wasn't thin; his coat was as glossy bright as his eyes, so glossy he might have been brushed, or even bathed, a feat Helma couldn't imagine.

She opened the door and Boy Cat Zukas padded into her apartment and stepped lightly into the wicker basket beside the door, as far as he was allowed to enter, and began to clean himself.

"Well," Helma said, standing back ten feet and looking at him. "Well."

Although she wasn't scheduled to work on Saturday, Helma left her apartment before Ruth awoke and drove to the Bellehaven Public Library, planning a full day in order to catch up on lost time. Before she left, she set a plate of cat kibbles beside the wicker basket, allowing Boy Cat Zukas to eat inside for a change, that is, if he wanted to.

She left the newspaper on the kitchen counter for Ruth, open so the headlines were clearly visible: "Hopeful author arrested in women's deaths," it read. "Plagiarism suspected motive."

A single line in the story stated that Pepper had also confessed to an attempt to break into Tanja's office in the Hopewell Building but had been thwarted by a counselor working late who'd called the police. Helma shook her head, remembering Pepper pulling them from the building in such a panic. No wonder.

The library hadn't yet opened to the public, but as soon as she entered through the loading dock, Helma heard women's voices and rounded the corner past George Melville's empty desk to see Glory Shandy and Ms. Moon in an animated conversation.

"Oh, Helma," Ms. Moon said when she saw Helma. "Are you scheduled to work today?"

"No," Helma told her. "I believe I'll sort through some of the Local Authors submissions."

"Can I help you, Helma?" Glory Shandy offered. "I know you're behind schedule and I've studied all the criteria; I even have a few suggestions I think you might find helpful."

Ms. Moon beamed at Glory, nodding in encouragement.

"I'll definitely ask if I need your help," Helma said. "Excuse me."

"Aren't you glad it wasn't one of our authors who turned out to be the murderer?" Glory asked Helma.

Ms. Moon frowned as if she were trying to make up her mind, and then her eyes cleared and she held up a page of creamy pink stationery. "Although this has nothing to do with the Local Authors project, Helma, I'd like to share the generosity of one of our regional authors who obviously read my interview in the *Belle-haven Daily News* regarding our recent deaths."

"Oh yes," Gloria breathed. "I'm sure it was picked up by the wire services."

Ms. Moon humbly touched her heart. "This letter's from Angelique d'Boudier, the bestselling romance author, can you believe it? She noticed *us*? What an honor. And she's such a moving writer. She understands women's hearts, their unspoken desires. She knows about love, true love." She closed her eyes and sighed, then added, "Although I've never read her romances, of course. I prefer the classics."

"I've never read them, either," Glory hastily added, shaking her head in little no-no no's.

"What does the letter say?" Helma asked, and without thinking she shifted her bag behind her. It held

Boyd Bishop's denim shirt, which she intended to return to him after work.

"She's making a very generous donation to the library. *Very* generous."

"Very," Glory echoed.

"Listen to what she told me," Ms. Moon said, em-
phasizing the word *me,* then reading from the creamy
paper in a subdued voice. "Writing is an honorable art,
filled with heartache and personal searching. My hope,
in accepting this gift, is that you will celebrate the glo-
rious pinnacles of the writing craft and not bring to the
attention of our faithful reading public the more sorrowful or seamier aspects of recent local tragedies."

Ms. Moon folded the letter and sighed. "You can tell
Angelique is a true lady."

"In every sense of the word," Glory added.

"She cares only for the enhancement of the writing
life."

May Apple Moon turned briskly to Helma. "So naturally, Helma, we won't be needing you to create a display for the deceased authors after all."

Helma pulled one book truck of Local Authors submissions close to her desk—the heaviest loaded of the
three awaiting her attention—and began sorting books
into piles of No, Questionable, and Yes. Most of them
would need further investigation by checking on the
author's residency or the publisher's validity.

"Hi, Helma." It was George Melville, dressed in
jeans and a sweatshirt. "You're not working today after
all the excitement, are you?"

"Just catching up," Helma told him. "Have you
come in to work?"

"Not a chance. I left some bowling coupons on my desk is all." He considered the stacks of books for the Local Authors collection and whistled. "Quite the job you've got there."

"It will take longer than I'd planned to sort through them," she conceded.

George nodded. "Lots of people with axes to grind write books," he said, reading out titles: *How to Spot a Lie, Taken for Granted, Get What the Government Owes You*.

Exactly what Helma was thinking.

"Don't stay a minute longer than you have to," George said before he left. "The sun is still shining."

As Helma lifted a book titled *Living Alone and Loving It*, an envelope fell to the floor, address side down. It wasn't unusual to find letters, notes, even uncashed checks used as bookmarks and left between pages. Helma picked it up, intending to return it if there was an address on the front, or toss it in the trash if there wasn't.

The envelope, the size of a greeting card, was sealed, and on the front was written *Miss Helma Zukas*.

It might have been from a local literary hopeful, but Helma recognized that angular and clearly legible penmanship. Her letter opener was out of reach so she clumsily tore open the envelope with her index finger, ripping the front across the grain so the envelope tore roughly in half, and giving herself a small paper cut she ignored.

It was a birthday card. Roses on the front. She swallowed hard before she opened it.

Inside, Wayne Gallant had written, "Dear Helma, After our long friendship and association, I hope you are interested in discussing a future with me. If you are, meet me tonight before the launch of your Local Authors project. We have reservations at La Bonita at 5:30. I'll be there, waiting for your answer. W.G."

She read it twice, then twice more, turning the card over as if more information might be hidden on the back, then finally released her breath.

When Wayne had stopped her in the police car, he'd asked if she'd thought any more about his suggestion, and she'd thought he meant to stay out of police business. She closed her eyes and remembered: she'd told him she had no intention of contributing to his explorations!

How could this have happened? Her birthday had been Monday and today was Saturday. Helma noted the titles from between which the card had fallen: *Living Alone and Loving it* and *Papier-Mâché Jewelry*, bringing the books into mind and remembering how they'd arrived in her cubicle.

Finally, she rose from her desk, holding the card in her hand, and entered the public portion of the library. The doors had opened to the public twenty minutes earlier, and Glory sat at the reference desk, smiling at the populace.

"Excuse me," Helma said in a not-to-be-denied voice, holding the torn envelope with her name toward Glory, "but why didn't you tell me this card had arrived when you brought me that stack of books on Monday?"

Glory's mouth opened. Her eyes moved rapidly left to right and she raked her fingers through a tangle of curl. "Oh, didn't you see it? I'm so sorry. Terribly sorry. I set it right on top of the pile I put on your desk so you'd find it, but another book must have landed on top of *it*. I can't apologize enough."

"And later you assured the sender that you'd delivered it to me," Helma said, seeing again Wayne Gallant standing with Glory the night of the Local Authors launch, Glory nodding her head in assent to a question from him.

"Well, yes, I did," Glory said. Her gaze now steadily met Helma's. "Because I *had* delivered it to you. I promised I would see that you got it and I did. I put it right on top. Oh, I hope I didn't cause any trouble, that's the last thing I'd ever, ever want."

"I see," Helma told her and returned to the workroom and her desk, where she picked up the telephone and dialed the police department. She remained standing while she spoke to the receptionist.

"This is Miss Helma Zukas. I'd like to speak to Chief of Police Wayne Gallant, please."

"I believe he's with—"

"Please tell him I'll remain on the line. Thank you."

"But—"

"I will wait," Helma replied and finally the woman said, "One moment, please."

Helma stood stone still until she heard his voice. "Helma, what's wrong?"

"I just discovered the birthday card you sent me. It was not delivered to me."

"But I understood it was . . ." He was too much a gentleman to claim that Glory had lied to him. "I'm sorry."

"You concluded I had merely chosen to ignore your invitation. To not even respond, that I'd allow you to simply believe I'd rejected your request without a word?" She hesitated while he silently listened, then told him, "Frankly, I'm surprised."

"Helma, I thought . . . I was afraid . . ." She heard him take a deep breath. "Please, I'd like to discuss this with you."

"I need to think about it."

"I was wrong," he said. "Can we talk?"

"It would be more appropriate if you phoned me at home."

"I'll call you tonight, Helma. As soon as you get home."

"That will be fine," Helma said, adding, "after seven thirty, though. I have an appointment right after work." And hung up.

She sat at her desk for a long time, surrounded by books from local authors, now seeing that not only were there titles that dealt with the sorrows of life, its griefs and limitations, but there were even more that had reassuring and positive titles: *Recovering from Grief, Raising Loving Children, Growing Beautiful Gardens, Making a Difference in the World, How to Love,* and *How to Forgive.*

Check out librarian of excellence, Miss Helma Zukas. She's left her tangled Lithuanian family in Michigan to forge a life of order and certainty in Bellehaven, Washington.

But far is never far enough. One by one, they find her, beginning with her outrageous artist friend, Ruth. Murder finds Miss Zukas, too. But what might throw anyone else for a loop doesn't faze Helma Zukas. She is a professional.

Armed with prodigious library skills, she's a match for the craftiest of criminals. And if life sometimes tosses her an oddball question, she may not know the answer, but she definitely knows how to find it.

Miss Zukas and the Library Murders

Introducing Wilhelmina (Helma) Cecelia Zukas—that's Miss Zukas to you. Sure, Helma Zukas lines up her pencils and never shouts in public. But Miss Zukas understands the power of knowledge, whether she's facing a library patron or a murderer. She caresses the library wealth at her fingertips. She has a book and she knows how to use it. Go ahead: make her day.

Who better to research a body discovered in the Bellehaven Public Library than the premier librarian of the Pacific Northwest herself? When the murder weapon turns out to be a piece of library history, and the clue a bit of her own Lithuanian heritage, Miss Helma Zukas's skills will not be denied. Chief of Police Wayne Gallant enters the scene, and the attraction between them can neither be denied *nor* accepted. With the aid of Helma's not-so-proper best friend, Ruth, a six-foot-tall bohemian artist, the two are soon in hot pursuit of the truth.

Chapter 1

Murder. Murder in the library.

Helma allowed herself a dismayed shiver and then she firmly put the horror of it out of her mind. It was done. It was too late to alter what already existed. Only the facts could be dealt with now.

A yellow plastic tape stretched across the ends of the fiction stacks, separating the crime scene from the rest of the library. It read: POLICE LINE DO NOT CROSS

Helma lifted the tape with one hand and smoothly ducked beneath it.

Four uniformed policemen and two men in suits stood talking beside the green-sheeted bulk on the floor. A redheaded policeman cleared his throat and caught the others' attention, nodding toward Miss Zukas, who had invaded their cordoned area.

"May I look?" she asked, stepping closer to the body.

It lay on the gray carpet under the green sheet, one dirty-knuckled hand peeping past a hem.

There was a man, a murdered man beneath the green sheet. Helma paused, swallowing when there was nothing to swallow. No, it was no longer a man. It was a body, just a body. Inanimate.

"The janitor will have a difficult time removing that stain," Helma observed, motioning to the deep red stain that curved beyond the sheet like a setting sun.

An ambulance attendant browsing through *Lolita*, looked up and said, "Probably have to replace the carpet."

"Ma'am," the red-haired policeman said, reaching for Helma's arm. "This is a police . . ."

"Excuse me," she told him and pulled back the green sheet.

The dead man lay on his stomach with his head turned to the side, toward Helma. "I've seen this man before," she said to the policeman reaching for her arm, dropping the sheet so it billowed and settled back over the body.

They all turned their cool, detached policemen's eyes toward her. She felt the stillness of their attention, their unblinking scrutiny.

"Yesterday afternoon he asked for one of the reference materials we keep behind the desk."

"Which reference material?" the chief asked.

Helma tried to remember. It had been a very busy day. Rainy days frequently drew the public into the library. "I'm sorry," she told him. "I can't recall right now but I may later. I frequently do."

"Can you remember anything he said?"

"He requested a quarter to make a phone call."

"Did you give it to him?

"I never give money to strangers," Helma assured the chief.

Miss Zukas and the Island Murders

An anonymous note in the morning mail reminds librarian Helma Zukas of her long forgotten promise to plan her twenty-year high-school reunion. She meant what she said and she said what she meant, so now Helma transports her class from Michigan to an island off the Washington Coast for a celebration "to die for." When fog descends, classmates die, and old animosities resurface, it's up to Helma, along with an assist from her raffish friend Ruth, to save the stranded group.

Chapter 14

Droplets adhered to Helma's hair like a fine spray. Dense fog fingers swirled lazily into the light, forming eerie shadows that took shape and then, just when she thought she recognized them, dissipated.

Beside her the door opened and Ruth slipped through. "Helm?" she whispered.

"I'm right beside you," Helma said.

"Geez!"

"Shh," Helma cautioned her.

"I hope you have x-ray vision," Ruth said. "This could be our last ride together. End up in the drink."

"All we have to do is follow the road," Helma assured her. "No turns, just stay on the road."

Gravel crunched beneath the tires and the car began to roll, first slowly, then alarmingly fast.

Helma left the headlights off and steered by the feel of the tires in the worn ruts.

"Are you trying to kill us? Slow down."

The sound beneath their tires changed and Helma hit the brakes. Ruth braced herself against the dashboard. "Now what?"

"We're at the road. You have to drive."

"I'm not driving."

"You have to."

"I can't. Why do I *have* to?"

"Because I left my driver's license in our room."

"Oh, for pity's sake, Helma. That's the last thing in the world we have to worry about. There are no police here, remember? And if there were, we'd be *grateful* to see their little flashing light behind us, believe me."

"I'd feel better if you drove."

"I don't drive without my glasses."

"I thought those were just sunglasses."

"Well, they're not 'just sunglasses,' okay?"

Helma turned on the engine. "It wouldn't matter. You can't see anyway."

Miss Zukas and the Stroke of Death

When she reluctantly agrees to resurrect her canoeing skills for Bellehaven's annual Snow to Surf race, Miss Helma Zukas finds herself paddling through a murder that points to her flamboyant friend, Ruth. The "Snow to Surf" is based on the Ski to Sea race in Bellingham, Washington, a torturous 85-mile relay race from the slopes of Mount Baker to Bellingham Bay during a seven-to-eleven-hour period every Memorial Day weekend.

Chapter 16

Helma dashed toward her canoe and employed a maneuver the cousins had used as children to launch themselves onto their sleds. She grabbed her canoe by the gunwales and pushed it and herself into the river, landing stomach-first on the center thwart, slapping the water with a smack, splashing, barely brushing the rocks.

Her canoe tipped but held, the bow end catching the current and turning before Helma had righted herself. She loosened her paddle from beneath the seat and dug awkwardly into the water, splashing backward but swinging the canoe straight. She began paddling downriver in long, efficient strokes, her knees out and braced, getting her bearings.

The little canoe sped along the river's surface. Ahead of Helma, a brown canoe as thin as an arrow rounded the bend, bent paddles flashing in unison.

Then Helma firmly put the other canoes—those

ahead and behind—out of her mind and concentrated on the river, its currents and eddies and obstacles. She focused on her paddling and the breeze and the position of her body and shoulders, envisioning it all as a single whole, a unit, movements orchestrated to perfection.

And in her concentration she failed to notice the spectators lining the bridges and parked beside roads as the canoeists passed beneath, didn't notice how the crowds went silent as this solo upright woman, her hardwood paddle cadently flashing, her strokes a piece of poetry and her canoe a work of art, passed by as swiftly and timelessly as a vision from a James Fenimore Cooper novel.

Final Notice

Aunt Em is the only sensible member of Miss Helma Zukas's boisterous extended Lithuanian family, an aged, calm and orderly woman. When Aunt Em suffers a mysterious "brain incident," just before a visit to Helma, the aunt Helma picks up at the airport is more akin to her bawdy friend Ruth than the aunt Helma has known all her life. Mysterious deaths, robbery, and chaos now accompany Aunt Em, along with a past Helma never could have imagined.

Chapter 4

"Who's Lukas?" Helma asked.

Aunt Em set her glass down so hard, whiskey sloshed onto the counter. Helma wiped it up with her napkin.

"I don't know any Lukas," Aunt Em told her.

"You said that was his suitcase, with the flamingo."

"I did?"

Helma nodded.

"Long ago," she said slowly, as if she were forcing up memories, "he was a good friend, the best of friends." She clasped her hands together and tightened them once to illustrate. "Like you and Ruth, only he was a man, but we didn't . . . you know." She made incomprehensible motions with her fingers.

"In Michigan?" Helma asked. "A friend of yours and Uncle Juozas's?"

"No," she said, picking up her glass. "Before that. Before Michigan."

Aunt Em had lived her entire life in Michigan; how could there possibly be a "before Michigan"?